TOM'S TRAIL

A WESTERN ADVENTURE

NOEL HODGSON

PRODUCTIONS

Published by DS Productions

ISBN: 9798841231110

❀ Created with Vellum

1

PART 1

RIDING NORTH

Sarah Torrance stepped closer to her husband. He was slumped in a chair at the table with his back to her, resting his elbows on the wooden top. In a sweat stained shirt, he sat glumly gazing at the wall in front of him, his shoulders hanging with weariness and defeat. She laid a hand on his arm.

"Don't take it so badly, Tom," she comforted him. "We'll see it through."

"W' need rain, Ma, lots of it," he said flatly, inclining his head to answer her. "The crops w' planted have dried roots an' the young leaves are curlin' for want of water."

"We've had drought before, Tom, and rain's always come again," she reasoned.

"Sure, but this time it's different. A Spring drought is worse. Look at the valley how it's already yellowin' with grass fading off, and we're only just into April." He got up slowly and turned round to face her, taking hold of her hand. "It's real serious, Ma. We can't afford t' just wait an' hope. We have to do somethin' soon before it's too late and everythin' is lost. We got t' make some decision about it, fast!" he concluded forcefully.

"Like what?" she asked, an anxious frown appearing.

"Well, Jim and me have been talkin' it over, but we're not yet sure what's best-" The sound of running feet interrupted him and they both turned to see their son, Johnny, appear in the open doorway.

"Look here Pa," he called, holding up a cluster of withered stalks with knotted roots. "Amelia an' me were down by the lower fence when we found a patch like this!"

Tom Torrance went over and took hold of the bunch and examined the infested roots. His grim expression remained unchanged. "It's clump root," he sighed, and immediately he strode out of the house into the fierce sun, heading towards the six acre field which was fenced off from cattle and horses. A little distance behind him his wife and son followed, watching him closely as he went hurriedly through the gate and down the outside row of small maize plants to the far end where his fourteen years old daughter, Amelia, was waiting for him.

The family gathered round the lifeless patch of diseased plants. Tom stepped towards some healthier looking ones and pulled them up to discover that they too were infected. He threw them down and turned round. Emotion creased his face with a kind of fierceness that made him look younger than his fifty two years. In an odd sort of way this confirmation of ruin made it simpler. At least now the uncertainty of foreboding was over and his fight was straightforward. He removed his hat and used his fingers to comb his long wispy hair to one side.

"What is it?" Amelia asked cautiously, her wide straw hat shading her young, pretty face.

"It's a fungus, hang it!" he said bitterly.

"Can we stop it?"

"Nothing w' can do, honey," he muttered dismally. "Nothing in the world now it's set!"

Showing him support, Sarah, his wife, stepped closer and gripped his arm. Looking up into his strained, craggy face, she felt his desperation with a sense of unease. In this mood he was a different man, vehement and restless, like when she first knew him in his thirties arriving in town riding shotgun for the stagecoach. "We'll get by Tom, you wait and see," she offered. "We've got some money saved and possessions we can sell if need be."

"Sure Ma," he replied dully, then straightened up to put his hat on again. "But w' can do more than that. We've near two hundred cattle here in the valley with the creek nearly running dry already. There's no time for us waitin' and hopin' for deliverance. We need to act!"

"You can't sell them all off!" Johnny argued. "We've got a breeding herd started!" At sixteen he was now as tall as his

3

father and worked just as eagerly. He felt he had a right to protest at what he suspected might happen.

"How are w' going to feed them and us, Johny? We're running out of grass and gonna lose what we've planted. Aa'm afraid w' don't have any choice," he replied directly.

"Rain can come anytime! You sell the herd and in a couple of weeks the drought breaks, so what then?" Johnny retorted, his blue eyes widening in consternation.

Tom hesitated, holding down his irritability, grasping to reconcile his son's fears. "Either way it's a gamble son. Your way w' lose all or gain all. My way we don't win but w' don't lose." He paused briefly for the right words, and gazed out along the valley. "Aa'm sorry but Aa'm too old t' lose it all. You're not, you and Amelia, but we are, your mother and me, and w' sure ain't trustin' in fate, or God."

"Don't say such things Tom," his wife admonished him. Although ten years younger than him, she stood her ground when she thought fit. "God's been good to us and you know it!"

He gave her a kindly, wry look and grinned. "Well let's hope he ain't gonna change his habit now, huh?"

The touch of humour cleared the tension between them and their loyalty to each other was fixed with open smiles. Johnny gazed at his father. "Okay Pa," he said simply, acknowledging his father's wisdom with a look of reservation. "But how are you plannin' t' do it."

"We need to talk with Jim Houseman about it. He has some notion of a cattle drive being rounded up in the region.

If w' can manage to hold on to about forty of the best young cows with a bull or two and sell the rest for the drive, w' should see the year through okay."

They paused, together, for a few moments in which to contemplate the possibility before starting to walk back to the house. Nothing else was said. The remorse and misgivings which a short while ago had assailed their thoughts were now pinned back by fresh hope, trusting in a positive move, and for a short while it was best felt in silence.

Back inside the house they drank water thirstily then got ready to leave, with Johnny and Amelia going off to hitch the horses. Alone in the house Tom and his wife regarded each other solemnly.

"You seem sure it'll work out okay, Tom?" she asked quietly.

He shrugged his shoulders. "Can't vouch for it, Sarah, but Aa've no intention of lettin' anyone think different!" he replied stubbornly. She gave him a faint smile and turned her attention to her basket into which she laid a meat pie to take with her. Before long, the family gathered at the front of the house where Amelia and her mother climbed onto the buggy, Amelia taking the reins. As soon as Tom and Johnny were mounted on their horses, the four of them set off together, leaving two dogs standing at the rail waiting in vain for a signal to follow.

A dirt track ran along the flat centre of the valley floor with the sparsely wooded, stony hills rising either side. It was mid afternoon and hot, the thin air as dry and clear as glass. Many cattle had sought tree shade on the slopes and were lying or standing, listlessly waiting for the sun's decline before they would wander off again in search of grass to nibble.

A mile from the west end of the valley where their farm was situated, the road curved following a creek which ran down from the hills behind them above the valley. In the ditch there was now only a trickle of water, a level normally seen in late Summer, not at the beginning of April. Staying near the creek they headed towards the lower end of the valley where the Houseman's place stood, a short distance from the pass where the stream and road sloped out of the raised valley. On lower ground the same stream joined Johnson Creek which later fed into the Guadalupe River, near a settlement called Ingram, eight miles west of Kerrville, Texas.

Reaching Houseman's place they rode up to the house to be welcomed by Jim's wife, Rosemary, an attractive looking woman, and her four young children who bounced happily on the porch steps. The youngest was a girl of three to whom Amelia rushed to pick up in her arms. Tom dismounted to assist his wife down from the buggy, then looked about.

"He's up on the hill someplace hunting hawks," Rosemary answered Tom's gaze. "W' lost two chicks this morning. I saw a hawk before noon circlin' near the barn and thought no more of it until I went to feed them."

"Aa'll go find him," Tom said.

"Can I come?" Johnny asked keenly. His father was inclined to say no, but the boy's willingness caused him to relent and remounting they trotted away, the others going inside out of the sun.

They guided their horses up the first hill behind the house then climbed more steeply towards the bluffs of the next. They found Jim's favourite black horse, called 'Star', tethered to a tree and climbed down to tie their mounts beside it. Now on foot, carrying rifles, they walked quietly up through brush and trees towards the rocky ridge. Spotting Jim ahead, crouching behind a low branch, Tom and Johnny slipped into hiding as well, out of view of the hawk sweeping now and again across the cliff face up above.

Rifle aimed, Tom waited until Jim had fired and missed before he pulled the trigger. Swooping away, the hawk suddenly lurched and tumbled down onto the rocks below.

Jim Houseman jumped up and looked round. Unable to see anyone he called out. "Only one fellow shoots that good round here - old eagle-eye Torrance himself!"

Tom and Johnny stepped out of cover and Jim started to walk towards them. He was an agile man with a powerful build. Clean shaven with thick, brown hair, he grinned cheerfully at them. "Now what's all this creepin' up and spyin' on a man so he has no excuse to offer for shooting badly?"

"Who says it was the second shot that hit? Could have been a delayed reaction from the first," Tom argued.

"You wanna bet on it?" Jim countered.

"Reckon not. Aa learned a long while ago that when it comes to bettin', Jim, you're a far better shot than me," Tom mused.

Johnny gave a chuckle. Despite the twenty years age difference between the two men they were solid friends, and their verbal sparring was well practiced. They had met as valley neighbours fifteen years earlier when both had set up home and since then the respect and regard both families had for each other had developed through cooperation and loyalty and liking. Over this time they had shared land and each other's problems generously, and now that this severe early drought confronted them both, they faced it as one. Ready to talk they moved to sit down on rocks in the shade of a sprawling oak tree.

"Just as I feared, we've got clump root disease in the maize and it'll soon be rife through the whole field!" Tom announced, candidly. "Aa guess now we may as well do what w' talked about, selling off all the cattle save a few. Have y' seen anyone, Jim?"

"A cowhand in town told me Aa'd have to meet with the trail boss himself," Jim answered. "Seems like they've gathered over two thousand already, so if w' want to sell ours to him w' better move fast before they complete their tally. They're camped out near River Bend, but the man said his boss would be in town Thursday noon if w' wanted to talk with him then. Aa said we should visit him before that and asked the man to pass on the message."

"What happens if he don't want them?" Johnny dared to ask.

"Somebody else will," Jim replied sharply, revealing his anxiety. "As the drought wears on more and more will sell up. There'll be drive after drive headin' north," he bemoaned.

Tom stood up, propping his rifle over his shoulder. "What sort of price will we likely get?" he asked carefully, gazing across the hillside.

"Cowhand said it depends on the cattle, Tom. But one thing for sure next month they'll be payin' less."

Johnny stood up beside his father. He frowned. "Those cattle are worth fifteen to twenty dollars each. W' don't want anythin' less for them!"

Jim stood up too. "Well we ain't exactly holding the aces, Johnny, but w' can deal. Now," he brightened, "if you boys can't smell coffee an' grub down the hill, the nose on my belly sure can. Let's go, huh?"

Turning to walk down to their tethered horses, he and Tom exchanged a cautious look, not wishing to discuss the matter further in front of Johnny.

―――――――

Early next morning Tom rode alone into the low burning sun, as he headed back down the track to the east end of the valley. His bay coloured horse, called 'Rusty', was flecked with silver, while his second one behind was a big, dull grey, named 'Rock'. Jim was already waiting, seated on 'Star', with another black one named 'Mack' as his spare. The two men greeted each other dourly before setting off down through the pass leaving their valley. The dry hard ground drummed with the horses hooves and a cloud of dust trailed them every time they broke into a run. Winding through hilly country following the stream they passed through Ingram and then journeyed down river along the bank of the Guadalupe. They reached Kerrville well before noon where they rested briefly in the main street canteen before riding for another half hour on their spare horses, to find the trail outfit camped down river, away from the herd.

They had come to talk business and introductions were formal. The trail boss, slightly older than Tom, was bearded and military in his manner. In a glance Tom and Jim knew they were dealing with an experienced and astute man. His name was Henry Mathias. His assistant, a big, surly cowboy called Fletcher, joined the three of them on the river bank a little distance from the camp where an other six men were seated round the chuck wagon, drinking coffee.

"How many cattle you want rid of?" the trail boss opened smartly, declaring in his words that the advantage was his.

"Together, we'll have around three hundred," Jim answered carefully, hands on hips. "Better than most you'll find."

"Keeping some back?"

"Sure," Jim said.

"And if the drought don't break?"

"We'll sell them too."

"If you can?"

"If we need too," Jim asserted.

Henry Mathias nodded his head slightly, as if the answers had been adequate and he approved of Jim's controlled reasoning. Now he turned to Tom. "We've got twenty one hundred and seventy head already, so addin' another bunch like yours would be about enough to get us goin'. Aiming to go up a new route to Abilene, Kansas. Heard of it?"

Tom nodded.

"If we're lucky there we might average out twelve to fifteen dollars a head. But we'll need to be lucky! There's likely to be an overspill supply with a long drought threatening and getting them there in sale condition might prove tough."

Tom showed no reaction. Despite the man's smart approach to a deal, he was straight and trustworthy. "So what do you reckon on payin' us for our cattle, huh?" Tom posed for a figure.

"Five dollars a head and no more." It was clear that he meant it.

"Without seeing them?"

The boss shook his head. "When Fletcher here has seen them and is happy that's what Aa'll offer. With the situation as it stands I consider it a fair price!" he stated.

Tom looked at Jim and saw him seething. "I'd like a chance for us t' talk it over first before we give you an answer," he replied grimly, showing his own dissatisfaction. Then he turned away and strolled with Jim along the bank side to where they could discuss the deal in private.

"Cow's belly, he ain't gonna rob us like that!" Jim groused.

"No he ain't, and that's the trouble," Tom answered with irony. "He's telling us straight the market'll be slumped in anticipation of rush selling."

"You reckon?" Jim stared.

Tom nodded.

"Then Aa vote we keep them a little longer and pray for rain. Far better than havin' them stolen from us at that measly price!" Jim argued fiercely, expecting his old friend to . agree with him.

Tom paused, then took a few steps away and gazed across the slow-moving river. Jim waited, slightly confused by the hesitation. Five dollars each was absurd. If only a quarter of their herds survived they could get as much for them later as what the trail boss offered for them all now. They'd be mad to accept.

"Hear me out first, Jim, before y' say anythin'," Tom commenced calmly, still looking across the straggling water of the shallow river. "Instead of him paying us five dollars a head we'll pay him four instead, just for the privilege of us taking our own cattle along with his. That way, when we reach Kansas then they'll still be ours to sell. Even at a lowly twelve dollars a head we'll get eight dollars which'll be a sight better than what he's offering now!"

Tom turned to regard his younger partner and met a

stoney stare which slowly softened and began to glisten. "Why not try him for three dollars a head instead of four?"

"One dollar below what he offered is tempting. Anything less would be considered foolish to a man like him! It also gives him a chance of raisin' it to five - the price he said he'd give us."

Jim allowed a huge grin to spread across his face. "Hey Tom, you're a crazy man! Aa swear, in all my life Aa've never heard o' such a crazy idea!"

"Aa mean it, Jim," Tom said frankly.

Jim chuckled. "Surprised you don't think w' should take them there alone, just you and me!"

"You know that ain't possible," Tom reproved him, without a trace of amusement. "But Aa'm sure in hell serious about the other."

"Reckon y' are. Only hope he says 'No'!" Jim wailed, his eyes beaming with the wonder of Tom's scheming.

They wandered back to the other two and Tom put forward his case, also arguing that both he and Jim would ride un-hired without pay yet under orders like the other cowhands. Also, they would provide their own string of horses. To end his proposition he stressed that which ever way they saw it, the deal favoured them more than the one before. It was," he pointed out, "money without risk!"

Fletcher, the big man, shuffled irritably. He disliked it at once, suspecting some sort of trickery, but he was unable to counter the deal with any sound logic. Mathias, the trail boss remained silent until his opinion was necessary. Before he

spoke he looked hard at the two strangers, particularly Tom
who he guessed responsible for the plan. Behind it, like the
man's face, he read a shrewdness that he could not help but
admire. However, even though the nerve and enterprise of
the plan intrigued him, he knew good business was not
founded on feelings or personalities.

"I'd want five. That's what I said at the start. Anyhow,
what if every stockman decides to deal this way? We'd turn
into a bunch of hired guides and our profits would be
severed!" he challenged.

"The way Aa see it, your profits would be assured!" Tom
argued. "Y' get money straight away and any losses on the
trail make no difference to it. You don't stand t' lose a cent."

"An' we ain't speaking for anybody else," Jim cut in. "This
is a one-off arrangement with nobody but us!"

"Don't do it, boss!" Fletcher interrupted. "We ain't done
nothin' like this before. W' favour them and word gets round
we're easy t' persuade!"

"Nobody ever thought of it before, that's why," Mathias
stated with a slight grin. He looked critically at Tom. "It's
original and Aa admire the idea, but the trail is arduous and
sometimes dangerous. Now your buddy here is young and fit
looking, but your older and slower and doin' a regular
cowhand's work you're likely to tire quicker. Sure, you're
doin' it for free, but how capable are you t' see it through?"

"Able enough to do my share," Tom answered cooly.

The trail boss paused to continue. He didn't doubt it at
all, but it was important for him to probe. "Also, if we run

into trouble Aa don't want either of you runnin' scared. Can you both shoot straight?"

"Cow's teeth," Jim chuckled, "I can shoot straight! But him here," he gestured, "he's good enough t' aim round corners!"

Henry Mathias raised an eyebrow at the adulation. Tempted to have it confirmed, an idea formed in his mind. "That good, huh?" he said glancing at Fletcher.

Jim nodded. "He sure is! An' if you're a bettin' man, Mr Mathias, which I believe you are, four dollars a head says he is!."

"Well now," Mathias began, cagily, "I'm not in the habit of givin' ground, but we believe one of our boys is as good as there is. So if Tom here can prove us wrong then the deal's on, you payin' us four dollars a head. If he don't, it's off, but with you payin' me a hundred dollars for the pleasure of saying 'No'! Now what could be fairer than that?" he exclaimed, amused with his own cunning.

Jim looked at Tom and knew by his glare that he disapproved of the boast which had led to this. "It's up to you?" Jim said as an apology.

Tom pondered, tight lipped, before answering. He nodded helplessly. "Aa'll go get my rifle."

Meanwhile, Fletcher ambled across to the wagon to talk to the other men and soon a young cowboy walked back with him carrying a rifle, while the rest of the group followed.

"We've got a marksman here, Wes. W' want to see how good he is."

"Whatever y' say, boss," the young hand muttered.

Mathias waited until Tom returned. "Boys, this here is Tom Torrance. Tom this is Wes Hardin."

Tom nodded and the other responded accordingly, both swiftly assessing each other with a brief, concentrated regard. Despite the young face, Tom perceived in the other's eyes the flame of those men he knew different from most others; relentless, wilful, moody types, all of them shooters.

"Why rifles?" Hardin demanded.

"Nothin' better," Tom promptly replied.

"You're carryin' a pistol," Hardin noted.

"Just for appearance," Tom quipped, casting Jim a light hearted look.

"Well, rifles it is!" Fletcher declared. "When you two are ready, step out here."

The two went with him and after simple instructions Fletcher made them gamble for choice of order with a pebble hidden in one of his two fists. Young Wes won and elected to shoot first. As instructed, the old white whiskered cook stood some distance off with a tin of eggs, ready to throw them, one by one, up into the sky slightly ahead of the two marksmen.

At the drop of Fletcher's hand the cook hurled in turn each of the three for Hardin, everyone of them spattering in mid air. Afterwards, he repeated the exercise for Tom who equalled the feat, despite having to reload after each attempt using his older single shot rifle.

Approval for both marksmen was muted at the moderate difficulty of the test. But after cook added five strides to the distance and they repeated their success, appreciation grew. Then Henry Mathias stepped forward, shouting to the cook to throw up five for each rifle at the new distance.

"These eggs weren't free!" cook protested.

"The' may as well have been," the trail boss joked, "the way you beat down that old lady's askin' price! Now do as Aa say, Elias!"

Grudgingly, Elias stepped out another five paces then turned to wait for Fletcher's signal. The onlookers fell silent and watched in amazement as Wes hit the first, third and fourth egg, missing two. His fellow hands shouted their praise then quietened down again as Tom took position.

Jim's attention was fixed, willing his friend's aim. The first egg flew up and began to arc down when it shattered. He hit the second slightly earlier, then the third as well. Jim felt a grin unsealing his mouth. The score was level with two shots left. The fourth egg sailed upwards and Tom fired carelessly without aiming, and he did the same again with the last one.

Bemused, Jim quickly confronted his friend. "What in the heck was that for, Tom?" he appealed. "Y' could have won!"

"The main thing weren't t' lose, Jim," Tom replied calmly, still looking ahead watching Elias striding to them.

Jim was not content. He felt robbed of victory. "Y' didn't even aim. Y' only had to hit one more!"

Tom turned and slowly smiled. "Would you have bet all the money you got that Aa would have?" he answered.

"Cow's teeth, Tom, Aa never understand you," Jim moaned.

Tom turned his attention to the trail boss. "Is that good enough to get t' ride with you?"

Henry Mathias nodded pensively. "Good enough, I guess. Okay with you Brad?" he said to Fletcher.

The big man raised his thick black eyebrows. "Guess so. But what's so bad about tryin' to win?" he griped.

"Well," Tom explained, "Wes and me will be ridin' and workin' together for some time. It's ain't a bad idea to start out equal. Right, Wes?" he ended, looking sideways at the younger man.

Hardin stared back at him with uncertainty, not knowing what to say, his thoughts and feelings astonished and confused by the older man's idealism. To cover himself, he nodded and then turned to walk away followed by two companions, one about his age, skinny and sly looking, and the other slightly older and taller with shoulder length hair.

Elias, the cook, a white bearded, crinkly faced old man in his sixties, took a long hard look at Tom. "Aa reckon Aa know you from someplace, Mister. Where you from?" he asked.

"East Texas."

"Full name?"

"Tom Torrance."

"Means nothin' to me," cook shrugged. "Good shootin' though. Only it's gonna be hard to forgive you for wastin' those last two eggs, not even tryin' t' hit them. If w' run short on the drive you'll be the first t' miss out!" He chuckled loudly and wandered off back to the wagon.

The remaining two cowhands were pleased to shake

hands with Tom in appreciation of his marksmanship. The first, a good looking, friendly man in his late twenties named Travis, and the other, a cheerful Mexican cowboy in his thirties, called Mex, was smaller but broader chested. When these two had walked away Henry Mathias reached out and gripped Tom's hand.

"The deal's on," he affirmed. "Bring your cattle and the money day after next. We're holding the herd two miles down river and leavin' early Saturday. You be there!" he concluded respectfully. He shook Jim's hand too, and then on the point of walking away with Fletcher, Mathias paused before adding his final thoughts. "Liked what you said, Tom. In my time Aa've seen two or three men shoot as good, but none of them were capable of sayin' that. See you Friday at the latest!"

A little later, riding away, Tom and Jim said nothing to each other until they slowed the horses to walk about a mile from Big Bend.

"How we gonna explain it to Johnny an' the women?" Jim demanded.

"Won't be easy."

"W' can always pull out!"

"Yeah, but we won't."

Jim gave a laugh. "Not after doin' like you did!"

"Aa didn't set out to prove anything. Remember, it was your mouth!"

"Yeah, but it sure was convincing."

"Y' reckon?"

"Y' had him beat. Why didn't y' do it?"

"It wasn't important."

"He deserved it. He ain't a man yet but he acts tough. You should have brought him down to size!"

"To do that you'd have to kill him."

"Jim gazed sideways at his friend. "You mean that, Tom?"

Tom kept looking straight ahead. "It ain't safe t' cross his kind," he advised.

"How d' you know?"

"Aa just see it."

"Is that why y' didn't beat him?"

"Could be," he replied. "But then again it was better t' miss the last two without trying than to miss takin' aim!"

Jim gave a laugh. "If y' keep talking to me like that Aa'm goin' to end up crazy like you!"

They smiled faintly at each other then spurred their horses into another run.

News of their plan was received at home with a sense of bewilderment and disagreement until its merit was clearly understood. Even then, when they met at the Houseman's place that evening, both wives were still openly fearful of the perils which might confront their husbands on their long journey. Johnny, however, was full of admiration for the plan and was desperate to go with them on what he imagined to be a great adventure, despite his father's assurances of its

hardships and weary routine. In the end it was only his position of responsibility at home - to be caretaker of both
steadings and families, that persuaded him to stay. Tom and
Jim knew too that Henry Mathias would never agree to
include him, but they never used this argument, preferring
one that would boost Johnny's self esteem rather than
scorn it.

"If y' weren't needed here we'd have y' ride with us," Tom
admitted.

"Sure thing," Jim agreed. "Anyway, work here ain't gonna
be easy. And any decisions t' be made is yours!"

Johnny stared at Jim, fully realizing the authority he'd
bear. "How long y' reckon t' be away?" he asked.

"It's gonna be about eight to ten weeks, Aa guess," Tom
replied.

"That long?" Amelia asked.

"On the trail we'll be lucky doin' fifteen miles a day," he
replied.

"You been on one before, Pa?" she said.

"No, Aa just know it."

"Kansas is a long way from home," she said wondrously.

"Anywhere away from home is a long way," he replied.
"We're only goin' 'cause it's necessary. We ain't that well off
now we can afford to be poor! T' get only five dollars a head
we'd be better giving them away and still be able to hold up
our heads with some pride!"

His final statement registered accord, asserting the just-
ness of their plan. Now that it was final there was no more

doubting it. After the youngest ones went off to bed they sat together and discussed arrangements for tomorrow's work. The cattle were already branded, but to be in time to join the trail herd on Friday they needed to round up again and draw off those to keep back. To achieve this task and prepare for their leaving everyone had to be involved. It was, therefore, with a strength of purpose and unity that the two families at last ended their meeting and the Torrances were ready to set off for home under the light of a clear, full moon.

Early next morning, Jim arrived at the Torrance's home and he and Tom and Johnny rounded up a herd of almost two hundred cattle. They drew off those too young to travel with some good cows and a bull, thirty nine all together, then released the others. After a noon-day break they started to drive the loose cattle down the valley leaving them mid way, and started again, with Amelia joining them, to round up the rest of the cattle at Jim's end of the valley.

During the afternoon they sorted this herd at Jim's corrals holding back about thirty and letting loose one hundred and thirty four. Although weary and hot, with their clothes damp and dirty with sweat and dust, they paused long enough for a cold drink before setting off on horses again to gather the first herd bringing them along to join and mix with the second bunch, a total of two hundred and ninety four cattle altogether. This done, the lot were then left to roam and feed at the lower end of the valley, making it easier to round them up early next morning to set off.

Unlike the other cowboys on the trail that would have

horses and mules provided, Tom and Jim had agreed to take their own string with them. This had been Amelia's morning task, collecting the best eight geldings, including their favourites, and having them ready in a corral at the Houseman's with rigs and saddles waxed and polished as new. Meanwhile at home both Sarah Torrance and Rosemary Houseman made up both men's bed roll, wrapping up in the tarp and quilts a few extra clothes and personal items carefully selected for the trip.

For more reason than mere work, it proved a strenuous day for both families, their emotions stretched by consternation over Tom's and Jim's absence. And so, at sunset, there was enough time for a warm bath and a family supper in each household before they went wearily to bed, and even then, thoughts of parting and of uncertainty clouded everyone's sleep.

Nevertheless, before dawn, both homes came abruptly to life, breakfasted and made ready. Tom hugged his tearful wife and daughter, then he and Johnny rode down valley to where Jim was waiting with his family. They rounded up the cattle at the top of the canyon and while Jim returned home to say his farewell to his wife and kids, Tom and Johnny started the drive, their two dogs swinging left and right behind the herd.

Jim, bringing the spare horses, soon caught them up and they made good progress through the morning before the heat of the day heightened to slow them down to a crawl. Mid afternoon the cattle were halted at the river's side for

Tom to visit town to collect money and to inform friends who would keep an eye on both families. When he returned they made the final push covering the last four miles in under two hours. At Big Bend, Fletcher was waiting for them with some men, to count the beeves over the river and to receive the eleven hundred and seventy-six dollars, as promised. His attitude to the deal had not changed. He checked the money formally then told them gruffly that Mr Mathias was holding a meeting after supper to tell everyone their duties and what was expected. Then he rode off to camp leaving his men to assist Tom, Jim and Johnny tracking the cattle into the larger herd half a mile downriver.

As well as Travis and Mex who they'd already met, there was a tall, lean, long legged rider called Stilt Rodgers, and a friendly, bright eyed, black cowhand named Jacob. Unlike Fletcher, all four cowboys appeared glad to see them and meet Tom's son.

Later in the evening, after the meal, the meeting was held round the fire as they drank coffee. Mr Mathias, in a military manner, outlined the journey and the daily routine which involved positions of responsibility on the drive and the roster for night watch duty. Each cowhand had already drawn their string of horses and he demanded good care of them. His rules of conduct were simple; respect for each other and themselves, and complaints to be expressed openly to him, rather than fester among themselves. For any behaviour which he considered detrimental to work or morale, a fine would be exacted on end-of-trail wages. A serious offence could result in punishment or dismissal. He finished by saying that their choice was a simple one; either accept the rules or pack their belongings now and be gone!

Nobody objected or had any questions, so the trail boss thanked them all and mounted up to go round the herd with Fletcher, Mex and the young, long haired cowhand called Scott who, Tom noted, had yet to utter a single word.

Johnny had been allowed to listen at the meeting and afterwards to sit with Tom and the rest, talking round the fire. However, it had been a long wearisome day for him and feeling too exhausted to stay awake any longer he went and lay down and fell asleep before Tom and Jim had unrolled their quilts.

Early next morning they were noisily awakened, as with everyone, to cook's shouting and banging of pans. And then in silence, Johnny drank coffee and ate biscuit before walking with Tom and Jim to where the young wrangler, Reuben, hardly any older than himself, had saddled one of his two horses. Biting on their emotions, they quickly hugged him farewell, then he rode off by himself with the two dogs chasing after, as Tom with moist eyes, stood still, watching his son ride into the distance.

"Come along, partner," Jim tugged his arm. "We're movin' out!"

Tom slowly turned and followed him over to the horses where young Reuben was listening to cook's instructions. As they approached, the fair, curly haired youth grinned at them before departing to loosen some young ponies hobbled down near the river.

"Bit simple when it comes to thinking," Elias confessed, " but he's as willin' as the world's wide when it comes to work. He'll learn too if he heeds a wise old owl like me." He lifted his white stubbly chin. "Believe you boys both ridin' drag the first week, huh? Don't envy y' at all!" the old man squawked.

Jim gave him a half grin as he mounted his horse. "It's men's work, I guess!" he called as he and Tom set off to catch up with the others.

"Devil's work, I'd call it!" Elias hollered after them.

For the first few days of the drive, the cattle were hurried along with cowboys whistling and shouting and swinging ropes. In doing so the herd created a line, three or four abreast and as their friskiness was run out of them the natural leading steers came to the fore. Out ahead of the animals rode the trail boss, Henry Mathias, who determined their course looking out for water and grass. Sometimes Fletcher would join him, then ride back to relay instructions to the two point riders. Occasionally he'd travel back further past the swing and flank riders that held the line intact to the rear or drag end. Here, where the slower cattle needed constant urging, the dust was thickest, particularly during the initial period of trail breaking.

With their mouths and noses covered with their bandanas, Tom and Jim worked assiduously, along with Wes, his skinny friend called Parker, and Scott McNeil, the long haired, silent one, knowing after the first week they would move up the line. Apart from his lead cowboys who were Travis, Mex, Jacob, and one with a patched eye called Selby, Mr Mathias liked to rotate the drag and flank riders, keeping them, as he explained at the meeting, 'interested and grudge free'. What made it still harder at first for Tom and Jim was what was considered the worst night duty as well; two and a half hours before dawn, on the first and second nights. By the third day their eyes were red and swollen with dust, strain, and lack of sleep. Fortunately, like their resolve, their humour persisted.

"These boys look like they been with us two months already!" Elias cackled aloud serving them supper on the second evening. The rest gathered about the chuck wagon grinned knowingly.

"W' can look a lot worse than this," Jim replied.

Cook shook his head. "Maybe it's all that men's work you're doin', huh?" he quipped.

"The devil it is," Tom muttered, smartly.

Approvingly, Elias gave him a pat on the shoulder.

"Reckon Wes could out shoot him now!" said Travis, next in line.

Tom nodded amiably and moved on taking a seat round the fire. Travis followed and sat down beside him. He put down his mug of coffee on the ground in front and after his first mouthful inclined his head towards Tom. "Where did y' learn t' shoot that good?"

"Used t' hunt a lot when Aa was young," Tom said quietly, aware that the others were listening.

"Well me and the boys are sure pleased to have you on our side," Travis said cheerfully.

Tom smiled slightly. "But since Jim here likes to boast for others not himself, I think you should know he handles a rope as well as anyone Aa've seen."

"Thanks partner," Jim mumbled, his mouth bulging.

Travis grinned. "Guess y' know everybody now." he said.

Tom cast his gaze round. The outfit comprised fully of fifteen members, including themselves, and apart from the boss and Fletcher and Scott, who were still with the cattle, the rest were all present, including Wes who raised his eyes momentarily. The only member that they hadn't spoken to was a latecomer called Red, who was a swing rider.

"You worked for Mr Mathias before, Travis?" Jim asked later.

"Sure. He's the best."

"He's a smart man. A Colonel in the war too. If we'd had more like him we would have won!" chipped in Selby, picking his teeth .

Elias chuckled. "Makes no difference to you Selby. If the Rebs had won you'd still be here now eatin' my food and workin' like a slave for thirty five bucks a month, just like Jacob over there!"

The black cowboy grinned widely. "Sure thing Elias. It

ain't much but a whole lot better than workin' for nothing. In fact anybody doin' this for no pay's got to be crazy!"

His reply was deliberately loaded and instantly heads turned towards Tom and Jim. Jim hesitated, on the point of speaking, but without anyone knowing Tom checked him with a slight click of his tongue.

"Is it right you're both workin' for nothin'?" Red dared to ask in an abrasive tone.

"If you want t' know our business y' better ask Mr Mathias. He's in charge," Tom replied directly to the ginger bearded cowhand.

"I'm askin' you. You're either one of us or you're not!" Red objected, in a sharp, unpleasant voice.

"Y' heard what he said," Elias interrupted. "It's not our business so let it be. Right?"

Everyone seemed to pause at once and silence stretched across the circle of men until Jim, with his usual knack, had words to break it. "You know something, Elias," he drawled, "If I bend over my eyes would drop out. So if anyone here thinks me and Tom are goin' through this for the fun of it, Aa'm tellin' y', they got t' be crazy!"

Cook gave a little chuckle and a sense of amusement spread round the group. Now Jim had eased the atmosphere, conversation continued in a convivial manner and turned to other matters. Afterwards, holding mugs of coffee, Tom and Jim rested in the glow of the evening fire and while listening to Mex playing harmonica they dozed off, only to be wakened soon by Travis who wanted them to fetch their bedrolls for proper sleep.

———————

Long hours in the saddle under a hot sun was wearing and the pace of the trail slowed as the column of cattle snaked unhurriedly out of the brush covered hills onto more open ground. The creeks and rivers were low and crossings were easy yet tedious as the herd filed leisurely over, allowed time to pause and drink. But morale among the cowboys was good. They had settled into a routine and had encountered no real difficulties. Friendships were forming and except for Wes and Parker who made no effort, the outfit mixed contentedly, even with Red, a born grumbler.

As cowhands, Tom and Jim worked willingly and slowly gained popularity for their skills and quick wittedness. During the second week they had ridden flank and now in the third they moved back to the drag. It was here that Tom rode alongside Wes and unlike many of the other men who were cautious of the young man's moodiness Tom tried to be sociable, without concern, chatting sometimes with him.

One noontime as the cattle were stopped to rest, Tom saw Wes tipping up his canteen to find it empty, so he offered him water from his own. With a look of surprise Wes accepted it and afterwards when handing it back he paused to speak.

"You shoot good," he admitted.

"No better than you," Tom replied.

"You could've won."

"No way of tellin'," Tom said.

"You good with that too?" Wes continued, pointing at Tom's revolver, a Colt Navy.

Tom smiled slowly. "Once. Now it's only for rattlesnakes and cleaning. Guess that's a Remington Five shot conversion model you've got there?" he enquired, looking at the other's holster.

Wes brightened. " You're a knowledgable man, Mister. But why d' you carry an old type rifle like that when one of these up to date repeaters is better to have in times of trouble?" He patted his Winchester.

Tom nodded. "Guess so, but this is what Aa got used to. Here, you hold it and see for yourself." He unsheathed his rifle and handed it over; an act of personal confidence which was intended. Wes raised the Sharps '63 Model and looked along the barrel, lowered it and felt its balance in his grip.

"Feels good, but heavy," he commented, handing it back to Tom to take back. "Now try this!"

Tom took hold of the Winchester and examined it thoughtfully then returned it. "Fine gun," he complimented.

For a brief moment they exchanged a look of approval, then hearing steps they both turned to see Jim on foot leading his lame horse towards them. It was a white coloured one named 'Sugar'. "Got worse, huh?" Tom said.

"Sure has. Can y' take him back to the remuda and change him for 'Tricky' or 'Mack'? Aa'll wait here," Jim replied.

"Either way," Tom suggested. "But Aa'd just be as happy stretching my legs out here as you. Anyway, it's better that you take him in yourself and see the cut gets kerosine on it right away!" Tom climbed down and let Jim mount his own ride, a dark brown, long legged gelding named 'Locust'.

"Won't be long gettin' back," Jim said, then glancing over at Wes who had remained grimly silent, he added jokingly, "Only listen to half of what Tom says and believe half of that!" With a chuckle he turned away pulling the reins of his lame horse as he led it away.

Standing, Tom took out his pipe and struck a match to draw smoke. He waited on purpose for Wes to speak first. He had sensed, with instinct, the young cowboy's wariness of Jim. For no matter how Jim tried to cover up his feelings, his contempt for Wes still breathed out.

"Been friends long?" Wes muttered, chewing jerky meat.

"About sixteen years, I guess." Tom answered, cleaning the rim of the bowl with his finger nail. "You're not sure of him, Aa reckon," he added openly. Wes said nothing. "How old are you?" Tom continued.

"About nineteen," Wes answered.

Tom pouted smoke. "Old Sioux Indian prayer says, 'Never judge a man 'til you've walked in his moccasins for two weeks!' It's worth rememberin', Aa reckon!"

Wes stared blankly as Tom sat down on a low flat rock. Then Tom looked up and grinned slightly. "He won't cause any trouble, I promise."

"Maybe not," Wes replied drily, then roughly turning his horse he rode off to catch up with the cattle.

———

After supper that evening, a group of men sat playing cards near the campfire, while at the wagon-side, Tom, Jim, Travis, Jacob and Mex were listening to Elias talking as he waited for Reuben to finish scrubbing out the cooking pots. His complaint was simple. He feared the early drought would continue and ruin many a hard working farmer. And in the end cattle too numerous to sell would perish in their thousands. He'd seen it happen years before. He himself had known a cattleman who had shot himself because of his misfortune.

"Can't understand anyone doin' that kind o' thing," said Travis.

"Me neither," Jim agreed.

"A man gets down so low and miserable he can't see anyway back up, that's what," Tom explained.

"Look what happened in the War, an' how many soldiers unable to stomach what they'd done or seen, turned the gun on themselves," Elias stated. "O' course the army never said it. 'Killed on active duty' they reported. Making it easy for themselves and the families left behind!"

"Did you fight, Tom?" Jacob asked.

"Neither me nor Jim did, and nobody asked us to. " he answered honestly.

"Well you saved yourselves a lot of wasted time," Travis muttered. "I rode west with Baylor, joined up with Sibley, went to Tuscon with Hunter and returned to Texas without firin' any more than three rounds. Most of the time we just sat about waitin' for orders."

"Well you can count yourself lucky, Travis, 'cause it weren't like that for many," Elias frowned, then looking up saw Fletcher approaching and addressed him promptly. "You want somethin', Brad?" he squawked.

"Boss wants to speak with Tom," he announced, solemnly.

"You want coffee too?" Elias added.

"Sure," Brad replied, and waited for Tom to get up and leave before he sat down in his place.

"Apart from some Comanche spying us out once or twice, the trail's goin' smoothly," Jacob said towards Fletcher, who merely glanced up.

"We've hit no snags yet," Travis admitted, "and the herd's as docile as any Aa've known. But I'd like some rain to cool things down a bit."

"Don't bother me," Mex muttered with a rolled cigarette between his teeth. "I prefer to sleeping on dry ground!"

"Got a long way to go yet," Fletcher insisted. "Indian Territory's comin' up and we hear from Fort Griffin there's a young band of Kiowas broken out on the rampage into Texas."

Elias handed him a mug of coffee. "A week ago when me and Reuben went into Mason for supplies we heard the same, but it don't pay to tempt trouble by too much talkin' of it!" he groused.

Fletcher leered up at him. "Nobody's talkin' about it so quit your snacking! Anyway, you know it'd be dumb t' ignore any warnin'!"

"Aa know it as well as you, Brad, but Aa see no reason to raise hackles until it looks like happenin'!" Elias retorted.

Fletcher gazed at steam rising out of his mug. "Ain't goin' t' argue with you, Elias, but we'll keep it in mind and watch out," he muttered.

Tom had walked from the wagon across to where Mr Mathias was sitting alone, furthest from the fire. In the three weeks on the trail the boss had maintained a slight distance from the campsite gathering where his authority did not overshadow his men, giving them space to curse and rail and joke naturally, just beyond his hearing. But he was, nevertheless, as Tom himself had mentioned to Jim, there at hand, available and aware of mood and feelings. In the course of their chat Tom's initial assessment of the man proved to be true. Mathias informed Tom of his satisfaction for his and Jim's hard work and good natured influence with the men. He was also, he said, heartened by the respect which the men had for them, and in particular the regard that Wes Hardin showed him – Tom.

"He's got a bad streak in him and Aa was concerned he'd resent you!" the trail boss admitted.

Tom puffed on his pipe. "Got a hunch he's on the run!"

"Probably, and not the only one either," Mathias added, confidentially.

"Guess so," Tom answered.

"Anyway," Mathias continued, "Aa need t' talk with you about Indian Territory. We may have some trouble, even lose some cattle."

"I know it," Tom replied. "Things can go wrong."

The trail boss stroked his pointed beard. "Just thought I should mention it, Tom. And Aa'll do my best for you."

Tom was slowly nodding his appreciation when voices from the card game loudened angrily. Both of them got up from sitting and walked towards the group. By now the men were standing and Red, holding Parker by the collar, was threatening to strike. Suddenly Wes leapt forward and booted him in the thigh. Taken unawares, Red buckled. Charging forward Fletcher grabbed Wes before he could add a second blow and slung him off his feet to the ground. "Enough!" he bellowed, and on the point of moving towards Red, Parker held back his punch. In a rage Wes jumped to his feet and seemed poised to be going for his gun when Elias, rifle raised to shoot, hollered his warning. "Leave it there, Wes, or else!"

Hardin froze.

Mr Mathias strode between them. He glowered at young Wes. "You ever draw on any man here while we're trail driving and I'll have the skin of your hide whipped off you! An' that goes for everyone!" he roared, and let his eyes circle, settling briefly on every face to confirm his threat. "Now, what happened? Somebody accuse somebody of cheatin'?" he cried scornfully.

Red pointed a finger at Parker. "He tried to signal t' Hardin what Aa was holdin'!" he growled.

"It's a lie, boss!" Parker spat onto the ground, his face twisted with spite.

Mathias shook his head. "It's always a lie! Anybody care to add anythin' what they saw?" No one spoke. "Right," he continued, "I'm fining you three ten bucks each as I said I would with trouble makers. If Aa change my mind at the end of the trail it'll be your own doing and nobody else's! Understand?" In turn, he glowered at Red, Parker and Hardin, square in the face, and each one bitterly lowered their eyes.

Mathias blew to calm himself. "Now things have been nice and peaceful until now so let's not spoil the fine job we're doing. Sure it's hot and dry and turnin' into a slow trail but there's a way to go, likely even the hardest part. So let's keep morale high and discipline as good as it's been." He softened his tone. "As I informed you at the start, this is a different route and gettin' the cattle safely to Abilene is a big enough fight without doin' it among ourselves! Now, it's getting dark so those of you on first guard get movin' and the rest get your bed rolls down. Day after tomorrow we should be crossing over Red River into Indian Territory!" he announced finally, then set off back to his own spot, glancing at Tom as he passed him.

Tom waited until the night watchmen had started to move away before he ambled over to the front of the chuck wagon to join the end of the line. When everyone else had gone, he gathered his roll and circled round to the tail end where Elias was stacking tin plates and sorting out ironware.

"If Wes had drawn would you have got him in time?" Tom asked lightly, concealing a serious interest.

"Maybe," Elias replied lowly, continuing his work.

"Wounded him or killed him," Tom mused.

"It worked out fine the way it did," the other commented, then stopped and regarded Tom curiously. "Aa don't figure things the way an old shootist like you does," he added, raising his chin with a wily squint. "Guessed at the start Aa knew you from some place even when you said y' came from east Texas, but Aa weren't fooled. No sir. Aa been rattlin' my head t' remember when an' where it was, and Aa got it figured now!" Glee deepened his wrinkled face. "You were younger then, without the heavy moustache, but round San Angelo no one messed with Tom Tileman. You changed your name, okay, but the man's the same!"

Tom chuckled, shaking his head. "Never heard of him, Elias. Sorry to disappoint you, cook, but y' got it wrong. Sure Aa can shoot rifle, but that don't tie me to anybody else with a reputation. Yep, Aa rode stage gun for a while but never made a name for myself."

Elias twisted his eyebrows, taking time to speak. "If you'd

been me an' Wes had drawn, would you have killed him or wounded him, huh?"

"Given the same chance as you, Elias, Aa guess Aa would have done the same," Tom replied, cleverly.

Elias started to wipe down the table board. "Go easy with him, Tom, he's a man killer!" he confided in a whisper. "And even though he shows you some respect he'd think nothin' of pulling the trigger on you if it came to it."

Gratefully, Tom patted the older man on the shoulder, then turned and walked away from the chuck wagon to find a place for sleep. Already some of the others were snoring like bull frogs. Before he closed his eyes he heard Mr Mathias and Fletcher and Elias turning the wagon tongue towards the north star, ready to direct the next day's drive.

Starting out from the Llano river the route which Henry Mathias had chosen was not yet recognised, or would be until they joined the latter part of the Chisholm trail near Newton, Kansas. However, a year or two later, this way was initially close to what became known as the Western cattle trail to Dodge city. With the early drought, finding enough grass and water was vital for the herd's condition, and so without competition and constraint from other herds, Mathias, with shrewdness and sensibility, had managed so far to sustain the herd, holding their weight.

Every day with the sun lying on their shoulders like a hot,

heavy hand, the cowboys sweated as they moved the line of cattle slowly forward across the shimmering wild prairie. Their working days were long and tedious and Red River was looked for with gladness, for here the men could wash off the grime glued to their skins and with Texas behind them be assured that they were close to half way there. On every trail north the rivers alone acted as reliable distance markers, as well as being hurdles to overcome.

At other rainy times under the threat of flood and quick-sand the following day's crossing might have caused a flutter of dread in each cowboy's chest. But not so now. With low water and dry banks it was a simple and patient matter for Henry Mathias and his herdsmen. That same evening after bathing and washing in the river the men enjoyed steak, gravy and beans, with the pleasure of feeling clean, as well as that of achievement.

Although the warning of hostile Indians was not taken lightly, these Texans were tough men and well armed, each cowboy possessing at least one pistol and rifle with plenty ammunition. It was customary to carry spare weapons too, and Henry Mathias had for emergency use another half dozen Remington rolling breech loading rifles tucked away in the chuck wagon. The only admission to the Kiowas threat was two other men, plus Fletcher, scouting forward with the trail boss. And Mathias insisted that one of these always be Wes Hardin or Tom Torrance, his best marksmen.

Three days after crossing Red river a patrol of eight soldiers from Fort Still arrived at noon camp where most of the crew were gathered eating. Cook gave them coffee and the young officer in charge explained that they were out looking for a band of renegade Kiowas, about twenty of them led by a warrior named Lone Wolf. On a hunting spree over the Red river border into Texas they had ambushed six freight wagons bound for Fort Belknap killing several teamsters. In a report from Wilbarger County they had been seen heading north back over Red river onto reservation land.

"We've seen no hostiles," Fletcher told the soldiers.

"You wont either, sir, until they strike," the lieutenant declared. "They're a scheming bunch!"

"Well if the' know what's good for 'em the' better just keep out of our path," Selby declared, throwing a chewed bone into the fire.

"What made them run?" Jim asked the officer.

"Discontent! We give them land and rations and they want more. Simple as that!" he replied, sardonically.

"More what?" Jim asked.

"More land, more guns and ammunition, more supplies, you mention it and they want more," moaned a thick necked sergeant sitting nearby.

"So what's the solution?" pondered Jim, directing his question back to the officer.

"They're going to have to change their ways. They can't just go huntin' where they please. There has to be a limit," he replied, earnestly. "And breaking out to thieve from settlers and kill when it suits them makes it harder to reason with!"

"It's hangin' they want not reasonin'!" Selby exclaimed,

his one eye shining. The callousness of being a soldier in the war had never left him.

"Well, if the' tangle with us they're gonna wish they hadn't!" Red growled, boastfully.

Three horses approached carrying the trail boss, Tom, and the tall cowboy, Stilt. They climbed down and joined the gathering. Fletcher passed on the news with the lieutenant adding details.

"Any idea where they might be headin'?" Mathias enquired.

"More than likely up the north fork of the river. It's hillier country and easier to hide out. Do you want us t' stay close by for a day or so?"

"Thanks Lieutenant, but we're intending moving a little to the east of there, so we don't want to waste your time."

"What's your route?" the officer asked with authority.

"Up to the Cimarron and on into Kansas to join the Chisholm run," the trail boss said tersely.

Tom sniffed. "Lieutenant, is this all the men you've got?"

The Lieutenant smiled condescendingly. "Don't worry, Mister, there's another twenty five ahead of us."

"Then they need your support more than we do," the trail boss advised.

The young officer raised an eyebrow at the other's confidence. "Whatever you say, sir" he replied, getting to his feet. He signalled to his sergeant to rouse his soldiers. "Thanks for the coffee and you all ride careful," he said aloud. They shook hands and the cowboys watched as the patrol mounted and moved out under command.

Tom collected his tin plate and mug and on his way to sit with Jim, he paused to speak to Wes, asking if he'd noticed the rifles the soldiers were carrying.

Wes shook his head.

"Springfield-Allin, single shot!" Tom said, with a grimace. "Even we're better armed to fight Indians than they are!" He moved on to take his seat. "Maybe that's why they wanted to come with us, for protection!" he stated wryly, causing a round of sniggers.

During the afternoon a breeze cooled the day, and once underway, the herd responded picking up pace so that by the time light was failing and they were ready to bed down, they'd added eight miles to the six in the morning. The breeze continued through the night like an endless murmur, ruffling and disturbing the cattle, so that it was necessary to double guard them in case of trouble. Next day the wind blew gustier and the wild grasses and brush flapped noisily making the cattle jumpy as they pushed forward bellowing and huffing with a nervous energy.

"They're acting queer, boss," Fletcher cried as Mathias rode back towards him to check on the their mood.

"Then let's drain it out of them," he blasted. "Keep the line but let's hurry them on 'till they're eager for restin'!"

Fletcher conveyed the orders down the line himself speaking in person to every man so that each knew his duty. When Jim on 'Star', riding drag with Parker and Scott, heard the instructions, he turned to the other two and offered words of comfort. "Well boys, look on the sunny side. If the beeves make a break they sure won't be comin' our way!"

Scott, shy of his stammer, gave a little grin, while Parker simply snorted, displeased by the hard dusty work in store for them.

And so it proved. Goading the herd faster with whistles and shouts and the swish of their quirts, the cattle trotted and walked continuously mile after mile for the rest of the day, passing between huge hills of granite, until they grew exhausted and their pace dwindled to a desperate crawl. Finally, at a selected area, the jaded herd was held up together and allowed to feed and drink at a water hole before they were settled down for the night.

Leaving some riders behind on watch duty the rest of the men made their way wearily to camp where the remuda of horses and the chuck wagon were stationed. Coffee was already heating on the fire and while young Reuben stirred beans into the meat stew cooking on the rail, Elias filled the men's mugs with the steaming black liquid and spoke words of encouragement.

"You boys done a fine job keepin' them goin' and holdin' the line. So what you looking grumpy for when you ought to be proud? Now get this coffee into your bellies and thank the Lord Aa'm here to provide! And here's another man you should thank," he cried, filling Tom's mug. "Here's the hunter that killed the antelope that you're all about to enjoy. I tell you no other outfit eats stews as tasty as mine. He paused to give credence to his following words. "An' y' know it's no lie 'cause Aa never tell anythin' other than what Aa know to be true!"

In this manner cook chatted, sparking them to listen and raising both their humour and appetite until their mood brightened. As much a preacher and teacher as a cook, this was him fulfilling his role. Henry Mathias knew his importance, and in Tom Torrance he saw the same virtue in another mould. The character of his men varied greatly, some more honest and decent than others, but as long as their trail driving work was dependable he valued them. What men of experience like Elias and Tom offered, especially for an outfit, was to keep heart when it was easier to lose it. As a leader of soldiers and cowboys Henry Mathias prized their type.

With the fire burning and the stew cooking in the pot the men were content to sit and wait, drinking coffee and munching biscuit which Elias ordered Reuben to hand out. At sixteen he was a strong, hard working youth. He cared for the horses tirelessly, and was eager to please, his face always bright and open. Elias bossed him with affection and prevented him from mixing too much with the men, particularly those who were foul mouthed and drawn to violence. No one knew exactly his circumstances, other than Fletcher who had known his dead parents and got him the job on the trail last year when he had acquitted himself well enough to be hired again.

"Bet you miss your boy and girl back home?" said Travis to Tom as they watched Reuben stirring the stew with a long wooden fork.

Tom took his pipe from his mouth. "Sure do. And my wife," he admitted.

"Must've been a big decision for y' to come away leavin' them behind," Travis said.

"Yeah. For me, an' Jim. He's left behind him four young kids and a pretty wife."

"What's it like been married with kids?" Travis asked. "Aa'd like t' do it someday."

"It's easy and it's hard," Tom answered, "and nobody in the world can tell you how much of either but yourself when it's done. You have a women in mind, Travis?"

"Sort of, but this ain't the kind of work women want their men doin'."

Tom nodded. Sitting on Tom's left, Mex came in on the conversation. "One day I get married but now I enjoy my freedom. When Aa'm as old as you Tom I'll have children too," he said with a grin.

"You bet," Tom added, "for to be old without family could be the loneliest feelin' in the world, huh?"

Mex grinned at Tom with understanding then took out his harmonica to blow a tune everyone knew as 'Honey Haired Girl From Houston.' Holding the pot between them, Elias and Reuben set it down off the fire and with plates ready they called the men to line up as it was ladled out. Under the darkening sky the men ate ravenously and half an hour later with their bellies full they started to bed down, eager for an early sleep. By the time Jim and Stilt and Jacob arrived at camp from guarding the herd they found only cook awake ready to feed them and young Reuben keen to take charge of their horses.

Dead-beat, the three men slumped to the ground beside the wagon to sit and drink coffee while Elias filled their plates.

"Have the beeves settled?" he muttered.

"Most," Jacob replied quietly. "But there's still some fidgety even though the wind's dropped."

Jim sighed. "We've just been ridin' round and round holdin' them in one place and hummin' and singin' like mother hens, but they're no nearer to lyin' down than when we started. There must be somethin' in the air ticklin' their noses!"

"Might be coyotes!" Stilt drawled in his slow deep voice.

"You hear any?" Elias asked, handing him food.

"Yeah."

"And you know the difference between coyote and Indians?" Elias said.

Stilt pondered, mouth open. "D' you?"

"Sure," Elias replied, "when Aa can see them!"

Jim snorted slightly at the old man's smartness but was too tired to humour him.

Jacob yawned. "Well, whatever it is something's spookin'

them. Let's just pray they settle down so we can get a night's sleep."

Elias poured him more coffee. "Is the boss stayin' out there all night?"

"He said he'd be comin' back as soon as the beeves are all quiet. Aa guess he's anxious that they don't run."

"Well if he's not back in the hour Aa'll send Reuben out with some meat. He's got to be worn out too."

"He could be too, Elias, but when he's got that look in his eye, what he's thinkin' or feelin' never shows. You know what Aa mean," said Jacob.

Cook nodded. On the big trail last year they lost days waiting to get over swollen rivers and the men got miserable and wet as the rains lashed down. For one week they were hardly dry but dare not complain, for Mathias himself was in the thick of it and had least rest, though not once did he grumble or moan. Finally when the sun shone through he broke the rule and gave them each a measure of whiskey from a newly opened bottle, showing what a reasonable boss he was as well as gutsy.

After their grub the three of them gathered their rolls and went to bed down under a star filled sky with a half moon. Meanwhile, out with the herd, Mathias, Fletcher, Selby and Red, remained on guard duty, humming and singing softly trying to quell the few agitated cattle still disturbing the others. After midnight when their patience seemed to be succeeding a coyote suddenly started barking closer to them than earlier and a number of cattle that had

48

just lain down got up nervously and paced round. Affected by them others sprang up and a great murmuring spread through the herd echoing panic. Mathias promptly ordered Selby to ride quickly back to camp to wake the outfit for help, while they remained circling the cattle trying to prevent any sudden break.

Naturally the news depressed the men as they dragged themselves groggily from sleep. Boots on, they ran hurriedly to saddle their horses and in a matter of minutes they were riding away into the darkness apart from Elias, Reuben and Tom, who remained at camp with rifles loaded in order to keep watch over the remuda horses and wagon in case of thieving. A band of Indians on the run would kill for extra horses, supplies, and particularly arms and ammunition. After the warning of hostiles by the soldiers, Mathias decided wisely to arm those men who carried only a pistol with the spare Remington rifles.

By the time the helpers reached the herd, a bunch had already broken away and the rest had become a bawling, swirling mass, on the verge of stampeding after them. Cutting them off proved hopeless for they simply dashed with alarm in other directions, until suddenly, a huge gap opened and they charged out, hooves crashing with unstoppable force. Racing after them in the moonlight the first riders attempted to overtake the leaders, but no sooner were the steers turned than they tore off again. Finally after four attempts the riders managed to wheel the bulk of the herd round, swirling them into a mill which eventually slowed them right down. In the confusion of near darkness the cowboys surrounded the cattle and eased them to a halt. Remaining mounted, they waited patiently for the herd to settle.

It was during this time that word circulated that Selby was missing. No one knew for sure but Mex thought he had seen him chasing ahead after the final run. Ringed round the herd, the men feared grimly for him while Travis and Fletcher went searching back over the ground covered by the stampede, about two miles. Half an hour later they returned to report no sign of him and there was a general feeling of disquiet among the riders as they continued to keep guard, worn out and desperate for morning and an end to this troublesome night. Only in daylight could damage be assessed and missing cattle rounded up. But foremost in their minds was the mystery of Selby's whereabouts, aching them like a wound.

At sun up they followed instructions, methodically rousing the cattle onto their feet to lead them towards the nearest creek for water and grass, leaving the ground they covered open to view. Here, they discovered Selby's fate. In the mill his horse had fallen - a gopher's hole - and he and the horse had been trampled to death. His body smashed so badly it was hardly recognisable. As others stared in disbelief, Jacob, his closest friend, climbed down off his horse and stepping forward knelt at his feet, touching his boot, his head drooped in silence. Mr Mathias approached on foot and standing beside Jacob put a hand on Jacob's shoulder to comfort him.

The trundle of the chuck wagon turned their attention. Elias slowed the mule team to a halt, while behind, Tom was helping Reuben to bring up the spare horses. Like everyone else, the three of them were shocked by the accident.

Elias came forward to join the trail boss and the black cowboy. Then the whole gathering fell silent, contemplating their loss and waiting for words to express it.

"He got no wife or kids. The only relative he spoke of was a sister in San Antonio," Elias announced, solemnly. After a pause he continued. "Selby Logan was a fussy, serious man, but he was a skilful and honest worker. He was also some-one, the more y' got to know him the more y' liked him. Don't let of any of us ever forget him. God rest his soul!"

It was a tribute rather than a prayer, but it drew a mumble of Amens.

Leaving Jacob and Stilt with a shovel to bury Selby, the others tracked the herd as they made their way slowly towards water. Although the men were exhausted they resolved themselves to the task of gathering strays and bringing the whole herd together at the nearby creek, by which time Elias had stationed the wagon and hurriedly built and lit a fire to boil coffee and cook breakfast.

After a long tally it was believed that something like a hundred cattle were missing. Another, more careful count confirmed it. So after breakfast the trail boss called a meeting.

"Brad and Travis reckon it's got t' be the first bunch that broke away before help came," he said. "It's gonna take time t' get them but we want them back quick, which means no rest for five of you men just yet!"

Glum faced at the thought the crew sat motionless as Mathias paused, looking round at each one, reading their expressions. "Red, Parker, Wes," he exclaimed, "here's your chance to make amends and cancel out your fine! Jim, you say some of your own steers have gone! You go too! Brad will take charge. Any questions?"

"Sure," Tom said. "Aa've got cattle missing too. Let me go with 'em!"

"Can't spare any more men!" Mathias insisted.

"If he's got good reason t' go he sure in hell can take my place!" Red offered foxily, then sniggered at his ruse.

Tom turned sharply towards him, vehemence in his eyes. "You're right. Aa got more reason than you Red. Aa raised some of those longhorns from calves. My whole life savings are in them. If they're lost Aa get nothing. For most of m' life Aa've had nothin'. That's fine when there's only yourself, but like Jim Aa've got a family to consider and they're a real good reason for me t' go in your place!" His jaw slackened, regretting his forthrightness. He appeased it hurriedly. "Another reason t' go is that Aa don't want to stay round here lazing about, drinking coffee, sleeping, and having cook feed us more than w' can eat."

Henry Mathias allowed himself a grin. "The way you put it Tom, Aa can't refuse you. Go in place of Red." He turned his head and stared sternly at Red's pink, stubbly face. "Okay, y' get your way this time but we'll find other work for you later t' pay off your fine."

"Whatever you say, boss," Red answered sourly.

"You're damn right it is!" Mathias replied irately, reasserting his authority. Red was a good enough cowhand but he prickled too much and needed to be put in his place. Then Mathias waved a finger. "Right, you five, come with me. Aa need t' talk with you! he ordered."

A little distance from the others he turned to face the group. He told them at once that the herd would be held here until they got back, but no longer than two days. He warned them to watch out for Indians and on no account to risk their lives. Also, if they bumped into any soldiers they should ask for help. He ended playfully by ordering them away, adding that the sooner they got going the sooner they'd be back! Then he walked away to his horse, mounted and rode off towards the herd lingering across lower ground near the creek where trees offered shade.

Having made quick preparations, the five riders selected their mounts and set off, each with a spare horse tagging behind carrying light supplies. Despite their lack of sleep their expectation of a short ride, perhaps only a day, made them confident and alert.

Keenly, they journeyed back to where the break had occurred and quickly found tracks and signs of the missing cattle as they peeled away flattening brush and grass. Following this trail was easy, and eager to proceed Wes and Parker pushed ahead at the front while at the rear, Tom on 'Rusty' took his time swinging out from right to left tracing the ground. After a while Fletcher and Jim stopped to wait for him to catch up.

"What is it, partner?" Jim called, sitting on his dark horse, 'Mack'.

"Nothin' yet," Tom replied, drawing closer. "But it would be helpful t' know if the' were any Indians about."

"You reckon they were here?" Fletcher demanded.

"Aa reckon Aa want to know for sure. No good blaming ignorance when you land in trouble."

Jim gave a little snort at Tom's candour. "Do y' want us t' help y' then?"

Tom raised a doubtful eye. "Help yourself, boys. It ain't just for me!" he exclaimed, irony in his tone.

Fletcher sniffed. "If y' could talk as straight as y' shoot Aa'd like you a whole lot better," the big man said bluntly.

Tom wiped his mouth with the back of his hand. "You got your style and Aa got mine. An' Aa'm too old for changin' the way Aa am!" he grinned. In a moment's regard Fletcher's dourness lifted from his face and he almost smiled.

"Now y' both understand each other, can w' get back t' work?" Jim sighed. "Aa want t' round up those cattle today not tomorrow!" Breaking away, he rode off to the left and with Tom heading off to the right Fletcher started to cover the middle ground.

As soon as they caught up with Wes and Parker who were waiting ahead, looking bored, Fletcher ordered them to join the line.

"What for?" Parker moaned. "W' can easy see which way the' went!"

"We're looking for what we don't know!" Tom replied, simply.

Parker squirted tobacco juice from his mouth. "Wha' d' you mean by that, Mister?" he challenged.

"It's necessary, Parker. Just do it," Fletcher said wearily.

A mile further on, with still no sight of any cattle, Jim whistled aloud for the others to come. By the time they gathered he was out of his saddle on one knee examining a pony's hoof prints. Walking about they found more, coming in behind the herd as they ran past. Remounting, they grouped together now to discuss the stealing of the cattle and the menace that the Indians posed.

"We've got t' see where they're holdin' them first before w' know what's best t' do," Fletcher advised.

"The main reason they'd steal cattle is t' bargain for horses and guns," Tom said.

"Aa say w' go back and tell the boss," Parker said carelessly.

"Tell him what?" Tom scowled. "That w' think some Indians stole them, but we're not sure where they are and what they're doing with them! Aa don't think he'll appreciate that."

Parker's eyes filled with resentment. "Y're only worried 'cause some of them are your cattle."

Tom glared at him. "You bet right, Parker. But Aa reckon it ain't for you t' speak out about!"

"Hey, old man, Aa got as much right as anyone t' speak up and say what the hell Aa want!" Parker fumed. "Don't get smart with me, Mister!"

Tom narrowed his eyes, staring, then deliberately and slowly gave a nod. Not knowing whether this was a sign of concession or intent, Parker hesitated, wetting his lips with the curl of his tongue.

"Aa guess in some way y' do," Tom said, slowly, his eyes still drilling him. "But Aa didn't come this far to turn tail at the first sign of danger."

"You callin' me scared?" Parker uttered, self consciously.

"Only if y' go no further."

Parker shifted in his saddle, his self esteem forced into a corner. "Aa do as he says," he exclaimed, pointing at Fletcher. "He's boss here, not you!" he jabbed, glancing across at Wes for approval. But Wes wasn't interested, his eyes focussed on Tom, impelled by his abrasiveness.

Fletcher leaned forward. "Tom and me are of the same mind. We go find them first and weigh up the situation. If w' can't do anythin' then we head back t' the outfit and get help. It makes good sense t' me." He paused, glancing at them all in affirmation. "So let's go, huh?" He wheeled his horse about and spurred him into the lead.

Tom and Jim were last to move. "I haven't seen that look in your eye for a long time, Tom," Jim said.

"No," Tom replied, "and it did me no good then either."

"Aa was kind of hopin' you'd get a chance to blow his brains out!"

"Jim," Tom said sternly, looking ahead, "In all the years Aa've known you, Aa've never seen you draw on any man and you've never seen me. Now, as Aa said before, he and Wes have killer blood in them and they're not for the likes of us to tangle with. So why don't you turn your mind away from them and remember why w' came on this drive, and why w' need to get home again!"

Jim paused, watching Tom set off. "Hey partner, if that's your best advice, Aa'm listenin'!" he hollered cheerfully and chased after him.

Riding alongside, Jim's mood changed. He turned his head. "Tom," he said earnestly. "You told me about yourself long ago. Now y' often give me good advice an' right now it's my turn. No matter how hard you try it's still there, the confidence and instinct. Parker sensed it and was nervous. Wes is wary of you. You ain't changed completely, Tom. In their company you're another man. It's in your bein' and y' can't hide it, so don't fool yourself."

Tom turned and observed him with a probing look. "Aa know how to play the game, Jim. It's you that bothers me. You could just be dumb enough to go and get yourself killed!"

Jim dismissed it with a quick laugh and protested. "Have no fear, partner, Aa promised myself that Aa'd see y' get back home and that's what I aim to do, dead or alive!"

Amused by Jim's lack of modesty, Tom shook his head, then they spurred their horses on to catch up with the others.

———

They rode southwest quickly for another hour until the sun was high then looked for shade to rest the horses as well as themselves. They found some trees near a shallow water hole and with Fletcher staying awake to keep watch the others soon dozed off, stretched out on the shadowed ground.

Fletcher sat chewing jerky meat, thinking sombrely. He knew what to expect. Near to where they were holding the cattle the Indians would be waiting for them to talk of trading. On that score there would be no surprises. To agree or not depended upon advantages. The chance of soldiers arriving in time to scare off the Indians was remote. The most likely outcome would be the exchange of horses and guns. At worst, an attempt at trickery and fighting for more than was bargained. He'd dealt with Indians before, two summers ago, when they traded five horses for eighty stray cattle. This time, however, was different. Since more than quarter of the missing bunch belonged to Jim and Tom, their interest was also at stake and this added to his cares. From the start of the trail Fletcher had been against the deal which involved them bringing their own cattle. As men, he trusted them both, but he regretted the boss's decision to gamble with the business. Gazing round towards the knuckled, sun worn hills into which they were heading, he brooded over his predicament.

After half an hour Tom woke up and offered Fletcher a chance to sleep. Fletcher delayed scratching his stubble beard. Tom lit his pipe and remained silent, waiting for Fletcher to say what was on his mind. The big man remained sitting, staring glumly ahead, occasionally brushing away flies.

"Don't know how things'll work out," Fletcher croaked.

Tom thumbed his pipe knowing what to say. "You're boss here. Parker's right. What you say goes!"

Fletcher reacted to the fact by taking a deep breath and blowing it out forcefully, letting himself relax. After a few minutes his head started to drop and Tom observed him as he dozed off to sleep, still sitting.

Ten minutes later when he woke up, Fletcher immediately roused the others. After slapping water onto their faces to freshen up, the five cowhands saddled their second horses and set off again pursuing the cattle's tracks towards the granite hills.

On new mounts they travelled fast for three miles then slowed, sensing with caution that the hostiles were near. Remaining in the open where an ambush was useless they rose steadily, with eyes and ears alert, up a rough, stony slope, reaching the top where they could view the area.

Suddenly, on another ridge, two braves appeared on horseback, allowing themselves be seen, then disappeared. The same thing happened again shortly afterwards, then once more later. Dropping down onto a wide, flat strip, the group followed tracks of cattle towards a stack of rocks, beyond which lay an entrance to a small, steep sided canyon. At a point where they could smell the cattle they pulled up. Ten Indians appeared on the sky line. The five cowboys formed a line then at Fletcher's command they swiftly circled the outcrop of rocks dominated by a single tall column and took cover. Clearly the band of renegades hadn't the strength to hold it as well as the canyon where the cattle were penned.

While Jim secured all ten horses the others took up positions with their rifles ready. Almost immediately a lone Kiowa walked his pony forward stopping mid way between the rocks and the foot of the canyon, about thirty five yards from them. Fletcher asked Jim to bring him a horse and proceeded to go out by himself to meet the messenger. Their conversation was brief and they soon parted, returning to their own. When Fletcher climbed down and tied the horse the others could tell he was aggravated.

"They want rifles and spare horses! Aa said it was too much! Then he said they would kill the cattle if we did'nt agree, but Aa told him we would need to talk it over. He said they would not wait long. Just a kid too! He couldn't have been more than sixteen years old."

No one spoke. In this situation, their demand was heavy.

They could sacrifice the horses, but without rifles they would leave themselves vulnerable.

"The' want a quick answer!" Fletcher rasped.

"Maybe with soldiers out lookin' for them they don't want to hang round any longer than need be," Jim explained. "Cow's belly, Aa say give 'em some horses but no guns!"

"Yeah," Parker said and spat out more juice.

"What about you both?" Fletcher said, turning to Wes and Tom.

"Aa don't trust them," Wes said morosely.

Tom took off his hat and brushed his wispy hair with his fingers. His eyes were hooded in thought. "If they press for guns w' can give them six shooters, but no rifles."

Fletcher scratched his whiskers. For a man whose manner was normally glum and defensive he seemed unabashed by the decision he had to make. "They're young braves. Aa say let's put them t' the test. They can have three horses, but the' get no rifles! Let's see how they respond to that, huh?"

"You crazy for a fight?" Jim grinned.

"No," the big man replied, "But we know from the soldiers that they number only twenty. What's more they won't waste ammunition shootin' cattle and then have us going after them too."

"How come you're so sure about it?" Parker demanded.

Fletcher looked at him coldly. "Because Henry Mathias put me in charge, and one thing he'd do for sure would be to call their bluff with another!"

No one argued, so Fletcher climbed back onto his horse and walked it out into the open again to wait for the indian to show alone before moving out to the centre. They covered him with their rifles. Once again their meeting was brief, ending abruptly with the indian rider swinging round and galloping away, while Fletcher returned slowly and calmly.

"What'd he say this time?" Jim asked, as he dropped down off the saddle.

"Nothing. He just stared at me and then took off like he was bitten," Fletcher explained, securing his horse, then he continued. "He'll either come out again to speak or they'll start shootin' at us for a little while to try and scare us into talking again."

"Thought you didn't want trouble?" Parker grimaced.

Fletcher smirked. "This won't be trouble, Parker. It's all part of the contest. Only they don't know we're holdin' two aces already." He inclined his head in reference to Tom and Wes standing to his right. "Them there!" he explained, "are worth four extra guns!".

"What have you got in mind?" Wes asked, curtly.

Fletcher allowed himself a tiny grin.. "If w' can get you both up there out of sight," he pointed to the tall rock pillar, "I reckon if it comes to shootin' you got the best chance of any of us, up there, to pick some off."

They looked up at the column of rock. "There's a slab at the front which'll give you cover as well. I got a good look at it riding back," Fletcher admitted.

"Think you can climb it?" Wes challenged Tom, mildly.

"I'm no hero for heights. You toss down a rope for me when you get there," Tom replied, craftily.

Wes snorted in amusement, then started to climb the rock with the rest watching carefully his every move. It required agility and nerve, so no one spoke or moved until he succeeded in hauling himself over the top. Once he managed to turn round Jim swung up a rope for him to catch and secure around a rock before Tom started to pull himself up by it, using his feet against the wall. Nearly there Wes reached down and grabbing Tom's arm dragged him over the final edge. Once their rifles had been hoisted up Tom and Wes lay flat on their backs behind the slab and without even a glimpse towards the canyon they waited restfully, their hats shielding their faces from the sun's glare.

"What range has that old rifle got?" Wes muttered, looking up at the sky.

"Four to five hundred yards," Tom replied. "But since Aa can't see that far I'd settle for anythin' under two!"

With an expression of surprise Wes turned his eyes towards him. "You kiddin' again?"

"Wish I was."

"You say y' can't climb and now y' can't see far. Why d' y tell it?" Wes complained.

"Habit, Aa guess. Anyway you'd have quickly found out Aa couldn't climb and, sooner or later, that Aa couldn't see far off," Tom replied.

"Well, if there's any long shot to be taken leave it to me," Wes said, slightly mocking.

Tom chuckled. "Will do, but you'll have to use my rifle. That Winchester of yours ain't got the legs!"

Wes huffed and said no more. In their silence they drowsed limply and sleep was threatening when a shot cracked and a bullet pinged off a rock below. They stirred at once and Wes rolled over ready to peer up when Tom grabbed his shoulder.

"Stay down. If they know we're up here they'll stay hidden. Wait for a better chance!"

Lying on their stomachs, heads down, they listened to the exchange of gunfire. Down below they heard shouts, telling each other where the enemy were positioned. Wes was content to let Tom decide for them and removed his hat as suggested in order to reduce their size of target when the moment came.

"Nice and slowly now," Tom said at last, and raising their rifles they peeked cautiously above the slab towards the rocks at the entrance to the canyon.

"Take aim," Tom said. "One–two–three!" Both fired and two braves tumbled. As Tom slipped in a second cartridge Wes fired again and smirked with success. Tom waited for another one to rise and shoot, and timed his hit perfectly seeing the body rolling down the bank side. By now the other Indians were aware of their position and sunk down ceasing their fight. Below, Fletcher gave the command to hold their fire as well. A period of silence hovered above the small valley like a bird of prey, no one moved, risking death.

Parker claimed to have definitely struck one too, making

a total of five hostiles killed or out of action. Now the odds were better Fletcher knew he could strike a better bargain. He spat on the ground.

"There's about three more hours of daylight left. Aa want us and those cattle well out of here by then," he explained. Quickly he went and climbed up onto his horse and walked it into the open with his hand raised, indicating a desire to speak alone with the messenger again. This time, however, he had to wait a while before the young Kiowa appeared and then they both moved cautiously towards each other and halted.

"Keep your aim on him Wes," Tom advised.

"I'm doing it but the big man's getting in the way. Would of thought he'd have more sense than that," Wes muttered.

They watched intently. The hostile gestured desperately with his hands showing dismay. Fletcher consoled the argument with a raised open hand then continued to emphasise his case with fingers flicking up in an obvious counting procedure. The young Kiowa answered in a less agitated manner then appeared to twist round for a moment to check on his fellow braves and made a slow overhead waive with his front arm, as if an agreement had been reached.

Covertly, it was a signal. On turning back to face Fletcher he held a pistol that had been slyly concealed behind him and as he shot into Fletcher's chest a volley of rifle fire from the canyon side caused the cowboys to duck away. Before Fletcher hit the ground, the indian had turned and was fleeing to safety when Wes pulled the trigger. "Got the vermin!" he cried in triumph as the rider toppled, then he fired another bullet into the prostrate figure. Tom spied the riderless pony as it pulled up and returned to stand beside the body, unlike Fletcher's mount which had trotted back to the rocks.

All shooting ceased again. At first no one spoke, Fletcher's murder filling them with outrage and loathing. "If only Fletcher hadn't blocked my aim he wouldn't be dead," Wes cursed.

"What happens now?" Parker shouted, impatiently.

"You quit shoutin' for a start," Jim snapped.

Parker fell silent, watching Tom climb down the rope to join them on the ground. Wes stayed above.

Tom looked only at Jim. "Keep your positions. Aa'm goin' out."

"What t' do?" Jim asked, bleakly.

"To do what Fletcher wanted. To get out o' here as soon as we can with the cattle."

"Who said you're in charge?" Parker niggled.

Tom looked at him askance. "If y' want to take my place an' talk t' them instead, go ahead!"

"They'll shoot y' down like they did him," Parker retorted.

"Got a better way out of this thing?" Tom asked.

Parker said nothing.

"Just as Aa thought," Tom commented, then looked upwards. "Wes, if Aa duck to the ground shoot whoever's there!" he called, and turning to leave walked slowly on foot out into the open. Here he made a show of courage, dropping his rifle, but not his pistol, before he walked forward, stopping about fifteen yards to the side of Fletcher's body.

It was at least a minute before an indian, likewise on foot, walked out alone and showing he was unarmed crossed the ground slowly. As he approached the riderless pony beside the dead, young Kiowa, the animal started, then ran round him back into the canyon. The indian stopped. In a loud voice Tom asked if he could speak English. The other replied he could.

"You have six dead. We have one. You give us the cattle and we give you three horses. We go and you go, and there's no more dead!" he outlined, loudly.

"We want guns!" The indian demanded.

"No guns. You cheated and killed him. Now, no guns!" "Tom insisted.

"No guns. No cattle!" the brave barked, angrily.

"If w' don't get the cattle, then you all die! Soldiers might let you surrender but not us. We'll follow y' and kill you all!"

The indian stared at this cold threat, remaining silent. Tom went on. "So far, it's one white man dead for six Indians. For two of us it'll be twelve of you! Three for eighteen! Give us the cattle and y' get three horses and no more dead!"

"Five horses!" the indian cried, glancing at Fletcher.

"Three horses!" Tom shouted. "You killed the deal when you killed our man! We take both his horses back with the body."

The indian paused, staring again at the unflinching determination in the older man's face, then raised his right

fist in front of him and beat his chest once, a sign of agreement. Tom copied him, then they both turned and walked
back to their own group.

For a short while the cowboys remained at the rocks,
keeping watch. Jim had selected remuda horses to hand over
and roped them in a line. When at last the cattle poured out
of the canyon running rapidly past, he mounted 'Star' and led
the three steeds towards the same Kiowa who approached on
horseback. Before they met, Jim let go of the horses then
rode across to be joined by Tom on 'Rock' who helped him
lift Fletcher's body over the saddle of his own spare horse.
Having tied him securely they set off after Wes and Parker
chasing after the cattle.

At pace, they guided the longhorns out of the hills onto
the flat prairie and drove until dusk thickened and darkened
the ground. Gathering the cattle near the shallow water hole
they had visited earlier, they chewed jerky meat and watched
them drink and feed on patches of grass while night closed
in. When at last they were rested enough they started off
again into the night on course with the stars until about
midnight stopping to rest again. Staying on horseback they
walked round the cattle, passing each other and speaking to
keep awake. An hour later, they set off once more, moving
steadily until dawn.

Throughout their journey, the excitement of rejoining
the outfit was dulled by the event of Fletcher's death. They
knew their welcome would be swiftly muted with regret and
grief for his loss. Despite his gruff, no nonsense manner he

was a straight, hard working assistant boss, and his loyalty to Henry Mathias and the job was immense. There were numerous stories about his strength but the most popular concerned a fight defending Jacob from a gang of four 'nigger haters'. With his fists Fletcher knocked out two then hurled another against a wall breaking the man's arm while Travis had grabbed the last one and kicked him out of the saloon door. For a man to have such a rigid sense of fair play, his death was a cruel and shameful end.

At first light they started to yelp at the steers, goading them from a walk into a gentle run for about a mile. At sun up, as the air warmed, they slowed again in sight of the main herd, arriving eventually in time for early morning camp.

Exhausted, relieved, and sorrowful, Tom explained to the gathering how they found the cattle and what had happened. Bitterness and sadness silenced the men as they breakfasted and afterwards Fletcher's blanket covered body was buried with his few possessions. Henry Mathias recited a prayer then spoke briefly in praise of a friend, a man of size, large in strength and heart, concluding aptly with words he recalled from the Book of Psalms, 'For he knoweth our frame; he remembereth that we are dust.' There followed a lengthy silence, and then in a final act of respect, Elias stepped forward to the grave, paused, then walked away. One by one, the rest of the crew did the same, paying individual homage as cook had done.

Apart from Tom, Jim, Wes and Parker, who were to be given time to catch up on sleep, the rest of the hands started to saddle up preparing to begin the morning's drive. It was at this time that Tom was summoned to see the trail boss and had to drag himself over to where Henry Mathias was talking to Travis.

"Won't keep y' long, Tom, but me and Travis just want to talk over what happened. We lost a good man."

"Aa know it," Tom sighed, "but it happened as Aa said and we could do nothin' about it. It was a cowardly trick but we were in no position t' do more than we did."

"And afterwards, you took the decisions, Tom?" Mathias continued.

Wearily, Tom removed his hat and put his hand through his hair. "Did what Aa felt he would have done."

"But you took charge?"

"No. I asked only myself to do somethin'."

"Don't jig me with words, Tom," Mathias rapped. "You took action and thereby assumed control!"

"Aa gave no orders," Tom repeated, quietly.

"God in heaven, you did fine! And when Aa asked Travis here to take over Fletcher's position, he said it should be you, not him."

Tom frowned at Travis "Thought you was a friend," he quipped.

"Sure, Tom, but y' know cattle and y' know men better than any of us hired cowboys," Travis explained. "The men would want you!"

Tom paused. "Aa'm not a hired man. They'd resent it."

"The arrangement was y' did everythin' a hired man would do, remember?" Mathias stated.

"Sure, Mr Mathias but there's a slant on it which makes a difference. Aa've got ownership! And no matter how friendly or hard workin' Aa might seem to be it don't make me one of them. Whoever takes the job has t' be that - one of them."

"You got ownership, Tom," admitted Travis, "but y' also got trust and that's all that counts!"

Tom smiled. "That's a compliment I'm pleased to return to both you men. However, Aa'm tied still not to take the job. One, for the reason Aa've said and secondly, because of Jim Houseman. As well as my friend he's my partner and my equal in this business, and I have no intention, now or ever, of standin' in front of him or above." He paused, rubbing his tired eyes. "I thank you both for your respect and your faith in me, but the answer has t' be no. Now Aa'm dead beat and need sleep, so if you please excuse me Aa'd like t' go now!"

Henry Mathias nodded. "Sure, Tom, you deserve it. Thanks for your time and your candour." Mathias extended his right hand which Tom shook, before striding back to the wagon where Jim, Wes and Parker were comfortably lying in its shadow, already asleep.

After the delay it was hard to fall back into the old routine and yet the herd as well as the cowboys were ready for motion. The trail was starting its fifth week with nearly four hundred miles behind them and not much more than another three to go. The loss of two experienced men, Selby and Fletcher, caused additional work for everyone, but it was shared out evenly and with the promise of an extra bonus payment at the end of the trail nobody complained. Toughened by work, dust and sun they doggedly continued their journey north wending slightly to the east across remote, withering plains, taking two days to reach the Washita river, another three to get to the Canadian, then four more to reach the Cimarron. In low waters the crossings presented no difficulty and cattle, horses and men, quenched their thirsts and cooled off at leisure – the cowboys washing clothes and bathing their bodies as happily as small boys.

Stepping from the shallows up onto the bank of the Cimarron, Jim wiped his face clean with his wet bandana then tied it round his forearm where a steer's horn had grazed the skin earlier in the day. On 'Sugar' he circled round the remuda to reach the chuck wagon where Elias had made fresh coffee. As he arrived he saw Wes leaving the fireside to go and stand with Reuben near the horses. It was a deliberate move. The previous evening Wes had angrily cursed Scott for picking up the wrong plate and in a fit of temper had pushed him away. Incensed by this treatment, Scott, who was normally self restrained, had opposed him and they had grappled briefly before being pulled apart by several men, one of them being Jim, whose iron grip Wes had struggled against with fierce resentment. After the trail boss had quietened everyone down and tried to resolve the matter verbally, Jim was the only one to speak out against Hardin's ill-nature. Afterwards, Henry Mathias took young Wes aside and gave him a final warning about his violence, threatening next time to dismiss him from the outfit. Since then, of course, the animosity between Jim and Hardin had visibly sharpened and neither was inclined to provoke it, thus avoiding each other's company.

After he had filled Jim's mug, Elias indicated that he wanted to talk with him alone and they ambled off to the other end of the wagon. Leaning against it, Elias opened the conversation with an unusual question.

"If one of your boys grew up to be a thief would you disown him or stick by him, hopin' he'd turn into a decent, honest man?"

"Of course Aa would. A son's always a son! I'd see him change. But why are you askin' when it won't happen that way with my kids!" Jim assured him.

"You sure about that?" Elias challenged, twisting his face.

"Sure Aa'm sure about it. It ain't in them!"

"But y' can't be certain they're gonna stay right for always?"

Jim frowned suspiciously at the older, white whiskered man. "Cow's teeth, people get driven t' all kinds of things, even suicide; but my kids are honest now and Aa reckon they're likely to stay the same!"

"Y' can count on it, maybe, but y' can't swear to it," Elias noted, chin raised with one eye half closed, as was his habit.

"Reckon not, but if the' get into trouble they're still mine and Aa'm gonna see Aa help them through!"

"Aa know it, Jim. Both you and Tom have high ideals for your offspring. Perhaps y' both learned from your past mistakes!" he added, wryly.

Jim smiled. "What are you gettin' at, old friend?"

Elias stared ahead. "What's your opinion of Wes Hardin?"

"Need y' ask?" Jim exclaimed, bemused by the question.

"Tell me."

"He's a son of a bitch!"

"That all?"

"He's bad, Elias. In fact, wicked is a better word for it! Some say he's already a killer."

"D' y' hate him?"

"Maybe Aa do."

"If he was your son would y' hate him?"

"Sure in hell wouldn't be proud of him. When he gets riled he goes crazy. You've seen him."

"But, would y' stick with him, hopin' he'd become a better man?"

Jim admired the way Elias had shaped his argument. He allowed himself another smile. "Guess if he was of my blood Aa'd have to."

"Well," Elias sighed, "his bitch of a mother was a younger sister of mine! So now y' understand why w' put up with him."

Jim stared at the other, speechless.

"He needed work and Mr Mathias gave him the chance," Elias explained.

"Aa'm sorry Aa said that about his mother, Elias. Who else knows you're related?"

"Only the boss. Fletcher did too."

"And you're tellin' me now 'cause y' don't want me t' stir any trouble between us? Is that it?"

"As a favour," Elias added.

"Is he hidin' from the law?" Jim enquired.

Elias shrugged.

"Okay," Jim replied, "Aa won't even notice him. It's the way Tom wants it to be too!"

"Tom's been good for him," Elias admitted.

"He's careful."

"You mean he cares?"

"No. If he needed to do it he'd kill Wes without a second thought. Only Wes don't know it 'cause Tom keeps him guessin' all the time!"

Elias pinched his mouth before speaking again. "Was he Tom Tileman from San Austin?"

Jim narrowed his eyes. "All Aa'm saying, Elias, is that he's as fast as Tom Tilemen ever was!"

Jim was on the point of turning away when Elias gripped him on the shoulder. "Aa trust you, Jim!" he added.

"You bet," Jim replied with a gleam. "Probably more than you do some of your own kin!"

Elias attempted a chuckle but his heart was not in it, and it faded as Jim walked away.

Continuing through Indian Territory the cowboys stayed alert, eyes ever watchful with the Remington breech loading rifles kept at the ready. However, since the encounter with the Kiowas beyond the North Fork of Red River, only a Cheyenne hunting party was spotted following them for a few miles towards the Washita River before turning round to go back. Apart from this sighting they saw no other humans but themselves, day after day for almost two weeks, on the dry, blighted, rolling plains under a desolate expanse of burning, cloudless sky.

And then it happened.

Two trail driving days from the border into Kansas, Tom and Mex were out hunting for food when they heard shots. Curious, they went to investigate and spotted three hunters firing at a group of about eighty buffalo further ahead. To avoid disturbing them at their work, they watched from a distance as two of the hunters, standing on the ground with their rifles propped in rests were taking aim at about three to four hundred yards from the animals. Instead of running away from the danger, the buffalo seemed bewildered by what was happening and simply gathered round those that fell, sniffing and mingling together, making them easy targets for the guns.

Finally, when less than a third of them were left, the herd suddenly panicked and raced off out of range, allowing Tom and Mex to hail their presence and approach the men

openly, declaring no threat. After a formal exchange of introductions, Tom and Mex learned that these buffalo runners,
as they liked to call themselves, were from Barbour county,
Kansas, and on their way home with their wagon load of
hides when they happily came across this small herd to add
to their pile.

Climbing down from their horses, Tom and Mex took a
drink of water from their canteens and showed a willingness
to talk for a little while.

The oldest of the three, named Jessie, a dark bearded
man with broad shoulders and bright brown eyes, told them
how the early drought was scaring farmers everywhere and
how the buffalo herds were starting to drift east towards the
lower, more fertile plains, where grass was thicker. Another
of the men, a smaller, cheerful fellow called Clem, was glad
to allow Tom to examine his powerful Springfield Allin rifle,
which he claimed could kill up to six hundred yards. The
third man, tall and fragile looking, carried a red birth mark
on one cheek partly hidden by a trim, brown beard. A step
back from the other two he let them do the initial talking, yet
his eyes switched from speaker to speaker with near scrutiny.
When at last he entered the conversation both Tom and Mex
were surprised by his moderate accent and educated tone.

"I presume you're destination is Abilene?"

"Sure thing," Mex replied.

"I trust you're aware of Marshal Hickok's appointment
there to replace poor Tom Smith."

"The one they call 'Wild Bill'?" Mex exclaimed.

"The very same. Hired by the Mayor himself, April 15th, to put an end to the lawlessness which has given the town such a bad name over the last year." He smiled. "You better warn your Texan friends about him before they get there. Apparently, he stands no nonsense!"

Tom grinned at the speaker. "That sounds like newspaper talk t' me, Mister."

He regarded Tom with raised eyebrows. "A wise man, indeed. I'm working temporarily through the Abilene Chronicle for a Philadelphia newspaper. My friends here allowed me to join them on their hunt so I can write an authentic account of what this hide business is all about."

"W' came down here specially to find a white herd," Jessie intervened, "but w' had no luck."

"A white herd?" Mex exclaimed.

"That's what w' heard rumoured," Clem shrugged. "But w' never saw any. Still, w' done fine, fillin' the wagon wi' hides".

"See any hostiles?" Tom asked.

"No sir," Clem answered. "We've only been down this far two days and smelled nothing of them."

Carlton Brewster, the newspaper man, enquired about the size of the cattle drive and the route they had taken. Tom suggested he aught to work along with cowhands on a trail someday to get to know what was involved in their labours. The fact that he didn't seem to mind getting his hands dirty, Tom pointed out, was the right way to be acquainted with ordinary men's work.

Brewster gave a thoughtful smile and Tom turned away

from it to speak to Jessie. "Guess this talking is stoppin' the work. Now Aa know you want those hides but the's a lot of meat going t' get wasted. So how about Mex and me helpin' y' skin some in exchange for some best Buffalo steaks?"

Jessie glanced at Clem, then grinned. "Aa was going t' let you boys have it for nothin' else than the privilege of talkin' wi' yous!" Then he turned up his hands and shrugged, displaying regret. "But since y' made the offer we're sure glad t' accept!"

Mex laughed, "Tom's heart is as big as his mouth!"

"You're darn right, Mex. When I want best steak Aa don't mess around biddin' for it!"

The rest chuckled. "I see you have a strong sense of humour, Tom," Brewster remarked, stroking his short beard.

Tom gave him a blunt look. "Mr Brewster, if you and me are gonna get along, you're gonna have t' stop pattin' me on the shoulder. Right?"

The tall man hesitated to reply. "I meant to compliment you, Tom, not flatter you!"

Tom's stare softened. "Maybe, but don't forget Aa'm just a cowhand. Nothin' more, nothin' less!"

Amiably, Brewster nodded. "If you say so."

Climbing onto their horses the five of them set to work. Clem rode away with Brewster to collect the mules carrying supplies as well as pulling the wagon of hides, while Tom and Mex went with Jessie to start the skinning. It was messy, fly ridden, smelly work, hacking and cutting along the legs and belly, then using a mule to tug off the hide leaving a

79

white, torn, naked carcass on the ground. With the extra help it took less than an hour to complete the lot, ready for pegging out to dry.

Cleaning his knife in the soil Jessie looked up and beamed. "You done us a big favour helpin' out. Aa guess y' can chose your own meat now, huh? Take some tongues too!"

"Will do," Tom replied. "Cook'll boil them up tonight."

"Nothin' tastes better," Clem assured him.

Taking their spare horse with them, Tom and Mex went to cut meat from a dead buffalo, while the other three started to stretch out the new hides to dry in the sun. Before Tom and Mex had loaded their supply, Clinton Brewster walked over to them.

"Mind if I have a word with both you gentlemen?" he opened.

"Why not?" Mex replied, standing up, while Tom remained on one knee, looking up.

"What chance have I of joining your outfit for the last stage of the trail? We're on our way home from here so Jessie and Clem won't mind."

"Y' want t' write about us too?" Mex asked, brightly.

"Not for certain, but let's say I'm interested," Brewster responded.

"We can't say yes or no, senior. It's up to our trail boss t' decide!" Mex replied.

"I appreciate that, but it's only for a short period. He may find some use for me too?" Brewster smiled.

Tom thought of the loss of Selby and Fletcher. An extra

rider would benefit everyone in a small way. And on a good horse, what he didn't know wouldn't matter. "Aa reckon w' can all but try, Mex," he suggested.

"Sure," Mex said smiling. "You can ride back with us, mister. If boss is happy for y' t' stay, then you stay. If not, you come back an' find your friends. Easy as that!"

Brewster was pleased. "Thanks for your support. I'll get my things together so that I'll be ready to join you soon."

When the newspaper man had gone and was out of listening range, Mex looked at Tom with a wrinkle between his eyes. "Y' think he fit in, Tom?" Mex asked.

Tom smacked at flies buzzing his head. "Why not? W' can do with a new face t' look at now and again. We're gettin' tired of work and tired of each other, so someone new and different around, to look at and talk to, might be just what the outfit needs."

Mex inclined his head, questioning Tom. "Ah, but, Mr Mathias, will he see it same?"

"Those are his very words, Mex. True as my wooden leg!" Tom replied, his eyes shining with honest humour.

Mex chuckled, showing his white teeth and then started to sack up a slab of hind meat.

A little later they gathered round to say farewell and Brewster shook hands with Clem and Jessie, arranging to meet up with them at a later date. Then he mounted his horse and rode off with Tom and Mex back to the herd, about six miles away.

As it turned out Henry Mathias had no objection to the educated newcomer joining up with them, and talked with him alone, explaining the system. Meanwhile, Tom and Mex were given a bite to eat by cook who was happy with their provision, then they joined the other cowboys at rest, telling them about the newspaper man who wanted, as Tom joked, to make them famous.

The afternoon dragged with heat and when the cattle were started they plodded forward at a slow, walking pace, heads down in solemn procession. Riding flank, Tom sat hunched in the saddle, his shirt damp with sweat and his senses barely alive to anything other than the perpetual sway of his brown, long legged horse, 'Locust'. Only when Wes rode up alongside did he surface from his sluggishness.

At first neither spoke a word, and sensing the other's irritability, Tom grew more determined to make him speak first. Eventually, Wes turned his head and his stare was dagger sharp. "Why'd you and the 'greaser' go and invite a reporter to join the trail?" he cursed.

Normally, Tom would have dealt with it lightly, but here and now he resented the accusation. "How long is it, Wes, that newspaper men bothered you?" he demanded, curtly.

"Aa don't like 'em. The' stick their noses int' people's business and cause trouble!" Wes retorted.

"Y' got something to hide, Wes?" Tom figured.

Wes glared. "Maybe Aa have!"

"And so has everyone else, sometime, someplace!" Tom replied, smartly.

For a moment, unflinching, they locked into each other's stare, remaining silent.

"All he wants t' know is the trail routine and how it's organised," Tom reassured him. "He's got t' do the work as well, so he'll have no energy left t' pry into personal matters. An' knowin' what the boss is like, he'll have already warned Brewster not t' turn over any stones."

Wes stayed morose. "Still don't like the idea," he argued.

"Then best keep it t' yourself," Tom advised, strongly.

Unhappy with Tom's rebuke, Wes glowered. "Thought you was a friend?" he said scornfully.

Tom paused, deliberately, straightening his hat with his eyes still fixed, unblinking, on the younger man. "Aa am, Wes," he said carefully. "And with Mex too!"

Wes felt the weight of Tom's remark. "Well, Aa don't like 'greasers'," he sneered. "Knife y' in the back if the' got the chance!" he ended, adamantly, with a spit to the ground.

"A lot of Texans are of the same opinion," Tom countered. "But by the time y' reach my age, Wes, you'll want t' make up your own mind about them, as individuals! Any of the boys will tell y' Mex is a top hand, an' you know it!" he declared.

Wes said nothing but his look was unforgiving. He was about to turn away when another rider approached in a hurry. It was Jacob. "Message from the boss," he shouted, pulling up to stop. "He wants us to get the beeves movin' quicker. Travis says there's good grazin' ahead about four miles on towards the Kansas border. At this pace it'll be dark 'fore w' reach there." Slapping his horse with his reins he rode past them both moving down the line to inform the other riders.

With a final, sour glance, Wes swung his horse round and galloped off to take his place. Alone again, Tom found himself thinking over what he'd said and felt more than a pinch of discontent.

With a big effort, whistling and shouting and waving of arms, the riders raised the speed of the herd. Two hours later they assembled them to graze near a creek fork where water surfaced only in small pools. For late May the drought situation was becoming dire; the ground severely cracked and plant life crusting under the heat's constant assault.

As hoped, Brewster's inclusion to the outfit proved as refreshing as a shower of rain. His voice was new and different and he used fancy words. When he spoke, ears turned in his direction. He answered questions patiently with detail and his own enquiries were pleasantly simple. Most of all he was pleased to take advice from anyone and accepted any joking at his expense with mild amusement. "You don't have to be a horseman to see I'm not one," he admitted to young Reuben. "I can ride but it's not natural, or indeed very comfortable!"

Tom waited with interest to see how he coped with Wes, if and when there was any contact. But Brewster was a man of instinct and tact and responded only to those he sensed secure with him. The likes of Wes and Parker, and to a lesser degree, Red and Scott, for reasons of their own, remained on the fringe of his audience, so he made no direct effort to include them, happy to be friendly with those wishing it, gleaning facts from them about trail driving, men's skills and duties, and their experiences on other trails. Two or three times a day, he scribbled a record of events and his impressions into a pocket notebook, but he did this discreetly, to avoid estrangement, knowing most of the men were illiterate. Later, if he desired, he would be able to use these notes to compose a lengthy newspaper article, as well as use them to write a fuller account, which, with others, he hoped to publish in a future collection: During long, tedious hours sitting in the saddle, his thoughts filtered into words.

'Joined the outfit on Wednesday May 22nd, 1871, just north of the Cimmaron River. Reception was friendly, although a small number of men, suspicious of my motives, kept their distance and were reluctant to speak with me. The trail boss, Henry Mathias, a confederate colonel during the war, was a just, imposing leader who wisely instructed me about daily work and of their untried route, reckoning on another three weeks to reach Abilene, Kansas.

During further conversations I learned of Tom and Jim Houseman's deal escorting their own cattle. In Tom's case this did not surprise me for I saw him as a shrewd, experienced, individual with a clever, versatile mind. It was obvious too that Henry Mathias held him in high regard. It also said a lot for Mathias that some of the outfit had served under him during the war and were still content for him to be their leader, years after.

Before my first full day was over I learned one absolute truth. For the most part, trailing cattle was dull, wearisome work, and for the scant wages the men earned it was monotonous, and sometimes dangerous labour. Now and again when a steer or two broke loose and they needed to be chased back into line, a horse and rider came alive. Otherwise it was nothing more than a long, slow, hot, daily slog. To sustain this work for two months required stamina, and a gritty, stubborn disposition. Over the next eighteen days, I learned to appreciate this bunch of Texan drovers and saw for myself the best and worst of their nature.

An older, grizzled man named Elias was our cook. In his own way, despite illiteracy, he was a character with innate intelligence. As a cook he was as good as any, so I was told, but as a story teller and people's philosopher he could not have been bettered.

"Mr Brewster," he said to me shortly after being introduced, "Aa got a feelin' you're an honest man. Is that true?"

"I believe so," I replied, slightly abashed by his statement.

"Good," he said, "because only a honest man can tell a decent lie!"

"What do mean by that, sir?" I asked, puzzled.

He twisted his face so that I couldn't tell if he was serious or scornful. "A decent lie is one that's better than the truth.

Like tellin' a mother she has a fine baby, when it's no better lookin' than a bug!"

I heard Tom chuckle behind me and I was amused. Elias stared. "Hey Mister, Aa'm being serious!" he declared vehemently. "When you write about us Aa'd like t' think you'll have a heart too!"

My face straightened. "No offence. What you said is valuable. I won't forget it."

"Right then, drink your coffee and get t' work. This idle talk ain't gonna patch my britches!" He stalked off and I turned to Tom who was waiting for the wrangler boy, Reuben, to bring him a fresh horse. I smiled.

"He's an extraordinary fellow," I said.

"No. He's just ordinary, like everyone else! Treat him otherwise and he'll turn nasty!" Tom joked.

Tom's new mount was a tan coloured gelding named 'Munch'. I liked the name. He advised me before trotting away, that Elias enjoyed nothing more than men gladly eating his food and any who didn't got persecuted by the sharpness of his tongue!"

Talk of this kind; acted, witty, instructive, open, inspired me to listen whenever I could, and since, each day, I was able to choose who to partner I tended to ride the line with either Tom, Jim, Jacob or Mex, and when invited, with Travis and Mr Mathias scouting ahead. A mile or so in front of the herd, they searched the way, looking out for good grazing and water and suitable campsites, yet always beware of any hazards likely to disrupt their progress. In fact, it was only on my third day, late afternoon, when out in front with them for the first time, that I encountered a shocking tragedy that would haunt me for the rest of my life.

Towards the ending of the day it was customary to look out for birds flying in a particular direction. A sure sign of water. Looking across the sky, Travis, assistant trail boss, spotted buzzards circling a mile to the west, and he and I were requested by Mr Mathias to investigate. Before we even arrived, a sense of dread stiffened our spines and as we turned into a dried out gulch we witnessed a spectacle that almost caused me to retch. Beside each other on their blankets, lay the mutilated bodies of my former companions, Clem and Jessie. As well as their bodies being hacked and sliced open they had also been scalped. The mules, horses, rifles and wagon load of hides were all missing. Aghast and overwhelmed by the horror of it, I stared with wrecked emotion at the terrible scene while Travis approached slowly on horseback before climbing down.

"Are these the two men y' rode with?" he called.

I nodded my head. Travis stared at me for a moment then kneeled down by Jessie's body, feeling his hand. "Killed this morning, or possibly at night while asleep!" He looked around. "Their pistols and boots have gone too," he added, then he stood up and began to wander about inspecting the ground, searching for evidence.

"Must have been Indians," I mumbled, still dazed with horror.

"Only Indians would do it this way, but Aa can only see boot prints round about. Could've been bushwhackers!"

"Might they not just be Clem's and Jessie's own footmarks?"

"You can see their boots have been taken, but Aa wouldn't rule out a trick t' put the blame on hostiles," he replied. "How many mules and horses did the' have?" he shouted, prowling further away.

"Three mules and four horses."

Only now was I able to walk my horse closer to the bodies. At a glance I could tell their throats had been cut. Dizzily, I climbed down and waited until Travis came back. "Can we bury them?" I asked, feebly.

"With bare hands?" Travis muttered, vacantly, preoccupied still with clues to the crime.

"We can't leave them like this!" I protested.

He looked down, sighing. "Nope, we can't. You're right." He went towards a starched, withered branch and stamped to break it. Selecting two sharp sticks he returned to give me one of them. "We'll scrape a bit hole the best w' can," he said.

Working hard until our hands were bruised we managed to carve out a shell into the hard ground into which we dragged both men. After piling loose earth over them we covered the heaps with stones. Tying both wood scrapers at an angle, Travis erected a tilted cross at the head of the pile. Now, without thinking sensibly, I was eager to turn away but not Travis who stood silently for prayer, head bowed with hands clenched. At once I returned to his side and did the same. Travis took it upon himself to recite the usual words then added thanks that I, myself, should be saved. Until that moment, gagged by shock and grief, I had not considered it. For a few moments more we stood in silence, and in the circumstance of their death, I shuddered to comprehend my own deliverance and the miracle of it.'

'On the way back we met the trail boss and Wes Hardin heading in our direction to find out what had delayed us. Travis told the news.

"Guess you should ride back and tell the men t' be on the lookout," the trail boss told us. "I'm sorry about your friends Mr Brewster," he said in earnest.

I acknowledged him with a nod then glanced at Hardin who was peering sideways at me. Maintaining a cold expression, he regarded my person callously. Having been warned of his quick temper, I was satisfied to disregard him, but discerned quickly that for one so young he carried vexation in an older looking face. Then I turned again to Mr Mathias.

"I thank you, sir, for your concern. Although I only knew them for a short time both of them were decent, honest men."

On reflection, I might have said a thousand other things, but didn't and maybe it was enough. I was still convinced it was an indian crime. By venturing into their territory there was always a risk, knowing how important buffalo were to the tribes. But their horrible death and my own lucky escape, would stay with me forever, along with the memory of Tom Torrance, who was in the first instance responsible for my transfer to the cattle drive. But then, of course, there proved in time much more to remember Tom by than this fact alone.'

———

'Alerted to possible danger, night watch was doubled, which meant everyone having to do a turn. The following day, more than anyone else, I could hardly keep my eyes open and only the fear of falling out of the saddle kept me awake. However, after a meal at noon camp, there was an opportunity to lie down to rest and with my hat over my face shielding off the sun I promptly slept for about two hours. Even still, the rest of the day's ride was a burden and there was no energy in most of us that evening for camp fire talk, content just to listen to Mex, on his harmonica, play the wistful tunes of border romance.

Before sleep I managed to scribble a further account of our work with the following lines; - The slowness of the drive is necessary to keep the steers in healthy condition. To avoid the main heat of the sun the day starts for the cowhands at the tinge of dawn and the herd is beginning to line out before half light on a steady crawl of seven or eight miles.

After a long mid day rest period we travel again, covering another few miles towards sundown."

Unknown to me, Tom had observed me working and was pressed to advise me. "Mr Brewster, Aa think it might be right for me t' talk to the men and offer your skills in writin' letters home for them. You see, it would be a courtesy y' would be admired for, an' it would excuse your own secret indulgence!" he implied with a sparkle.

I pondered his suggestion, hesitating before a smile. "You have my permission, sir!" I announced genially.'

'It was, naturally, with some relief and pleasure that the drive approached the Kansas border near where the Medicine Lodge River runs along it. At this point our hopes were lifted and expectations were focussed towards the final stage of the trail, roughly a hundred and forty miles, less than two week's ride.

Almost visibly, spirits were raised and an air of pride straightened backs in the saddle. Although I had not experienced what the rest had endured from the beginning, I sensed the anticipation in them; the thrill of money to spend, heated water and a proper wash and shave, new clothes, drink, and indeed, the company of women, a soft bed, and most of all the prospect of work completed and the well earned pleasure of idleness and rest. The very thought of it reduced scowls of irritation, and a sort of smugness crept into grins and laughter.

Mr Mathias, himself, observed it. "They can sniff the edge and get ready to jump. Aa've seen drovers spend everythin' they've earned inside a week!" he admitted.

"If y' paid them more it would take longer!" Tom teased.

The trail boss squinted at him uncertainly, then huffed. "We pay better than most. Up to fifty dollars more," he claimed.

"Aa know it," Tom said. "That's why they shouldn't get paid in cash but in investment, like me and Jim. What we earn goes back into raisin' more cattle. We can't afford t' go spend-crazy!"

I chuckled at his notion. "So you believe in responsibility as a moral solution!"

"Sure do, Mister. Moral, more moral and most moral! Call it what you want!" His eyes were bright with the thought of debate.

Everyone there laughed, Mr Mathias, Travis, Jacob, Jim and myself, all knowing exactly what Tom meant. A sound idea didn't need complicated words to prop it up.

"If Aa hired on that basis there'd be no takers," Mathias continued. "It may seem good sense, but can you imagine someone like Red hearin' me tell him he don't get his wages until he gets back to Texas, 'cause I don't want him t' spend it all at once?"

"Cow's teeth, he'd spend it all at once in Texas, anyhow!" Jim cried.

"Sure would," Jacob said. "He'd be a fool with money t' gamble any place he got it!"

"Okay," Tom admitted, "but in a way it would still be investment. For us anyhow! Kansas money spent in Texas is gonna benefit all back home. He buys a new hat, the shop-keeper has money t' spend so he goes and buys a big steak. The eating house needs more steaks and Aa've got cattle to sell!" He shrugged, glancing earnestly at us all, before grinning. "When it comes to it, Aa guess Aa'm just as selfish as the rest of you!"

In my travel notes, I described Tom's knack with words in the following way. "The man was humorous and made others laugh. But he kept them guessing. The crew always listened to him closely. Like a lawyer, he picked on words, turned them over, twisted them round and shaped them anew. And when he was silent, he listened and weighed up what to say, and was often happy just to say nothing. The rumour existed that he had once been a known gunman called Tom Tileman from the San Angelo region fascinated me. I'd heard Tom was still an excellent rifle marksman and saw it briefly when out hunting with him. As to his illustrious past, I have no doubt about it, for there was enough boldness and sense about him to be good at whatever he tried. But whenever he was asked if it were true, that he was that shooter, Tom merely frowned at the question as if it were ridiculous and chuckled lightly, shaking his head in dismay.'

'Anyhow, the herd was about to cross into Kansas and everyone was pleased about it and our tails were up when a bunch of riders, claiming to be 'protectionists', caught and roughed up Travis and Mex who were scouting ahead, demanding money for the cattle's safe passage into Kansas.

When the two men returned to report the incident and the threat they'd made, Henry Mathias scowled angrily, and saddled up. With Tom, Wes, Jacob, Stilt and myself accompanying him, we set off at once to talk business with the gang who were waiting, as arranged, for the trail boss to reply.

We met them at Medicine Lodge river; the water running between us. There was five of them on horseback, each well armed and desperate, mean looking characters. Both groups stared across at each other in silence until one of the other riders spoke first.

"Boys and me reckon you've got over two thousand head back there!" he yelled in a single sweep. "Four hundred dollars ain't much to ask for their protection, is it?"

Concentrating on him, it was at an instant, that I noticed the white patch on his horse's chest and knew at once it was Clem's horse. Loathing and anger boiled up into my throat but I restrained my disgust, staying quiet. Mathias stared across the river, his austere look steeled with resolve. "We don't need anybody's help t' look after them!" he boomed.

Their leader gave a high pitched chuckle. "Hey Reb, this ain't up for argument. You either hand over money or we start shooting tonight and your steers will run all the way back to Texas!"

Mathias turned to speak quietly to Tom. "If you've got anythin' to say, shout out."

"Mm. They're not bluffin', boss. Keep it straight with them now and it'll give ourselves time t' think it over," Tom replied quietly.

Mr Mathias sat upright in his saddle. "We want t' bring the herd up to the riverside for the night. Before we begin the crossin' tomorrow I'll send the money over."

"Told you w' want payment tonight!" the leader wailed, then the pitch of his voice lowered in threat. "You get it here before sundown or we stampede them!"

Mr Mathias snorted. "Hear that, boys," he cried aloud, half turning towards us. "He gets the money before it gets dark, so we fret all night hopin' he sticks t' his word. Aa ask you, men, what kind of deal is that?" Facing the rabble again, he stood up in the saddle and leaned forward to make his point forcefully. "My way, it's a safe bet we'll all be here in the mornin'. Us and you!"

On the other side they talked briefly among themselves before the leader replied. "Okay Reb, but remember we've got others with us back there who may not like it. Not unless we just make it five hundred for the delay! Yeah, five hundred!" he chortled, "or we damn well scatter you tonight!"

After a long severe pause Mr Mathias reluctantly agreed to it. "The morning, it is!" he railed, then he swung his horse round and we rode off hurriedly behind him, back to camp, not a word said.

Arriving at the wagon we dropped down out of the saddle

leaving Reuben with our horses and walked over to where the others were waiting. Standing gravely before everyone, Henry Mathias broke the news, recounting almost exactly what had been said.

"How many of them?" Elias demanded.

"Five at the river, but they claim there's more behind them."

"They're just a bunch of lyin' thieves!" Jim cursed. "Cow's belly, let's not give way t' them!"

"They're not just thieves!" I interrupted, deciding the time was right for the truth. All eyes turned towards me. "I saw Clem's horse. Their leader was sitting on him. They must have murdered the buffalo hunters!"

I felt the force of every stare. "Are y' certain about it, Mr Brewster?" the trail boss demanded. I nodded, then Mr Mathias turned towards Travis. "How many riders did you reckon at the killing?"

"No more than five or six," he answered.

The trail boss squeezed his nose in thought, then his hand fell. "Maybe, just maybe, they don't have any more men behind them. I half suspected it bein' no more than a ruse!"

"Why don't w' go for them right now?" Stilt blurted, his blood faster than his brain.

"They ain't dumb," Mathias replied. "We've got t' watch the herd and any shooting's going to send them wild. Anyhow, Aa've already lost two men on the drive, God rest their souls!" Mathias said grimly, then he looked away, beyond his men. "Our first job is t' get the cattle up t' the river

97

to quench their thirst. At the moment that's all we'll aim for. When that's done, we can talk it over amongst ourselves and decide if there's anyway out of this hole. Right?"

There was a mumbled response, then we set to work. Of course, all we did was go through the motions, particularly myself, with my mind continuing to glare at the sighting of the central figure on the other side of the river sitting on Clem's horse, and his blatant, sneering tone of voice. Naturally, dominating my feelings was an overwhelming revulsion and desire for justice. Like the rest of the crew, I was also against paying a ransom to cross over the river. It was sheer blackmail and to pay up was no more than an act of submission. But then it was not as simple as that. Like Jim and Stilt, my instinct for revenge or rebellion was passionate, but without a scheme to support it, any move was unlikely to succeed.

What happened that memorable night, I was later able to describe vividly from information gathered from our own men's versions of events. In all honesty, I can state that this account is as authentic as you can get; bare, straight forward and exact, untarnished by the gloss of time from which most stories are moulded.'

———————

'With riders posted along the middle of the shallow river to prevent cattle crossing to the other bank the cowboys let them fill up before moving them about half a mile back to settle down for the night. Red, Scott and Reuben were left on guard, while the rest, unable to relax and strip off and wash themselves as they normally did at rivers, headed for camp in a foul mood. At supper round the fire, opinions mustered towards retaliation, but Elias, Tom and Jacob, were doubtful. Still, it mattered little how the crew felt or argued, for when Henry Mathias came forward his mind appeared to be made up. He stated plainly that without a sound option, the money would have to be paid. Mutterings of protest were voiced but he raised his hand and beckoned them to listen further.

"I can't ask any of you to risk your lives more than what you've done already. They're dangerous men. Killers! And if we don't agree to their terms they'll stampede the cattle. For pride's sake, it's not worth the trouble or the risk of a shoot out!"

"Maybe that's what they reckon on us thinkin'," Travis said, cutely. "But Aa still don't like the idea of bein' robbed by a bunch of lousy Jayhawkers!"

"Me, neither," Jim cried. "An' if it's so easy for them, they might just as well turn up ahead of us at the next river too, askin' for more money! I say we've got t' stop them, boss!" he appealed. Most of the cowboys murmured their support.

"They think they've got us fooled over the size of their gang, but we're pretty sure there's no more of 'em!" Travis affirmed.

"An' we've got Texans here that can shoot faster than any of them!" Parker boasted, desperate to have a say.

"An' they murdered Mr Brewster's friends," Mex added. "W' can't let them get away with this!"

"Somethin' else too," Elias drawled, aiming to stoke up their fervour a little more. He raised his stubbly chin. "If w' think payin' those rattlesnakes is going t' prevent them stampeding the cattle anyway, then we got the brains of a tick!"

At once, like sparks to tinder, his words ignited a round of angry exchanges before all eyes fell again on the trail boss.

Henry Mathias folded his arms, secure in his authority. "I feel the same as you do! But we've got the cattle to look after. Unless somebody has a real plan in mind all this spite and lust for vengeance ain't worth the risk. And, Aa mean a proper, worked out strategy, not just some wild notion that spells disaster!" He emphasised this with a pointed finger punctuating the air before him.

Daunted by his insistence, nobody offered any of the suggestions which had previously been relayed round. There was a glum silence.

He moved his hands to his belt, hooking his thumbs. "Well now," he began slowly with a sudden mood of calm. "While you yourselves were debating it , Tom and me got a chance to discuss the situation and we've a bit idea I sort of like. When Aa've got my plate of grub and sat down t' eat, Aa'd like you boys to hear it? Right."

I smiled to myself at the man's tactic, thinking how he, Mr Mathias, had come to the meeting, appearing empty handed and downhearted, and all but ready to submit to the outlaws demands. And then he goes and lets his men declare their support, encouraging a fight, while all the time he's holding a trick card hidden up his sleeve waiting for the moment to show it! It was smart alright, and it was perfect! I glanced at Tom and he gave me the tinniest glint of a knowing eye.

As soon as the trail boss returned and sat down the silent crew waited eagerly for him to speak. Like an experienced leader he held them quiet for a few moments as he finished a mouthful of cornbread then took a drink of coffee to clear his throat. "The war's been ended some five years. We all have bitter memories of it. Most of us here lost family or a close friend. But it's done with and the country's one again." He paused to take another drink. "Earlier today when I listened to that bunch of murderin' thieves the word 'Reb' was used. It's been used before, but it was the tone of it which sticks in my gullet. The tone of a man who spits on a past enemy. A man who is unforgivin' and merciless today as he likely was then. Let me tell you Aa have no intention of lettin' that scoundrel go free!" he growled.

I swiftly observed the taut faces and harsh stares surrounding him. Cleverly, the boss's words had the desired effect of determining their anger. Now, he leant slightly forward to outline what Tom and he had schemed, as if it were for their ears only, which of course it was.

"What they threaten to do is stampede the cattle. They know we dread it most; the damage it can cause, losin' steers, wastin' time, the work and danger for us. This is what they depend upon to make us submit to their demand," he said, choosing his words carefully. "This and murder are their trade! But, we ain't soft bellies like they think, and what they don't know is that we suspect there's no more than the five we saw!" He paused, sitting back again as if he'd said what was necessary and important. For him it was. "Now, Tom'll tell you the rest - the idea we came up with which Aa believe can work."

Tom, smoking his pipe, looked up, puffed a little more then removed it to speak, as prepared. This was another astute move by Mathias, maintaining the force of persuasion with a different, popular voice.

Tom stood up. "They're probably camped not far off over the river, I guess, with one of them stayin' awake t' keep watch. But there ain't much moon tonight, so it's gonna be kind o' dark for seein' what's happenin'. Later on, if we, bein' real quiet, secretly drop back most of the herd a mile or two, leavin' about two hundred here near the river, they're gonna be none the wiser. Now then," he paused to accentuate his words, "with no more than six of us behind them, walking them gently, we can ease them across the water and head slowly towards the light of their camp fire. When w' get close, we jolt the cattle into a run an' they charge straight over them, with us comin' in behind shootin' anyone still standing!" Tom paused, taking off his hat to smooth his hair. "Yeah, boys! They threaten us with a stampede, so we give them one - right at them!" He looked round the group of cowboys, his face creased with a ruthless urge. "Timin' is real important, but w' hit them fast and hard and without warnin' and not one of them gets away!"

He allowed his words to penetrate in silence before his stare relaxed. Immediately, it was clear that everyone one of us had witnessed an aspect of the man that was awe inspiring. He left us raging within and now the trail boss came in to bolster the effect. "Only thing w' need t know is who wants to go?" he demanded. Hands raised quickly, mostly everyone willing. Mr Mathias allowed himself a smile. "You're good men! Tom and me'll talk it over with Travis and Elias before saying anything more. An' if any of you want to speak up now's your chance?"

"Sure do." Heads swivelled towards Jim. "Aa'd like to volunteer t' creep out after dark and spy out how many they got there. Seems kind of foolish to be assumin' there's no more of them than we saw!"

"We already got a volunteer, Jim," Tom replied at once.

Jim stared. "Sure about that, Tom?"

Tom lowered his pipe and eyed the other squarely. "Aa'm as sure as I want t' be, Jim, and that's all that matters."

Jim knew not to make more of it and said nothing, giving only a faint nod. No one else spoke so Henry Mathias summoned Tom, Travis and Elias away, walking past the chuck wagon to talk together while the rest of us remained at the fireside sipping coffee in silent anticipation.

After about five minutes they returned and the trail boss announced their decision that Tom, Travis, Mex, Wes, Scott and Stilt would go on the raid. The remainder of us, under his orders, would lead the main herd away and hold them safely at a distance. My heart sank. I wanted to witness the action, but knew like everyone else that the decision had been made and it would be useless to object. Even still, before events unfolded, I did later in the evening convey my regret to the trail boss who dismissed my argument bluntly.

"Mr Brewster," he said, "with me y' can be of some use. With them, you'd be none what so ever! Aa'm surprised you even considered to ask?"

I wanted to respond and could have made several claims, but his analysis was correct and he had expressed his opinion candidly without insult. In matters of shooting and killing I would have just been an observer and the situation could not carry a passenger. However, despite not actually being there with them, I was able to describe in detail what happened that night across the river. I was mainly grateful to Travis and Mex for this, who, under my interrogation for facts, later recounted their tale of the night.'

'The hours seemed to drag as the sky darkened and a half moon rose in the east hardening brightly alongside a few stars. Then almost quickening, night time descended darkly over the plains and a cooler air was suddenly felt in our faces. Soon after it was whispered round that Mex had left camp to spy on the enemy and we were anxious for news as we gently spread the cattle apart in preparation of the planned withdrawal from the river side. Ready on horseback, we waited at least another hour before finally learning from him that the opposition numbered only five – as we suspected. This known, the order to make the cut was given. Of course everyone's part was important and demanding, but first thoughts were lodged with the six chosen men and the danger of their undertaking. Doubts that had never existed sprang to mind, for if they failed the whole affair would prove calamitous.

In darkness and making as little noise as we could, we riders, with Mr Mathias in charge, guided the bulk of the cattle, ambling almost at will, in a peaceful trickle away from the smaller herd, held back by Tom and the others. For the time being, the chuck wagon was to stay put with the camp fire purposefully stoked and shining, and every now and again when we, the retiring riders looked behind, its glow grew gradually dimmer into the distance. It was a warm night but the chill of apprehension tensed my shoulders making me hunch in the saddle. I guessed the others felt the same, but I knew they weren't the sort to ever admit it.

We must have travelled about two and a half miles before word was passed round to let the cattle slow to a stop with each rider moving out wide forming a huge circle. In the next ten minutes the standing cattle bedded down quietly and peacefully as if they knew of the plan and were willing members of our subterfuge. At that stage, each of us knew this was where we would remain for the rest of the night, waiting and watching and listening, in tense, nervous suspense.'

'When the main herd had left, the six riders kept their steers near the river where they remained undisturbed. Each man was given full ammunition and a Remington breech loading rifle. Even Tom left his old Sharps in the wagon! Two men at a time were allowed back to camp for coffee, where Elias let it be known later that he had slipped a little whiskey into the pot, and each pair were allowed a brief rest. About two hours after midnight, when Elias and his wagon had already crept away to join us at a safe distance, the chosen six riders began the operation, slowly budging the cattle and walking them to the river, letting them linger first before nudging them across onto the far bank. As Tom had instructed, the riders followed in a wide arc quietly fanning the cattle together behind Mex on horseback leading at the front, guiding them forward.

Although the Jayhawker's camp fire was not yet visible, Mex was able to course the route over the slightly rising ground from the river, and before it levelled out he halted and Tom and Travis circled round to join him at the front as the cattle paused, as if sensing to wait. There, Tom and Mex stepped down and leaving Travis to hold their horses, the two of them crept forward onto the rise where they could peer ahead. Despite the glimmering light of a starry night sky the land was shadowy dark. They strained their eyes seeing nothing definite until a prick of fire light arrested their gaze, certifying the direction and distance from the enemy camp.

"How far d' y' reckon?" Tom whispered.

"Three to four hundred yards. No more," Mex replied. His voice quivered. "Should we hit them now?"

Tom studied the sky. "Sure. Another hour an' they'd see us comin'," he said tonelessly.

They sneaked back to their horses and together with Travis went round to join the other three where, still mounted, they grouped around Tom, sitting on 'Rusty'. He spoke precisely. "We're ready to go, men. They're straight ahead." He pointed the line to take. "You know the plan so let's get them rollin'!" he rasped.

They swung out into line again and barged into the cattle, hissing and growling and slapping to shock the cattle and to set them off running, gathering speed into a dangerous charge, bursting in mass towards their target. At the twenty second countdown Tom fired his pistol upwards and the others, waiting for it, fired as well, directing the herd even faster over the last hundred yards into the area. It was difficult to hear anything other than the clatter of hooves and their own shots but gunfire sounded from the other side but made no difference as the stampede swept directly over the Jayhawker's camp. At this point Tom, Mex and Stilt pulled up fiercely, leaping to ground, and while Stilt grabbed their reins and ran off to the left, the other two knelt down and aimed their rifles. Meanwhile Travis, Hardin and Scott had veered out to the right to do the same. And as the cattle crashed through the site and off into the distance, they wildly opened fire with the Remingtons, sending a spray of bullets into the shadows on either side of the ember fire. Holding onto the horses both Stilt and Scott waited in reserve, pistols ready.

In the lull that followed not a single shot was fired in return. All that was heard were the groans and cries of injured men until these too fell quiet. Furthermore, with the enemy's horses scared off, there was no chance of any left alive to escape. Up to now, everything seemed to have gone to plan.

For a full five minutes there was an eerie quiet with no one moving or speaking. Then Tom hollered. "We've got y' surrounded! If any of you are alive, stand up and walk this way with your hands high in the sky."

There was no reply.

"Okay, men, do what we planned," he shouted. "When we can see better we'll move in!" Mex left his side and stole away to the left beyond Stilt and the horses. At the same time, on the other side, Wes moved away past Scott who was holding their horses. As well as securing their position and keep guard of their horses it was also intended to confuse and discourage any survivor feigning death to make an escape.

The quarter moon gleamed down magnifying the stillness of the greying blackness. They continued to wait, listening and watching, fingers on triggers, strained by unknowing.

Then suddenly, the suspension ended with a swift exchange of firing and a yell from Mex. "There's one runnin'. I got hit!"

Tom jumped up and ran to find Stilt crouching. "See anythin'?"

"Got a glimpse. He went into the bushes there!" Stilt hissed,

Tom crept forward. "Mex," he whispered.

"Here," Mex answered and Tom found him sitting, rifle in his hands. "Nicked my leg. Nothin' serious. Should've got him!" he cursed. "He went that way!" he indicated.

Tom left him and started to creep towards the dark patch of bushes. Moving silently, he kept low, pausing often to listen before stalking forward again. The coarse bushes spread over a gentle down slope ending in a shallow, face of rock, like a long wall. Here he hesitated, deciding on his strategy, then hastily climbed up it onto open flat ground where he ran lightly in a circular sweep returning secretly to the edge further along. Lying down he waited above.

A while later, with dawn light threatening, Tom was on the point of leaving his spot when he suddenly heard someone approaching beneath the bank. He froze, alert, peering down. The top of a hat appeared. Tom lowered the muzzle of his rifle until it almost touched the man's head. "Don't move!" he rasped.

"It's me! Wes!"

"What are you doin' here?" Tom demanded, gruffly.

"Travis said to help."

"You could've got shot!" Tom hissed. "See anythin'?"

"No. Figured he must have come this way."

"Probably heard you and stayed in the bushes," Tom despaired.

"Another one gave himself up," Wes whispered. "He's wounded in the shoulder."

"What about the other three?"

"Dead."

Tom paused in thought. "Is the fire still alight?"

"Pieces smouldering, that's all. Why?" Wes queried.

"Because Aa want you t' get a flame and set fire to the bushes. If he's in there we're gonna find out easy, without gettin' shot at. I'll stay this side in case he runs this way. Tell Travis. He'll set your positions!"

Wes gave a gentle snort. "You got it all worked out, Tom," he uttered with appreciation, then turned and slinked away.

Alone again Tom lay on his side, peering into the gloomy contours of the immediate area. Visibility was steadily improving with shapes and lines defining themselves. His thoughts returned to Wes saying he had it all worked out, but he knew it wasn't that simple. You guess, that was all. But if you've guessed before, some other time, it helped. And if the fire didn't bring him out you guessed he wasn't there so you got on horses and went tracking. In his early days he recalled a hunt with a posse for two robbers hiding out in hilly country. They chased them for five days, eventually cornering them in a steep canyon. To force them out the sheriff had some men climb round to roll down rocks from above. They came out faster than they went in. Now, he mused, he was playing the part of the sheriff. Only it wasn't over, yet.

Tom saw the glow and watched the fire spring into a blaze. The roar of dry, brittle branches and leaves sent a gush of sparks into the air. Flames leapt wildly from bush to bush consuming the stretch. Suddenly a figure darted out towards the bank and vaulted up. Tom took aim and fired twice. The man staggered and toppled back over. "You got him!" a voice screeched. It sounded like Travis. Tom remained kneeling for a few moments then got up and walked forward along the edge.

Shortly, in the dying glow of the burning bushes they dragged the four dead men's bodies together. The wounded one had his hands tied behind and blood soaked his shirt where a bullet had passed through the outside of his shoulder. Tight jawed, he stood in bitter silence. It was he, they learned later, who had fallen asleep on guard, failing to warn the others.

"Hard t' tell if the' were trampled t' death or shot. Maybe they got both," Mex remarked aloud, limping to his horse.

"They ain't - so tough n - now," Scott said.

"Hell, it was easy," Stilt chuckled. "Got t' hand it to y', Tom, you sure got it planned right!"

Tom wiped his mouth. "You did fine, boys, just fine."

Travis walked up to the prisoner. "Guess it makes you want t' weep," he sneered. "Want t' tell us where the rest of your band are?"

The other stared down. Travis cocked his pistol and

pointed it between the prisoner's eyes. The man raised his head. "There's no more," he mumbled.

Travis seemed to turn away when he suddenly swung his free hand, smacking the man hard across the mouth and followed up immediately by kicking his legs away from under him. With a groan the outlaw crashed painfully onto the ground and he lay there, grimacing, panting fear. Travis turned round to explain. "It was him who hit me when the' first caught Mex and me!" he boomed, angrily.

"Why don't you just kill him?" Wes suggested.

"Let Mr Mathias decide on that," Travis replied, about to mount his horse. In the saddle he looked to Tom. "Reckon w' better get after those steers?"

"Reckon so," Tom replied with satisfaction. "We don't want 'em gettin' to Abilene before us!"

Travis nodded. "Okay all, we'll leave Mex with the prisoner an' go after them. With a bit of luck we'll get back in time t' eat breakfast wi' the rest of the boys!" he crowed loudly.

In the first light of dawn, the four younger cowboys rode off rapidly with a whoop of triumph. Unhurried, Tom mounted 'Rusty', acknowledged Mex with a simple salute and then started after them at an easy, comfortable pace.'

'Meanwhile, away from the action, we, with the big herd, listened and wondered with a terrible sense of unknowing. I recorded this time in my notes giving a fair account of what it was like for us.'

- While holding back the main herd, we were able to hear distant shooting and we were desperate to learn of what was happening. The cattle were in an idle mood so we had no difficulty with them, and when later, other shots were heard and the glow of a large fire was spotted Mr Mathias decided then it was time to send reinforcement. At first he chose only Jim and Jacob, but I appealed sufficiently to be included, so by the time the three of us set off, the night sky was fading fast with the eastern horizon beginning to gleam.

Towards the riverside we met Mex on horseback walking his prisoner towards us. He told us the good news and when Jim and Jacob galloped on to help the others to gather the scattered cattle, Mex and myself made our way back to camp with the roped Jayhawker.

In a silvery light we moved slowly. Excitedly, Mex recounted dramatically what had happened and I listened intently, thrilled by their daring. I quizzed Mex about the details of the raid and managed, later, to scribble brief notes. Shuffling in front of our horses the prisoner said nothing. Here, I have to admit my sense of joy was hinged on revenge for the murder of Clem and Jessie, the buffalo hunters, and I viewed the pathetic figure before me without any sympathy. I supposed he'd be delivered to the nearest town for trial.

When we arrived at camp, they cheered us in, delighting at the news. Mr Mathias rode in last from the cattle and a look of stern pride crossed his features as he listened to

Mex's account. He allowed the prisoner's wound to be cleaned and bandaged before questioning him and the surly silence of the captive melted in his stare. The outlaw blabbered that none of it was his doing. He'd ridden with them only a few weeks. Mathias listened glumly. I stood beside him. The other four were family, the man explained. They were all on their way to work on the railroad. We knew it was all lies and left him sitting tied to a wheel of the wagon.

An hour later in the crisp rays of a low sun we started moving the main herd back to the river. The warm night and tensions of the affair left us drained and the cattle also showed little energy.

We reached the river and set up morning camp to wait for the other's return and it was nearly another two hours before they trailed in, exhausted but happy, despite losing two steers which had been badly injured falling into a gulch. However, they had claimed the dead men's horses and guns which, in value, more than compensated for the loss. The reunion revived us and once again the successful raid was retold in similar versions as a late breakfast was served up to them. Typically, more than any other Tom was philosophical about it.

"We chanced our luck and was fortunate. Caught them cold, that was all."

"Prisoner said he was on watch and fell asleep," Mr Mathias stated.

"He just made it that bit easier," Tom grinned. "Instead of

being on their feet running they were just sittin' up when the steers hit them."

"How confident were you the plan might work, Tom?" I asked, pencil at the ready.

Tom made a deliberate act of rubbing his forehead in thought. I sounded too much of the newspaper man for his liking and he was about to penalise me. "T' tell the truth, Mr Brewster, Aa figured it was fifty-fifty. Either it worked or it didn't. But my confidence leaned towards the one that was gonna succeed."

I heard a few chuckles and I smiled too. "If you'll allow me to put it another way. Did you have any doubts it might not work?" I asked, politely.

Tom narrowed his eyes at me. "Doubts, Mr Brewster! Sure, Aa didn't want any of us t' get killed. But at a time like that y' don't entertain them! We planned what t' do if it went right and we planned what t' do if it went wrong. That's called being cautious."

I smiled again and scribbled down his words.

Jim had waited his turn to speak to Tom. He aimed his question right between the eyes. "Tom," he began, wistfully, with a hint of devilment. "We all wanted to ride with you. What made y' choose the boys you did?"

Tom pinched his mouth, trying not to smile. "Mr Mathias and me put your names into a hat an' pulled out the first five. Honest, Jim, that was it!"

"You bet it wasn't!" Mr Mathias interrupted, sharply "We picked the best men for the job and that's the reality of it. If y' want t' know the truth, Jim, we didn't pick you because you're too pig headed t' realise what a great friend y' have!" He tempered his insult with a wide grin and even Jim was amused. "Now let's cut out this yakking and think ahead. Apart from two dead cattle and Mex bein' nicked in the leg we've come out of it fine. We've got a prisoner t' deal with, but that can wait. Aa reckon w' can leave the herd here at the river t' rest until mid afternoon then start them movin' for three hours or so before sundown. We're all worn out and it's gonna be a long day so grab sleep when you can." He paused to change tone. "Aa'm kind of proud of you boys, all of you. We stood together and defended our rights as cattlemen, and our Texas name. My thanks t' you!" He turned and walked away to his horse to ride off to check the herd and inform those out there with them, Red, Jacob and Parker, about the day ahead.

As he was leaving Elias was first to speak. "Aa know how you men did your bit an' the boss praised everyone, but Aa want y' t' know how Reuben helped keep guard and did a man's job too. He's feedin' the prisoner right now, so when y' get a chance, mention he did fine."

There was a mumble of agreement. With a rolled cigarette dangling from his mouth Stilt muttered that for a bunch of 'rebels' we gave them a real beating! Around him, faces shone with satisfaction.

Travis wiped his mouth. "Mr Brewster, when y' tell your readers about this past night and how we came through it, don't forget t' tell them how we got riled up by their leader callin' us 'Rebs'!"

I stood up to reply. "You have no need to explain yourselves. They were murderers and villains and you fought them on that score, but no one can dispute the insult maddened you to fight!"

Elias cackled. "Don't fool yourself, Mister! Y' can claim what you want but Aa'm telling you the only thing that mattered t' most of us here was the fact that we wasn't gonna be robbed by a bunch of outlaws who thought they could scare us off. Calling us 'rebels' made no difference!"

"I think Travis has a point," I insisted.

"Sure he has. But don't make it sound fancier than it was!" Elias retorted, grabbing my empty plate.

Tom slowly grinned. "Elias, you and me both know it, but for those folks back east the whole affair needs to have something bigger behind it than sheer cowboy cussedness. Him calling us 'rebels' got us prickled an' they ought t' know it!"

"I agree with you Tom," I replied.

Elias spat on the ground. "Aa say it was no more than a fight about thievin'," he protested. "But if y' both want t' make it into a war thing then you're both stubborn enough to do it. So long as y' know it, Aa want no part of your lyin'!" Ending his outburst, he lifted a pot off the stand and carried it away, muttering to himself.

Jim chuckled louder than anyone else. "Cow's belly! An' Aa get called pig headed!"

"You got no need to complain, Jim. You been called a lot

worse by that pretty wife of yours," Tom said, moving away wearily to go and lie down in shade. Happily, the rest of us fell silent, ready to take our rest.

Shortly after, stretched out on the ground, I shielded my face with my hat and felt the weight of sleep sinking over me. Interestingly, before my mind closed, I held a vivid picture of a woman I'd never seen before with Jim standing beside her, his wide grin almost laughing. And indeed, she was pretty just like Tom had said.'

———

'About noon time, I wakened, hot and stiff limbed with a dullness of mind that poor sleep can give. I got up and looked round to see the others on their feet preparing to eat. "You got the look of a sick dog!" Travis called to me. "If Aa was you Aa'd cool my head in the river!" he laughed.

In the warm sun I wandered to the water's edge and splashed my face then went to join the rest.

In the shadows of a cottonwood tree the group ate their stew made with fresh wild onions and watched the cattle upriver as they lounged in and around the water. After grub, feeling brighter, I did a stint of watching the herd and got back in time for a brief nap before they would start moving the herd. This time I woke with a clear head to discover the men gathering round the prisoner, so I hurried over and quickly learned that Mr Mathias had ordered him to be hanged. The outlaw's face was ashen with fear. "Aa only rode wi' them this past week!" he protested. "Please, mister," he appealed to me directly, "don't let 'em do it!"

My heart tightened with emotion. "This is not justice!" I implored loudly. "We ought to take him with us into Harper County and have him face a proper trial," I declared.

The trail boss stared at me. "No, Mr Brewster!" he barked. "You be satisfied here and now that our way is right and best. He's a thief and a murderer an' don't be fooled!"

"It's not right. It's unlawful!" I heard myself cry out, looking round at the gathering. Not one expression flinched with doubt. All eyes were fixed on me, accusingly.

"Hell, what kind o' man are you?" Red scorned.

I ignored him. "Tom!" I appealed. "For heaven's sake this is not the way!"

"It's the way it is out here," he answered flatly. "And it's not uncivilised to think it's right!"

I shook my head, despairingly, and walked away to separate myself from the deed. With his wrists tied behind his back they mounted the condemned man onto a horse and roped his neck to a branch leaning out near the bank of the river. He screamed for mercy until the horse ran and his body jerked downwards, swinging out over the water's side, back and forth while the cowboys gazed with satisfaction.

Although I refused to spectate, this is how it was described on occasions over the following days. In fact, it seemed to me at times to be repeated purposely in my hearing. Later, when recounting this episode, I ended with a personal aside which reinforced my sense of despair at what is and always will be, an indecent act.'

- While this was carried out I was at the remuda preparing my horse to ride with the herd when Reuben returned from the spectacle. "Mr Brewster, let me help y'," he said, pulling the cinch underneath the horse's belly. He tightened it quickly. "Mr Brewster, that man was one of 'em that killed the hide hunters. Why'd y' want t' save him?"

I studied his blank expression. In his work he was a caring boy yet it was apparent that the hanging had not disturbed him in the slightest. "I happen to believe in lawful justice!" I stated sharply.

Unable to comprehend my meaning Reuben frowned. Immediately, I felt sorry for talking down to him. "What I mean to say is that I'm against a lynching without a proper judge passing sentence."

"But it would have happened anyways, Mr Brewster," he said with surprise.

"Maybe your right," I explained. "Only now we'll never know!"

He pinched his mouth just thinking about it.

"Have you ever seen a hanging before, Reuben?" I asked.

His eyes brightened. "Oh, sure, Mr Brewster" he exclaimed. "This is my second!"

In dismay, I climbed onto the saddle and left him looking up at me.'

'The indignation and scorn which my protest stirred in some of the men lasted through the remaining day. It would have continued longer if I had not decided to explain myself at the evening campfire in a serious but amicable discussion with the trail boss, Elias, Tom, Jim, Mex and Travis. Naturally it was overheard by Scott, Red and Parker, who were playing cards. Reuben was already asleep beside the wagon, while Wes, Jacob and Stilt were out watching the herd but would, no doubt, hear about it later.

I did not relent my opinion but I listened to their side of the argument. "I'm afraid I wasn't prepared t' lose one of my men taking him all the way t' some town someplace where he'd probably have t' wait t' give evidence at a trial, whenever that might be, t' see him hang anyway!" Henry Mathias declared.

"An' who's t' say it weren't a place where he had friends who rigged his defence, or else broke him out o' jail to escape? Cow's teeth, it's happened before!" Jim suggested.

"I know," I admitted, "but the principle remains, however justified you were to hang him, that it was not your right," I reasoned calmly.

"It wasn't his right to murder either!" Elias croaked.

"Bet your friends wish they'd been able t' see it. They got no second chance!" Mex pointed out.

"I'm not denying it. I wanted him punished. But how can we improve and civilise this frontier land by ignoring the appointed course of law and its methods?" I beseeched.

"Only when the method of law is satisfactorily established," Mr Mathias stated. "Until then it's goin' t' be a justice that's best at the time."

"Sir," I addressed him, "what is convenient is not necessarily acceptable!"

Mathias glowered at me momentarily then relaxed, maintaining the ease and orderliness of our discussion. "Out here, Mr Brewster, where hardship and danger are not imaginary threats but very real, convenience is not an excuse. Putting it straight, the man we hanged today was not worth the decency of our time an' effort."

A few heads around about nodded with glee and I knew better than to shake the branch of argument again. "I appreciate what you say and understand. But my view of things is not so much about today as tomorrow and the improvement we, as a people, can make towards a civilised future."

"It'll take time, Aa agree," said Tom suddenly. "And t' have an appointed hanging is a whole lot more satisfying in the eye of progress than one that's not. But, Aa guess, what really bothers you, Mr Brewster, is the dread that us, unlike you, showed no conscience." He paused to study his pipe, then continued. "We hanged a man who deserved it. There's no denyin' it. It was convenient too. It would have been proper for others t' have seen to it." He raised his eyes and fixed them on me clearly. "Maybe the best thing we could have done was to have given him a horse and let him go, hoping our kindness and forgiveness would make him a changed, good, and civilised man. Maybe one with a conscience!" he concluded with a kind, joking gleam.

I smiled back "Do you believe that?"

"Not me," he drawled. "But it's a tempting notion for the holy!"

Elias sighed and stood up. "Aa've heard a lot of talk in my time but this is turning the world upside down. Stoppin' crime by havin' no punishment is the craziest notion Aa've ever come across since you two paid t' take your cattle with us! The usual campfire talk about whores, horses, Indians and the like gets to be dull at times, but at least a man can rely on his hat on his head!" Grumpily, he picked up the empty mugs and went off to the wagon.

Mex prodded a burning log with the toe of his boot. "It's makin' no sense to me any longer either," he remarked, taking out his harmonica.

Jim elbowed Tom gently. "Guess Travis feels the same way too," he quipped. Head lowered, asleep, Travis's eyes and ears were shut to the world.

Wearily, I stood up as well. "Guess there's no more to add, Mr Mathias, other than it's been a pleasure talking with you. We may have different points of view but they've been aired respectfully and I'm grateful for the learning." The trail boss stood up too and shook my hand before he left to pick up his bed roll at the wagon. It was a warm star struck night and the moon was golden and as sharp as a shard of tin .

Lying still, with thoughts ringing as loudly in my head as the crickets in the nearby bushes, I gazed up to the heavens until my eyelids folded with the strain, and sleep promptly dumped me unconscious.'

'Early morning I wakened with a sore face, bitten during the night by mosquitoes. All of the crew suffered too. For some unknown reason a night swarm had descended on the camp and those on guard duty had been forced to pull up their bandanas to protect their faces. The herd too had been agitated and were in an jumpy mood. I was told, earlier on the trail when bugs had been prevalent, that Elias had made up a garlic smelling repellent which he advised everyone to smear onto the rims of their hats and shirts. But after two nights of use the men complained of its stink and rejected the practice. In spite of the dry conditions which reduced insect activity, Elias had continued to use the potion. It was therefore with the open glee of a healthy smile that he inspected our swollen faces as he served us morning breakfast.

"Guess you boys just got what y' deserved!" he chuckled loudly. "Y' ridiculed my ointment an' teased my hide. Well just you look now at the only face here without bumps and tell me again what an old woman I am!" He dolloped the gravy with a dash, whistling like a happy, dawn bird.

"One thing for sure, Elias," Jim replied. "These bumps are gonna die away long before that smell o' yours!"

"Don't worry me, Jim. None of us smell that good anyway. Mine's not just different, it's useful as well. Just remember it when you're scratchin' in the saddle!" he concluded and chuckled again as he stirred the coffee.

It turned out to be a different day altogether. As we were stopping at midday a long single black cloud like a huge boat passed overhead and a brief shower of rain excited the cowboys so much they took off their hats and let the water wash over them and run down their necks. Amazingly, for the Texans it was their first rain since well before the trail started and they whooped like daft kids and urged their horses to dance a little. The fun suddenly turned to raucous laughter when Stilt's horse bucked sideways throwing him to the ground. In a circus mood the younger hands started exhibiting a few saddle tricks running their horses over the glistening brown grass. Jim tried standing up and Scott sat back to front. Parker lay back over and then Scott hung out sideways. Forgetting to take himself seriously for once, Wes leapt from his running horse and holding on swung back up again in one movement. The rain splashed noisily and joining the show Mex and Red raced side by side towards Tom and myself who were happily watching the others showing off, and they skidded to a halt.

Parker arrived a second later, yanking his horse to stop. "Come on Mr Newspaper man, let's see what you can do without fallin' off," he cried sarcastically.

Red squirted tobacco juice from his mouth. "You ain't that good too," he remarked.

"Hell, Red, you're about as much fun as a one eyed skunk!" Parker hollered, gleefully, and spurring his horse into Red's nearly caused the little man to tumble off. Laughing aloud, Parker raced away.

Angrily, Red shouted after him. "Someone's going t' break your skinny neck one day and Aa hope to see it!"

In the rain Parker never heard it. Tom edged his big, dull grey horse, named 'Rock', closer to the fiery little fellow. "Take no heed of him, Red. He ain't gonna live as long as you, so why worry?"

Red scowled, still staring after Parker. "Keep your advice, Tom. He don't scare me!" he rasped.

"Well it sure scares me, Red. You and him!" Tom reasoned.

Nobody warned anyone. Everyone just sensed that Mr Mathias was riding our way and each horseman dispersed swiftly back to their duty, spreading the cattle out to graze. The rain thinned and the huge cloud soon slid by. All at once there was sudden sunlight, bright and hot, and the prairie around us shone with a startling sheen and began to steam. Pausing, I gazed through a rainbow as far as the eye could see and marvelled at the openness of a vast, misty, rolling land-scape. No man knows for certain how another thinks or feels, or how deaths of friends stain the mind, but here now in Kansas, with the job well through and the end of the trail looming, I imagined that it had to be a magical scene to anyone of them, even the least aware.

"What d' y' reckon?" Jim asked, coming towards me.

"Just glad to be alive!" I replied, glibly, in the bright haze.

"No doubt about it, Mr Brewster." He spat to the ground. "You'd have had your throat cut too if y' hadn't changed course and joined the trail."

"I don't think I'll ever forget it!"

"Guess so," Jim said. "As y' know we lost two of our own crew. It could have been less or it could've been more. One mornin' when a few cattle broke away spooked by a snake, I went after them and trying to cut them off my horse stumbled only it didn't go down. Cow's belly, I thought it was gonna be the end of me!"

"You never can tell what fate has planned," I replied. "Better to reckon if it doesn't happen it isn't worth worrying over?"

"That's how Tom figures it!" he chirped.

I smiled as Jim tilted his hat to speak. "Don't know if y' noticed, Mr Brewster, but ain't it a pretty sight, the colours of that rainbow an' the shinin', golden grass?" he added, giving his speckled horse, called 'Tricky', a slap to move on.

'By the time we had eaten at mid day, our clothes had dried on us in the hot sun. The lightness of mood had evaporated too when it was learned that Stilt's fall had caused him to break a wrist bone. He hadn't complained about it at first thinking it was just bruised. However, when Mr Mathias looked at the swelling he sent him off at once to Elias who realised it was worse and did his best to set it straight before bandaging it up. "Damn stupidness did it anyway," the boss chided. "The way you boys were actin' could've set the cattle stampedin'. Did nobody think of that?" He stared critically round him.

"Well, it weren't as bad as y' think, boss," Travis began, sounding apologetic. "After all, the beeves were downhill below us and the rain was splatterin' over them makin' more din than us."

Mathias puffed and sipped his coffee. "But y' weren't watchin' them! Now the trail isn't over yet and we've got an injured man due to some recklessness. I don't approve of it and that's all there is to it!" Softening tone he went on, "Right, if all goes well today we should reach the south fork of the Ninnescah by sundown, then tomorrow, the north fork, and the followin' day make it to the Arkansas river. A few days after that along the Chisholm trail should bring us to Abilene. When you get there and been paid y' can celebrate to your heart's content, but until then, you're employed t' do a job and don't let anybody forget it!"

Nobody argued and nobody had a right to. He spoke directly and it made sense. Most of all he was respected. Stories about previous years' trails were often recounted. Many liked the one which involved him disciplining a surly, violent, hand who had spat towards Jacob calling him a 'nigger head'! Mr Mathias had simply walked forward to the dead fire, rubbed charcoal in his hands from a blackened Mesquite branch then stepped up close to the bullish man and opened his palms. "What colour are these?" he asked calmly.

"Black," the fellow replied, sullenly.

Mr Mathias took hold of one of Jacob's wrist turning his hand up. "What colour is this?" he asked.

The man hesitated, looking at the lightness of the palms. "Brown," he replied.

"Good," Mathias exclaimed. "I'm pleased you're not colour blind as Aa feared, because it means Aa don't have t' get rid of one of the best cowhands I hired down in San Antonio."

The man paused, dumbstruck by the mixture of criticism and compliment. He scratched his beard, contemplating his boss's words, then replied in a low, humbled voice that he was wrong for what he said and what he did.

Accounts such as this of Henry Mathias's leadership qualities gave him an aura he deserved. Yet, and he admitted it often, he relied wholly on the support of his followers, which is why the death of Fletcher at the hands of the Kiowas had caused him such sorrow. The big man had been loyal to him for ten years, throughout the war and the trail driving seasons.

To our consternation, Stilt was prohibited from night duty and all of the outfit in some way were penalised for the period of high spirits by having to cover for him. In a mulish way, Stilt enjoyed the attention he got, although Elias had him doing extra chores to compensate for it. "Aa'm not nursin' you for nothin', Stilt," he told the tall, gangling cowhand. "Now get your lanky legs movin' over t' the fire and stir the pot good and proper!"

"Sure thing," Stilt drawled, pouring himself more coffee into his almost empty mug.

Elias huffed. "Since y' busted that arm Aa've brewed twice as much coffee as Aa made before!"

"There ain't nothin' wrong in it, Elias," Stilt remarked.

Elias twisted his face. "Not for you, it's not! But the crew are fed up with you goin' for pisses through the night and causing such a commotion doing it! You've got t' be the clumsiest critter on earth when it comes to gettin' up t' water the grass!"

Stilt guffawed like a jack ass. "Elias, you got t' be the funniest man Aa know!" Beaming, he ambled over to the fire and set his mug down.

For me, in particular, broken sleep was the hardest of all demands. Dragging myself from the bedroll was a sheer test of will power. Unlike the others I was never able or confident enough to doze in the saddle to make up for lost sleep. Even during rest time in the heat of the day I found it hard to sleep, my relaxation hampered by flies and the strong sunlight. "You'll adjust to it," Tom told me, "an' if y' don't you'll reach a point where it don't matter anymore. When you're fully worn out you'll sleep, even if you're next to a beehive!"

Tom had an aura which I recognised as similar and yet different to the trail boss. I saw it one way. In their dealings with others his cleverness of mind tended to be bladed whereas Mr Mathias's was pointed. That was the only description I could think of to compare them! And they were equally effective. In the case of a man doing wrong Mr Mathias was likely to say something like - 'It was stupid and you know it!' Whereas Tom might put it like - 'It was a mistake and you should know better!"

Just as Mr Mathias predicted, we reached each river at the end of every day and splashed in them happily to wash away the dirt and grime and sweat we had accumulated from the dust and sun which tagged us constantly. In many ways, Travis was heard to say, we were an unusually clean crew compared to most. Having spent a few days with buffalo hunters, I was well aware of his meaning. But then living the outdoor life body smells tend to be fainter, so I never felt any strong aversion!

I also came to appreciate that Elias's skills as a trail cook were numerous as well as vital to the well being of the crew. He was also a good barber and would shave those who wanted it. He even trimmed my own short beard as expertly as any professional. If Tom's smartness could be described as blade like and Mr Mathias's as pointed, then Elias had the cut of a saw! "Bet y' grew a beard to hide this!" he affirmed, prodding the birthmark on my face.

"I suppose I did at first but I liked the beard too," I answered.

"Don't blame y'. People would just look at it. Aa got a friend with a big wart thing on his nose and the only thing stoppin' him from cutting it off is fear he might bleed t' death. If it was on his cheek, like yours, he could hide it too.

Think yourself lucky, Mister, if it's all you got wrong with y'!"
he groused.'

'Crossing the Arkansas proved difficult. The water level had
fallen leaving broad sand banks in places which threatened
to bog the horses and cattle, let alone the wagon. While we
were held up, Jacob and the boss went up river to search for a
safer crossing place, while Mex and Travis headed downstream. Idling time away, Parker, Stilt and Scott, played cards
with Reuben looking on. Red and Jim were with the herd.
Talking with Elias as he tidied the wagon, I saw Wes coming
our way. Only then, when he realised it was me, he suddenly
changed his mind and turned to go and sit beside Tom who
was relaxing in the shade of a small tree on the river bank.

"It's apparent that Wes has some respect for Tom," I
remarked.

"Why shouldn't he?" Elias snapped.

"Well, he speaks to Parker and Stilt and Scott but rarely
anyone else, apart from Tom. Not that he spends long with
him. Just watch."

"Maybe he just likes t' keep t' himself."

"Perhaps. But I find it interesting that he seeks out Tom at
least once a day to exchange words with him."

"Some people might think bein' interested is being nosey,
Mr Brewster! You should b' careful what y' say. Somebody
might object!"

"I'm only telling you, Elias."

"Sure. And you're not the only one who sees it. Only nobody else says it! That's the difference, Mr Brewster," he grumped

"I only mentioned it to you, Elias, nobody else. There's nothing wrong in what I'm saying! It's to Tom's credit that Wes feels he can speak with him," I insisted.

"Why don't y' just go over there an' tell them both?" he rasped.

His irritability confounded me. "Why are you making an issue of it? It's an observation, nothing more."

Elias frowned at me, his bushy eyebrows protruding. "The boy's related, Mr Brewster. He's hot headed and been in trouble wi' the law, an' Aa want t' save him from people like yourself. He's edgy about you bein' around so Aa'm forced to tell y'. Get it?" he foamed.

I took a long breath. "I understand," I answered, carefully.

"You'll be smart if y' did," cook retorted. "Now get away from here so Aa can get t' work. And," he added, emphatically, but with a roguish spark entering his voice. "If you so much as mention anythin' about this conversation to anybody, next time I trim your beard, I'll snip off your big nose. Right?"

"Right," I replied, amused by his cantankerousness, and turning round went over to where the cowhands were playing cards. As an occasional player I sometimes enjoyed watching their game. But then I had hardly sat down when Scott suddenly stood up and pointed. We turned our heads and in the distance saw riders approaching in an open wagon. Having spotted them already, Tom and Wes and Elias walked over to join us.

It happened to be nothing more than a family of six; a man and a woman with two lank girls, surely twins, about Reuben's age, and two dirty faced younger boys. The family were miserable looking and gaunt faced.

"What can w' do for y'?" Elias shouted as they neared.

"We're settlers, farmin' a little land about three miles from here, an' seein' the dust your herd kicked up thought we'd ride over an' maybe sell y' some rations," the father said wheezily.

"And what is y' want us t' buy?" Elias demanded.

He coughed a little before answering. "We got eggs, corn, beans and some potatoes. Got some goat milk too."

Tom stepped forward raising his rifle, aiming it towards him. "Get out of here, mister, right now!" he ordered.

Horrified, one of the girls wailed in tears. "What way is that t' treat a poor family?" the man rasped. "What harm w' done you?"

"What is it Tom?" Elias demanded. Mystified, the rest of us were muted by his outburst.

"They're diseased!"

"Only a sickness," the mother bawled, grievously.

"For pity's sake, we're poor people!" the man beseeched, about to step down.

Tom jerked the gun. "Stay up on the seat," he ordered. "Turn the mules round and get out o' here. There'll be enough cow chips around when we've gone t keep your fire burning through Winter. I promise you we'll leave a cow or calf for meat. But turn the wagon round now and get out o' here. Do as Aa say, or Aa'll shoot!" he barked.

The man coughed again then glowered for a few seconds at Tom who aimed the rifle at him. While we stood watching in silence, the man followed Tom's command and they moved away; the sobs of a mother and her children gradually fading.

From behind him, we looked at Tom as he stood, shoulders braced, watching the wagon rolling further and further away. Then he turned to us and his eyes were dull with sorrow. "They've got typhus," he said. "They'll be lucky to survive."

"Darn me!" Elias cried. "Should've known it!"

"It's okay, nobody touched anythin'. But it was too much t' risk after comin' this far!" Tom explained.

"Do y' reckon w' should move the herd away a little?" Stilt proposed.

"No need t' worry," Tom replied. "We'll be crossin' the river as soon as the others return."

"Hope the b-boss gets b-b-back soon," Scott mumbled.

"Want me t' go and tell Jim and Red?" Parker said gravely.

Tom sighed. "Why don't you boys just get back to playing cards and quit scarin' each other. You ain't caught anything yet!" He gave a little grin. "But Aa'm pleased you're all thinkin' of your health. Means when you get to Abilene y' might think twice about visitin' those girls you keep talkin' about!"

135

"Have they got it as well?" Reuben frowned.

We strained not to laugh but we couldn't stop ourselves from beaming at his innocence. "Boy," Elias cried, "they're likely t' give you a double dose if y' ever let them get near you! Aa've known men nearly die just lettin' them sit on their knees!"

We grinned widely and Reuben reddened, realising he'd said something foolish and it had turned into a joke. "Never mind it, Reuben," Tom comforted him. "Go an' saddle 'Locust' for me, will y'? An' if y' want t' ride along why don't y' saddle one for yourself."

The young wrangler's face lit up. "Sure will, thanks. Where w' goin', Mr Tom?"

"To pick out an old cow or calf for that unfortunate family an' leave 'em hobbled. Will you cover his chores, Wes?" he asked.

"Aa'm no coffee boy," Hardin muttered, then glancing at Elias he relented. "But Aa'll keep an eye on the horses, this time."

"I'll help out if needed," I offered, instantly.

"Well thanks Mister Brewster," Elias opened. "I've got a burned pan needs scrubbin' and when that's done you can grease one of the wheels. Been squeaking all the time we've been standin' here."

The others chuckled. "It's a pleasure to be of use," I countered in turn. "Up to now my help has been seriously under-valued." Now it was my turn to grin.

"On other trails only me and the boss were the smart

ones," Elias bemoaned. "Now everyone's tryin' to be."

"Call it progress!" I asserted.

Elias twisted his face. "If you're aimin' t' pull me into an argument you're out of luck. My mind's still grievin' about that family and what's t' become of them. Darn it, when you tell those easterners about life out here, Mr Brewster, make sure y' mention them!"

"I will," I replied earnestly. "I certainly will."

"Like to know what else you're goin' to be sayin'?" Parker scoffed with a note of suspicion.

"Well, for a start if I mention anybody, I won't be using their real name. But there's nothing I'll be saying that should worry any of you," I retorted, tactfully.

"Don't care a hoot about it. I can't read anyway!" Parker declared, unashamedly.

"But somebody could read it to you?"

"What are y' gonna say that w' don't already know?" he jeered.

"Depends how much you know already," I replied, calmly.

"Know when it comes t' riding a horse and usin' a rope you're no damn good!" Pleased with himself, Parker grinned slyly towards Wes.

"If you teach me how, I'll teach you to read and write," I proposed, as a gentleman would.

"Don't reckon I could stand your company that long," Parker remarked, grinning round with a sneer. What could have been a joke was clearly meant to be a cheap insult.

Before I had a chance to answer him, Tom quickly

stepped forward and jabbed Parker, forcefully, in the chest. Parker recoiled, dismayed by the sudden aggression.

"Boy, you have no manners!" Tom growled angrily. "Get on a horse and get t' the herd right now out of my sight!"

Parker's indignation seethed up. "Aa ought to kill y' for that you old lizard!" His right hand hovered near his holstered pistol.

Tom was holding the rifle in his left hand while his right hand shifted nearer his navy colt and his eyes were drilled on Parker.

"Let it go Parker!" Stilt advised.

Parker glanced momentarily sideways and when his hand flinched, Tom whipped out his revolver. Parker froze, his hand stiffening alongside his undrawn gun.

"Get on your horse and get out o' here before Aa blow your ears off!" Tom rasped, his rage burning. Outdrawn and outwitted, Parker stared at Tom. He swallowed nervously and then slunk off.

Tom put his gun away and turning about went to the water keg to spoon himself a drink. Stilt, Scott and Wes slowly sat down to play cards while Elias nodded for me to follow him to the wagon. By now Reuben had brought the horses and without a word Tom and the boy left together. Soon after them Parker headed out as well, without a word to anybody. At the chuck wagon I lingered a while waiting for Elias to say something about it, and it was worth the delay.

"Been looking to see that all trail, Mr Brewster, and got t' thinkin' it might never happen! That cowboy was once upon a time the quickest and deadliest shot ever seen in Texas. Yes sir," he crowed, "that there was no other than Tom Tileman. Hell, Parker nearly shit his pants when he saw the gun pointin' at him! It was that fast!" he added with a chuckle.

"I'm surprised Tom lost his temper. He's always been composed."

Elias raised his chin. "He snapped, that's all. Patience gets sort of thin towards the end of the trail. Turnin' the family around had him on edge an' Parker's big mouth did the rest. But the skinny runt had it comin' from somebody and there was nobody better!" He gave a little chuckle, his eyes sparkling. "Made my day it did, just to see it. Had a hunch it was him and now Aa know it. As true as the sun coming up each mornin', that there was Tom Tileman!" he echoed, merrily, pulling his white whiskers in contemplation of it.'

'Three hours later we managed to swim the herd across the big river and started moving north towards Newton, Kansas, where needed supplies could be purchased. Out of general hearing, talk among the cowboys was centred on the incident with the squatter family and the confrontation between Tom and Parker. Those who had witnessed it were targeted for conversation by the others who were itching with fascination for a greater description of how quick Tom had drawn. Consequently, the tension which should have died away was

kept alive with looks and whispers, so that an air of
expectancy hung as thick as dust around camp.

Defending themselves from it, both Tom and Parker
remained distant and tight lipped, although Tom had
reported the event immediately to Henry Mathias upon his
return to camp from scouting up river. It was, therefore, not
surprising for the trail boss to gather us to a meeting as soon
as the day's trail was ended to settle the affair with well
chosen words. He explained that he had spoken to Tom and
Parker and both had regretted the occasion. He appealed to
us all to put the matter aside and be still conscientious of our
duties. "We've got a few days t' go to Abilene, barring accident. We're tired and sick of ridin' and desperate for some
comforts. Let nobody here spoil it by stirrin' up any trouble
or friction among us. You've done a fine job and Aa'm
prepared to give each of you a week's bonus pay when we get
there if you can hold to what I ask."

"An' what about that fine you still got over me?" Red
piped up.

"Aa ain't forgotten it, Red. Y' still have time t' do extra!"

Red squirted out tobacco juice. "Like what, boss?" he
persisted.

Mathias shook his head with a look of annoyance. "Hold
your tongue, man. This meeting was called for a more
serious matter. Elias, give him some work before he demands
it! Now," he looked around, "Travis, Jacob, Wes, Scott, Jim,
Parker, let's go get the cattle bedded down. Tom, Mex and

Red can take first watch. Mr Brewster, can you guard the horses after midnight? Stilt, you help Elias as best y' can."

"Help!" Elias cried out with contempt. "What he can do wi' one hand round a kitchen, Aa can do wi' none!"

Mr Mathias waived his hand in an impatient gesture. "Insult him as much as y' like but let me get out o' here first before you start!" he concluded, turning away.

In an instant his instructions moved us all to action. To get wood for the fire Stilt and I were sent over to a dry creek where some pale, shabby looking trees were stooping. He was in no hurry, so we sat on a rock out of view while I rolled him a cigarette.

"Boss said all the right things but it don't matter," Stilt remarked tediously. "Parker'll want even someday. Tom should've killed him when he had the chance!"

"Is that everybody's opinion?" I asked.

Stilt blew out his first stream of smoke. "Don't know."

We sat in silence enjoying the shadow of the steep bank behind us. Without a breeze to fan us the day's heat had been roasting. I removed my hat and wiped my face dry with my bandana before tying it round my neck again. My clothes felt grubby with sweat and dirt even though they had been soaked in the Arkansas river eight miles back.

"You've seen men draw. How quick was he?" I quizzed.

"About as quick as you're likely t' see," Stilt answered.

"But he's not proud of himself for it, is he?"

"He got mad, that's all. You saw it."

"He didn't need to. Parker was bad mouthing me. He shouldn't have interfered."

"Guess so. But Parker looked set to pull out his gun."

"Guess so," I echoed.

We sat a while in silence then Stilt stood up and scratched his chest. His dull eyes fell towards me. "Tom was a fool not t' have killed him. Parker's sly as a coyote."

"He did all he had to," I replied.

"Y' reckon?" he drawled.

I sensed he wasn't really interested in a reply so it was simple for me to just shrug my shoulders as if I hadn't figured it out. But I had. Tom, the family man, the shrewd one, the thinker, friendly, amusing, yet tough in spirit and outlook, had lost his self control in handling Parker. Up to that point he had always seemed in possession of himself, acting with a determined but responsible head. He may have won the argument, whilst exposing his past expertise with a hand gun, but after the event, at the wagon as he drank water from the keg, I perceived in the blankness of his stare a sense of shame and misgiving.

Nevertheless, it was better to shrug my shoulders at Stilt, for what he believed I couldn't dispute and what I believed, he'd see no sense or merit! For him and others, no doubt, Tom's only weakness had been to not pull the trigger. At the time I thought this view was stupidly short sighted. Later, I could only reflect upon it with a sense of irony!

Further down the creek we found a small, withered, willow tree and snapped off a few branches to add to the sticks we had gathered below it. On hearing Elias hollering for us to hurry, we set off at once at a quicker pace back to camp to fuel the fire that Mex had already lit. Lying nearby, Tom was already dozing, or appeared to be.

———————

'Next morning as we drank our first coffee there was a general lethargy and look of exhaustion on faces. It seemed that the pulse and turmoil of the previous day had taken its toll. After sowbelly, beans and biscuit for breakfast, we made ready to start and few words were spoken as we saddled up our horses in the pale light of dawn. In the east, the sky was flamed in expectation, and as we rode away from camp towards the herd the huge golden orb of the sun rising behind us cast long shadows, furrowing like ploughs before us through the dew-less, prairie grass.

Fortunately, unlike the crew, the cattle were alert and keen to move on, so little effort was required on our part to get them started. They readily fell into place without much commotion and the day's trail was underway, trickling as smoothly as a slow stream of water.

It so happened that the swing rider in front of me that morning was Jim Housman and I purposefully avoided catching him up for the very reason he had spent more time with Tom since the incident than anyone else and might suspect me of wanting to pry into his opinion about it. So when Jim slowed, I slowed, and when Jim stopped, I stopped, maintaining a gap between us. However, this sensitivity was made nonsense when, finally, Jim turned round and signalled briskly for me to join him.

"If Aa stink too much t' ride with for cow's sake tell me?" he called as I approached him, astride his speckled horse, called 'Tricky'. "It's not your custom t' stay back when there's a chance to talk to an intelligent, interestin' man like myself! God knows there ain't that many around here!" Jim joked.

"Guess I'm not that smart," I confessed. "But it was nothing more than respect. There's only one thing really to talk about."

"Sure, Aa understand," he grinned. "An' t' save y' bein' embarrassed I'll tell you without needin' t' ask!" He paused briefly to swig a gulp of water from his can. "Tom's okay," he began, wiping his lips. "He's sore with himself and grim quiet, but just the same. The old dog took a bite when he just needed t' bare his teeth and bitin' takes more recovery. That's what he himself said of it, if y' want t' know!"

I smiled. "Why did he draw?"

Jim gave me a droll look. "It seemed like Parker was about to an' before he did, Tom caught him cold, and rid the danger without needin' t' fire. It was the best he could do in the circumstance."

"Did Tom say that too?"

"Tom don't boast about gun play. Never!"

"But he showed that he was once a gunfighter, named Tileman?"

Jim grinned, shaking his head. "Elias has everyone convinced he is, but Tom don't admit it!"

"But he's fast."

"You won't see faster."

"Stilt figures Tom should have killed him when he had the chance. He says Tom was a fool not to have done it."

"Cow's belly, if Tom had shot him they'd be calling him a killer. He don't, an' he's called a fool!" Jim exclaimed.

"Stilt reckons Parker'll want revenge."

"Parker's got one friend, Hardin. Everybody else is for Tom. Parker's a loud mouthed, nasty son of a bitch, but he ain't dumb enough t' take on anyone faster than himself. An' now he knows Tom is, for sure. He also knows the rest of us will be lookin' out for him!"

I admired and accepted his argument but was eager to continue. "If Elias is wrong, why does he cling to the idea of Tom being Tileman?"

Jim blew as if puzzled. "Elias got the notion at the very start, when Tom and Wes were shootin' the eggs, an' the old buzzard can't let it go. You know how he is when something buzzes in him. He chews on it like tobacco and keeps spittin' it out."

"What do you know of Tom's life before he settled down."

"Not much. He wandered around and took work when he had to, sometimes ridin' gun with a stage. Just because he's a marksman and fast, it don't mean he has t' have been somethin' more. Reputations grow like melons in Texas. If y' kill one indian it becomes two inside a week. Guess it's the wantin' we have to appreciate who and what we are."

I automatically reached out and clapped him on the shoulder. "Those are fine words, Jim." I praised.

He smirked. "It's my line for a change and Aa like it as well!"

I chuckled with him and then Jim started to tell me how he and Tom were planning to turn round as soon as they got their money for their cattle and head straight home to their families. He had told me before about them, but I listened again imagining how joyful their return would be. At that time, myself a single man, I could see in them the joy and happiness of family life.

A little later, when some cattle behind us ran out off line, we parted company to return to our places. To offset the boredom of the long morning's ride across flat, treeless prairie, I consciously ran through each day since I'd joined the trail, reliving in memory the details of my journey and the dramas which outlined it. Although generally, my written notes were sketchy, my mind was brimming over with images and descriptions and dialogue, and I sensed again, not merely as a reporter, how blessed I was to be a witness of a time that turned out to be epic in the history of the American West.'

'Near the small town of Newton, Elias, Red and Jacob, rode in to get supplies for the last stage of our journey. When they returned at mid day camp the outfit heard about the town's busy development as a new railhead on a line down from Topeka. In a matter of weeks a cowtown would be established and businesses were setting up to prepare for a boom trade with free spending drovers. With this in mind, there was a distinct change of heart as the riders goaded the cattle off again on the late afternoon drive. Only two miles west of the Chisholm trail they felt destination bound. Directing the herd due north of Newton, Abilene was four days ahead, but now it suddenly felt within range and for those who had trailed there previously the route was familiar territory. And it had its effect, for it seemed that every cowhand's whoop was louder, ringing with a note of excitement!

Conspicuously, their exhilaration stretched more than just lungs! Indeed, I experienced it first hand, for an air of comradeship reached out so that irritations and grumblings faded in the face of hearty conversation. Despite his stammer, even the long haired Scott, who seldom spoke, was more inclined to do so, but most remarkable of all changes, the singing on night watch sounded sweeter! Was it possible, as well, that our food tasted better? In general, the monotony, weariness, heat and discomforts of the journey, at once seemed easier to bear, so that everyone had a bit more spring in their movement and lightness about their carriage. "Happens every time we're on the run in," Elias explained to me. "They get a sniff of livin' again and life don't feel so bad after all! Even you, Mr Brewster, look taller in the saddle," he remarked without a trace of scorn!

Naturally, it was fun to be round the evening campfires as the chat sparked wilder than the flames. Only one thing spoiled it for me; for there was less of Tom's company. Since the confrontation with Parker he had mostly retired from the campfire scene, spending his time with the trail boss, detached from the boys. It was clear that the two men's respect for each other had developed into a firm friendship, and to most cowboys it was understandable. Typically, Red seized upon it to goad Travis.

"Seems to me, Travis, that Tom's taken over your job. He rides out front wi' the boss all the time now."

Travis threw the dregs of his coffee onto the fire. "Reckon so," he replied, matter of fact.

"Well it ain't right. You got Fletcher's job!" Red insisted.

Travis snorted lightly. "Red, y' know as well as the rest of us Tom's place is where he choses to be. So hold your tongue and think of somethin' else to grump over."

"Yeah," Jacob came in, thrusting his hand of cards up for those of us not playing to see. "Like these you dealt me from the pile."

Red spat recklessly towards the fire but his spittle missed and landed on the outstretched toe of Wes's right boot. In a frigid silence Wes glared at him.

Red's mouth twitched. "Didn't mean it," he muttered.

With his mouth clasped in silent venom, Wes turned his foot and wiped it on the ground.

Jim was swift to make light of it. "If that's how good your aim is, Red, no wonder y' weren't keen to come with us after the Kiowas!"

Red snorted his disapproval of Jim's sarcasm. "My aim's good enough for Indians. Last fall, Selby, me and Jacob chased off half a dozen of them tryin' to steal horses down near Laredo. Ask Jacob here."

Jacob nodded with a sigh. "Are y' playin' cards here, Red, or are y' gonna yap all night? It's your turn t' show!"

"Good players can do both, Jacob!" Red fired back.

"Not with a poor hand like this, y' can't" Jacob quipped.

Stilt sighed too, weary of the jabbering and eager for the game to resume. "Only bad hand is this one here," he declared holding up the injured one, "so let's play some, huh?"

Stilt hadn't intended to be funny and that alone made the others smile. Red played an Ace of hearts and Jacob stared at it, wide eyed, deliberating.

"Mm, interestin'," he mumbled.

"Feel the hand getting any stronger, Stilt?" I asked about his injury.

"Good enough for pickin' his nose and scratchin' his backside," Elias croaked. "But no damn use when it comes to work!" He lifted the coffee can off the fire and started to refill mugs.

"At times you're a mean old bear," Stilt drawled.

"Darn right, Aa am!" Elias declared. "If Aa was nice you'd be expectin' me to tuck you in at nights!"

"That would be fine as long as you left out the goodnight kiss," Parker joined in, grinning, delighted to take part in the banter.

"Aa'd rather die of thirst than have t' kiss any one as ugly as you, Parker!" Elias fired back with scorn.

"Y' ain't so pretty either," Parker rallied.

Elias glowered at him, twisting his face. "Not now, boy, but at your age Aa sure was. And Aa had a charm too. But y' don't know what that means, Parker, 'cause y' ain't got one cent's worth of it in you!"

Parker tried to brush it off with a cheap laugh, but Jim seized the initiative to retaliate for him. "In case nobody's told y', Elias, you lost your charm when y' lost your looks!"

The men sniggered, brightening again in anticipation of cook's response, but Elias acted as if he didn't care about it, continuing his round until reaching Jim, where he deliberated to speak.

"Your right about it, Jim, I did loose it. Which is why I keep crunchin' horse flies onto your plate almost every time we eat."

Jim grinned uncertainly, but Elias kept a straight face. It was only when he walked off to the wagon that he began to chuckle, restoring the mood of humour!

"Okay, Mr Brewster," Travis began, rising to speak out, "time for you, me and Wes, to take over from the others out at the herd. Don't forget now, Jacob, you and Jim and Tom are next on duty so grab some sleep if y' can."

"Sure thing," Jacob replied without looking up, still intent on the game's conclusion. Then he thumbed his lips slowly, before drawing out a card to fling down. It was the Ace of Spades! "See you, boys," he called out as we were turning to leave, and his grin was plainly huge.'

'The following day we journeyed steadily over windless, hillier ground, a mile east of the Chisholm Trail where another herd was moving slightly ahead of us. However, after we had covered eight miles in the morning and six more later in the afternoon, we saw that we had edged in front of the other herd and felt pleased about it. What's more, for most of the day a spread of cloud had screened the sun and in its shade we felt less burned out at the end of the day than usual. With grass and water available to fill the cattle, our spirits soared at the promise of only one more day's ride to reach the Smokey hill river, two miles south of Abilene.

Mentally, it seemed that the drive was over, and an animated, yet relaxed atmosphere settled over the trail's final evening camp. As with endings, memories were sharpened, and while reminiscing, a tone of reflection carried the talk. Again the deaths of Selby and Fletcher were recalled with regret and respect for their qualities, and once more, the actions against the Kiowas and the Jayhawkers were recounted and verified.

It was a time as well to think beyond Abilene, when the cravings for comfort and pleasure would be fulfilled. In earnest, open voices, the possibilities were discussed: another trail or different work – the return home or the freedom to wander, seeing new places. Options were aired and debated, but still no one, this early, wanted to commit themselves to a decision, aware of luck playing its part! Nevertheless, it was enjoyable to question and reason, revelling in the range of choices before having to make up one's mind. Even I, who had a newspaper job to continue, considered the opportunities with the glory of a free will of my own.

Perhaps it meant more to me than others, but this was also the last evening the group would spend together as a crew, isolated from the real world. Separation was inevitable and the end of hard work welcome, but never again would it be the same, or return as it was now. Mr Mathias would organise other runs and most of the hands would join him again, but not everyone. Notably, Tom and Jim. And for most of us this would always be remembered as Tom's trail. Above everyone else he would be the individual that stood out most. Not to mention the question of his past - but his manner, his wit, his boldness and charm - that Parker lacked - made him greatly admired.

At this time, despite his absences from evening camp fire chat, Tom remained friendly without becoming involved. He said what he needed to, was cordial and interested, and while curbing his opinion on issues his humour was undiminished.

"Doin' a lot of ridin' alongside the boss, ain't y'?" Elias

squawked as Tom waited for his dish with the rest of us at mid-day.

Tom nodded. "That's right," he replied.

"Got a lot t' talk over, huh?" the old cook baited him.

"That's right," Tom repeated lazily.

"Well as long as y' both enjoy each other's company and do your work it's nobody else's business," Elias teased.

"That's right," Tom answered.

Elias scowled at him. "Aa remember a time when you'd be word wrestlin' with me by now, not keepin' agreein' like a soft cushion!"

"You ain't got a good memory, Elias." Tom said flatly.

"How come?" the other demanded, frowning.

"Aa never argued with you, Elias, until my plate was full."

Elias's frown fell and he cocked his head in thought, one eye nearly closed. "You mean to say Aa could grudge a man his share just for arguin' against me?"

Tom picked up his plate first, then nodded. "That's right!" he repeated, and with a twinkle he walked away, leaving the rest of us chuckling.'

'Cloudy again, we coasted through the last day, crossing the Smokey Hill River before setting up camp early evening. Despite having no fresh change of clothes, we river bathed to wash off the top layer of skin dirt and felt better for it. Some of the boys were anxious to go to town at once and Mr

Mathias advanced them a little money to break their thirst with the understanding that they returned before Ten in good order. Officially their employment ended only when the herd was handed over to the buyer's men. Until then, wages would not be paid.

After supper, Stilt, Scott, Mex, Red, Parker and Mr Mathias trooped off to town. The boss wanted to contact an agent he knew. The rest, left back at camp, had duties and enviously watched their departure. Later that evening, returning to the fireside from night guard, Jim and Travis joined us at the same time as the others returned from town. Sitting down while drinking coffee, they listened to the excited talk about the saloons and girls and good time waiting there for everyone.

"See or hear anything of Hickock, the sheriff?" I asked.

"Heard he's out o' town looking t' arrest a man in Solomon. They say he's just a killer himself wearin' a badge!" Red spluttered, a little drunkenly.

"Heard it said he's gonna have it made law no one's to wear shootin' irons in town!" Mex exclaimed.

Red whistled in dismay. "He's gonna need an army t' do that!"

"Got a reputation for doing what he says," I replied.

"Well good luck t' him," Jim said. "Alcohol an' guns are bad partners!"

"You mean t' say you'd let him take your gun from you?" Travis asked, eyes widening.

"If everybody else ain't wearin' them, what's there t' be afraid of?" Jim countered.

"Well some might just keep them hidden!" Red blurted.

"Then if everybody's got them hidden it's a dumb law," Jim argued.

It was too late and we were too exhausted to pursue the discourse, so Jim's line was a suitable conclusion on the matter and to the day. Shortly after, we gathered our bedding at the wagon where Elias and the trail boss were in conversation and left them there still talking. The full moon burned white like a forged coin and I stared up at the clustered stars while the others fell quickly into a snoring sleep. Once lifting my head I spied the distant glow of Abilene town's lights and smiled to think they we were finally and safely here, at the trail's end.'

'The following morning there was much coming and going. A buyer and two assistants inspected the cattle as the men ran them through the count of steers and cows. The buyer, a round chested, serious man wearing a light weight jacket, eyed the herd silently next to Mr Mathias who made occasional comments. Afterwards, while the two of them, plus Tom and Jim, rode back to camp to discuss terms, riders spread the herd out again on short grass further up river.

Those of the crew not needed to stay with the cattle left as soon as Travis gave the word, and by the time they arrived back for coffee it was already rumoured that Tom and Jim had refused the thirteen dollars per head which the buyer had offered, claiming their cattle to be in superior condition to the rest, which, it was true to say, was correct. At first the buyer refused to deal with them separately, but after a private talk with the trail boss he relented and generously agreed to pay them fourteen dollars, which they accepted.

Before noon a group of cowboys left camp to accompany the boss to town where the contract and finance was to be secured. While he visited the agent's office then the bank drawing money for wages, they browsed through stores for new shirts and pants, and afterwards, without so much as one beer, they returned promptly to the outfit.

Later in the afternoon the railroad's hired men came out to collect the cattle and the crew were finally relieved of their responsibility for them. Although a relationship with the animals had built up over the two months drive, I noted with interest that there was no sentiment or reflection shown in the least way by the cowboys towards the herd's departure. The front steers which had doggedly led the way controlling the others so sturdily, went off like all the rest without a moment's regard.

Back at the chuck wagon Mr Mathias presided over his last meeting, thanking all formally and handing over each man's wage and bonus. He warned against excess and extravagance and wished us good luck. "Camp'll be sitting here for a few days if any of you care t' use it. From now on your free men. Watch how you go, and if not, may the Lord do it for you!" he concluded cheerfully, raising a salutary finger. The cowhands cheered and swaggered off, the majority of them mounting their horses and galloping off to town, happily yelling.

Having packed my belongings to depart alone, I delayed a while longer to chat with Tom, Jim, Elias and Henry Mathias at the wagon, smoking a cigar which the trail boss had cordially offered.

"You're smart men," Elias said, arching his brow towards Tom and Jim. "Raising him a dollar more than us was fancy work."

"Guess w' have the boss here t' thank for that," Jim replied.

"Nonsense. He paid you an honest price," Mathias said.

"W' would have liked more," Tom continued, drawing on his cigar. "But he wouldn't budge again."

"It's going t' be a glut season, Tom. A herd two days before us only got thirteen dollars a head. We can't complain," Mr Mathias said.

"Well," Elias drawled, "Y' did a sight better than you would have done selling them to us at five dollars! Your gamble paid off, huh?"

Jim nodded with a reflective smile. "Aa guess so."

Tom stared at the smouldering end of his cigar then flicked off the ash. "The gamble's not over until w' reach home, Elias, an' Aa'm sittin' in my own chair under my own roof," he mused.

"Are you really leaving so soon, Tom?" I asked.

"Tomorrow morning, first thing."

"Just the two of you?"

"No. Scott wants t' ride with us."

"Back through Indian Territory?"

He nodded brightly. "At night if need be."

I looked at him, kindly. "Well, I'm due to stay in the Main Street hotel tonight. It would be a pleasure to have you and Jim dine with me this evening if you care to?"

"Be an honour, Mr Brewster," Tom replied.

Ready to go I stepped forward and shook hands with them all. "Trust both of you gentlemen can also dine with me tomorrow evening," I said, inviting Mr Mathias and Elias.

"That's a possibility," Elias said, "if Aa'm allowed a night off."

Mr Mathias smiled. "Aa can assure you he'll be with me, Mr Brewster."

Young Reuben had my horse ready. He was chewing a grass stalk. I thanked him and climbed on.

Reuben stared up with his eyes shining. "So long, Mr Brewster. You're a better rider now than you was," he added, genuinely.

I gave a laugh. "You gave me good advice on that score and I haven't forgotten it." I fumbled in my waistcoat pocket and found the five dollar note I wanted to give the boy. His face beamed as he held it open in his fingers. "Why thanks, Mr Brewster!" he exclaimed. "Thanks a bunch!"

"No more than you deserve," I said, setting off at a trot while Reuben ran excitedly to show others what he had received. Just then as I departed on horseback, I recalled what Tom said during one of our many discussions that it was right to reward the young for what they do well so they learn to live well! The thought made me smile. Most of what he said wasn't new. It was the common sense way he said it, that made an impression.'

'South of the tracks, the cowtown saloons were already alive with early evening custom when I walked my horse through the junction on Texas street, crossing the tracks, to enter the residential and quieter part of town where my hotel was situated. Before dismounting in my old, worn, sweat stained clothes, a sense of the wilderness stoked me with disdain for the social, conventional way of life I was about to re-enter. Instinctively, there was an immediate temptation to turn about at once and head back to the south side to seek familiar faces and talk that I'd become accustomed to. But the moment passed and I was forced to smile at myself for such an impulse; an impulse, I realised, that was nothing other than a kind of reverse vanity!

"W' know what we're used to and used t' what we know," was a line Tom expressed about people's attitude to change! My own instant reaction to the regulated, civil part of town was a case in point.

Before entering the hotel, I first visited a store where I bought new clothes. I'm afraid I did so without a great deal of interest, despite the earnest attention of the assistant who was glad to help me choose items to replace the old, grubby clothes I stood in.

An hour later, after a steaming bath, my only inclination was to lie down and rest upon the soft mattress of a bed where I quickly dozed off only to wake later with dusk filling the window. Hurriedly, I dressed in my new clothes and went downstairs to wait at the table for my guests while sipping a glass of red wine and reading through my note book.

Tom and Jim arrived and soon, together, we enjoyed the luxury of an ample meal and wholesome talk. They were interested in how I would write my articles and I tried to answer them specifically. We talked of the West and I mentioned my growing interest in the indian problem and my pessimism about it. It seemed to me absurd that in the development of our free, immigrant nation, the country's native was destined to be captive.

"So y' think reservations ain't the answer to them?" Jim asked.

"It's a form of captivity," I replied.

"So what's the solution?" he asked, calmly.

"Let them live as they do, independent and free. It's us, the newcomers, who should live round them, not them round us."

"It won't work and y' know it won't!" Jim affirmed.

"It's what we do, Jim, back home," Tom came in. "We know the local tribe and there's no trouble between us. If they want a cow or anythin' of ours we talk and make an exchange."

"But it won't stay that way Tom," I countered. "As other settlers arrive in the vicinity and build homes and farm the land, someone's going to object to them and then there's going to be conflict with the soldiers coming in to chase them off. That's how it's been elsewhere and how it'll be in the end, everywhere."

"Maybe," Tom said, with a glint in his eye. "Unless you and me own all the land in the area and stop anybody else havin' it but us and the Indians."

"Another kind of reservation," I hinted.

"Sure," Tom grinned. "But it's where they live and want to be anyway!"

"What if the Indians decide to build houses like you and breed and raise cattle?" I proposed.

"Fine. I'll sell them what they need." He winked, deliberately. "We'll do good business together! My knowledge and their ambition workin' hand in hand!"

We smiled about it, at the same time knowing, as Tom had implied, that it was an ideal invariably doomed by greed and mistrust, and to a certain degree, by the very nature of assistance becoming interference.

Towards the end of the meal I learned that they were to call upon Scott in one of the saloons, returning with him to camp for an early morning start. The idea of joining them for a final toast in one of the cowboy saloons appealed to me. It seemed like a perfect climax to the trip, and to our short lived, yet sound friendship.'

'While I walked alongside their horses, we crossed the tracks into the noise and lights of the south side. It seemed like stepping into another, vibrant town. We travelled along Texas street which was as busy and rowdy as these towns were noted to be, with the uninhibited sound of music and voices. We passed a group of young Texans howling with laughter at one of their number who was vomiting in an alleyway, and a short distance from them we circled past a raging pair of cowboys being restrained by friends, before, or even after, there were blows. At the door of another dwelling two girls smoking cigarettes waved, calling on us to come on in.

Outside the Bull's Head Saloon they hitched their horses and we entered the smoky, clamorous room, finding Scott and Mex at the end of the bar, near the door. While being served we spied Stilt, Red, Wes and Parker card gambling with another three men sitting round a large table at the other end of the room. Mex informed us that Travis was occupied with a girl, while Jacob, Elias, Reuben and the boss who had been in town earlier to eat, had gone back to camp to relieve them, Scott and himself, from horse guard.

"What y' reckon then, Mex, to this place?" Jim asked, sportingly.

"Good. But have to remember in here that me a Mexican, so Aa keep m' head down a little, huh?"

"Are you serious?" I asked.

"Sure. This is Kansas, remember. It's bad enough if y' Texan but for a 'greaser' it's worse!" Then he gave a grin. "Still, bein' a black man, like Jacob, is even shittier!

"He's r-right, Mr Br-ewster!" Scott asserted.

"You see now, Carlton," Tom came in, "why Indians don't stand a cat in hell's chance?"

I nodded, seriously, then brightened. "Are the women prejudiced too?"

Mex grinned again. "They see only the money."

Tom sniffed in amusement. "Do the' charge the same though?"

"You bet," Mex exclaimed, merrily.

Tom bought another round and we chatted amiably, glancing now and again across the room or at those coming in and going out of the door. It was full but not crowded and the barman had time to talk with us. He had eyes like a lizard, quickly checking and surveying what was going on around him.

It was his stiffening that made us turn our heads. Red was on his feet cursing his misfortune. He threw his cards down on the table and grabbing his bottle knocked his chair over moving away to the bar.

In a bleak voice, Hardin accused him of being a 'Turntail'. Red resented the remark and spun round. Wagging a finger at Hardin he scolded him foully as a trouble maker. Wes leant back in his chair and with a smirk mocked Red's lack of nerve for not going after the Kiowas. Red cursed him, adding he was a no good kid that needed whipping.

The room quietened.

Hardin's eyes filled with violence. "Get out of here y' damn lump of crowbait!" he fumed.

Emboldened by alcohol, Red was furious and spat onto the floor. "Damn if Aa will for a louse like you!" he blasted.

Slowly and blatantly, Hardin rose from his seat and poised himself for a confrontation. Men quickly moved out of harm's way leaving the two silently and tensely facing each other. Wes seemed to grin and suddenly, vexed beyond reason, Red rushed for his gun. Like a bolt, Hardin drew faster shooting him in the chest before Red could even fire, and at once he fell backwards and lay still, blood pumping out of his heart.

There was a brief, stunned silence. Jim marched forward. "Y' son of a bitch!" he cried.

Wes glared at him.

"You wanted it t' happen. You pushed him t' stand against y'. You're nothing but a dirty killer!" Jim ranted with disgust and indignation.

"Shut your mouth or you'll get the same!" Hardin muttered. His face pinched with fury.

"Y' don't scare me, kid," Jim snarled. "Aa say what Aa want to say!"

"Y've said it so shut up!" Wes rasped.

"Aa don't back off from the likes of you!" Jim flared.

Hardin stepped slowly sideways to take up a position facing Jim along the bar. The crowd moved again out of line. At the same time Tom slipped along the bar closer to Jim. "Enough of this," he protested. "Forget it, Jim. We're goin' home tomorrow!"

"Keep out of it, Tom!" Jim ordered him, keeping his stare on Hardin.

"Don't be a fool," Tom remonstrated. "He'll kill you!"

"Keep out of it, Tom!" Jim snapped.

Tom sneaked a hand round a bottle on the bar then suddenly swung it round, clubbing Jim on the back of his head and he dropped like a cut rope.

Tom stood over his friend and confronted Hardin. "You let it go now, Wes, and call it off or I take his place!" he stated, solemnly.

Wes straightened. "It's not your fight!"

Tom sighed. "No. But it is now if it's what y' want?"

Standing half drunk at the side, Parker could not hold back his feelings. "Take him, Wes. Y' can lick him!"

Still staring at Tom, Wes ignored the remark. "If Aa have to kill y', Aa will!" he vowed.

"You don't have to, Wes. Let this be an end to it between you and Jim and there'll be no gun play between us," Tom said cooly. "It's your decision, not mine."

"Don't let him get away with it, Wes!" Parker hissed.

"Aa've no argument with you, Tom. Y' shouldn't have interfered," Wes scowled.

"You're faster than 'im!" Parker rasped, his lip curled.

"Shut up, Parker," Wes rapped.

"If y' let him go word'll be y' were afraid of him!" Parker goaded him further.

"Make up your own mind, Wes. You're your own man!" Tom advised in a low, intent voice, his features glazed with concentration.

Hardin's expression never altered while the rest of the room, wrapped in silence, waited for his answer. At last, his stance relaxed. "Take him home, Tom," he muttered.

Tom acknowledged him with a slight nod then bent down and hauled his friend up onto his feet, supporting him with a clasp. Jim stood slumped, semi-conscious. Nobody else moved.

"Don't let 'im go," Parker's voice rang out as Tom turned round, slowly dragging his partner away. With all eyes on them, Parker pulled his gun out. Suddenly there was a shot and in the confusion Parker wheeled, clutching his side. Still standing, he gaped with disbelief and agony at Hardin's smoking gun, then he groaned aloud and collapsed to the floor at Red's feet.

Tom delayed long enough to weigh up what had happened and was set to turn and make his way out, carrying Jim, when in through the door marched a tall, striking, long haired figure wearing a sheriff's badge. Behind him were two deputies, armed with shotguns.

Hickock cast his eyes round the room, levelling them finally at the bartender. "Explain it, Thompson!" he ordered. The other told him exactly, making out the fairness of the killings. Hickock's eyes registered each player involved in the scene before studying Tom. Gradually, his regard widened in recognition. "Tom Tileman?" he uttered..

"Is that so?" Tom mumbled.

Hickock stared. "Met you once a long time ago in Santa Fe. Used to ride stage with Jeddle Bowrey. Remember him?"

Tom nodded.

"Anyway," Hickock continued, "y' best see t' your friend. Aa'll talk with you outside." He stepped aside to let Tom, with Scott helping him, support Jim out of the saloon into the night's fresh air. When they had left Hickock peered critically at Hardin. "You've killed two men and Thompson says it weren't your fault. What do y' say?"

"It's like he says. The first drew on me and Parker was about t' shoot Tom in the back," Wes replied in a chill, contemptuous voice.

Hickock asked another man that he recognised in the crowd if it was true. The man nodded. "Okay. Aa'll be back in here soon. Aa want all shooting irons put on the table in the corner there. You can pick them up when y' go!" he commanded loudly, then turned and went outside leaving his two assistants to carry out his order.

While Mex and Stilt began the task of carrying out Red's and Parker's dead bodies, Hardin made his way past them out of the saloon. I expected the officers to question him or at least take his gun but they said nothing, only one of them followed him out onto the sidewalk to observe his movements. At that moment I also sneaked out.

Next to the horses Tom was sitting on the sidewalk edge with Jim buckled beside him, holding his head. Hickock stood nearby. Openly, Wes approached them, while from over the street Scott walked his horse to join them, and I moved closer.

Giving a groan of consciousness Jim uncovered his face. Tom stared up at Wes. "Aa should thank y' for stoppin' Parker shootin' me in the back. But for killing Red, Aa don't ever want t' know y' again," he said bitterly.

In a moment of unease Hardin changed stance, wiping his mouth with the back of his hand. "He drew first," he answered glumly.

"You riled him to do it," Tom deplored, getting up to stand. Scott had now taken Jim and was pouring water over the back of his head and he shuddered, opening his eyes.

"Maybe y' ought leave town," Hickock instructed Hardin. Wes eyed him spitefully then glanced over his shoulder to see that the officer was still there outside the saloon with his shotgun, keeping watch. "An' stay out!" Hickock commanded. Wes glowered at him, then casting Tom a final, pensive regard he walked away.

Helping Jim onto his feet, Scott and Tom let him find his balance. He rubbed his head and raised his eyes gaining focus.

"Why don't you get him to a bed in town?" I suggested.

"He'll be fine, I promise," Tom replied, gently. He looked at me earnestly. "Right here, Aa guess it's farewell for us, Mister Brewster. Shame it's been a sad ending, but we've enjoyed your company!" We shook hands warmly and managed to smile. Tom saluted Hickock with a strong, knowing look, and then he and Scott helped Jim onto his grey horse, 'Sugar', and mounting theirs either side, they set off at a walking pace, Tom holding Jim steady by the arm. I stood motionless with the world, confounded by thoughts and feelings of wonder as I watched them go along the street, the image of Tom supporting his friend imprinting itself for ever on my mind.

"A'll buy you a drink, mister," Hickock invited me, and, eager to talk with him, I turned slowly to follow him back into the saloon.'

At camp the following morning Tom woke Jim gently to find him brooding with an aching head and a confused sense of regret and indignation. Nobody was inclined to mention the incident, leaving him to come to terms with it and speak about it when he wished. Elias served a full breakfast of biscuit, gravy, sliced ham and omelette, then he himself sat down and ate and drank black coffee with them, talking to Tom about their leaving, offering some advice as to their safety.

"If you're plannin' to cut across the Territory you'd be better travellin' at night. Three of you makes it worthwhile any Indians chasin' after you. You've enough to steal from and there's not enough of you t' worry them!"

"Not until Tom shows them how to shoot!" trumped Reuben.

"Boy," Elias grumped, "it ain't polite t' come into men's conversation without bein' invited!" He turned to Tom again. "But if Aa was you Aa'd choose goin' back down the Chisholm trail. I hear there's a stream of herds on their way up. You'll have Texans somewhere nearby, every day!"

"Well it makes good sense, Aa guess," Tom answered.

"S-s-sure does," Scott added.

Elias frowned at him. "Let me cut that hair 'fore you go?" he moaned.

"S-said Aa'd w-wait till Aa g-g-get home," Scott stuttered.

Tom grinned. He liked the idea of Scott accompanying them. He had an even tempered nature you could trust. And, if he started the journey with you he'd stay the course. On the trail not one of the crew ever doubted him. Although seeming self-conscious, they sensed in him a dauntless streak. For all their carping, Parker and Red were never heard to target him. And now they never would.

Elias poured Scott more coffee. "Lettin' hair grow that long ain't good for a man!" he blurted.

"Why's that?" Jacob asked with his mouth full.

"It weakens his mind so he don't think straight."

"He weren't hired t' think!" Mex said. He'd spent the night in town and only recently arrived back at camp in time for breakfast.

"He ain't hired now!" Elias sniped.

"But he still don't need to think," Mex retorted, grinning.

"How on earth is he gonna get home if he don't think for himself!" Elias raged.

"He got Tom!" Mex joked.

Elias dismissed it with a snort.

"He better take care o' me too," Jim mumbled. "Aa'll be lucky t' ever think straight again!"

Elias grinned and leant over to refill Jim's mug. "In a couple of days you'll be as pig headed as y' were before. Let's feel that lump." He stepped across to place his fingers above Jim's right ear.

Jim flinched. "Aa want none o' your ointments!"

"Don't fuss. It ain't worthy of any of them!" Elias exclaimed. "And if y' want t' know, Aa've seen bigger blisters on a man's hand!

Jim forced himself to smile and then regarded Tom who was looking at him earnestly.

"Aa did it for the best," Tom explained.

Jim nodded. "Aa know it Tom." He paused, his eyes warming. "But y' might've found a softer bottle!"

The group chuckled then turned their heads to see Mr Mathias approaching the fire. He stood before them and pushed his hat up revealing the front of his sparse grey hair. "Good t' see you're okay, Jim," he opened. "An' I understand your actions. They were honourable." He turned his attention to Tom. "Goin' into town soon t' see about burying Parker and Red and sorting out matters with the law. God knows, I'm real upset about Harding killing Red like he did." He paused. "Anyway, Aa know you're wantin' away soon, but I'd like to have a word with you, Tom, in private."

Tom had finished eating so he got up and the two of them went off together beyond the horses towards a tent where the trail boss slept and kept his belongings. They sat outside on a log, their backs to the low morning sun. From the town's direction came the noise of a steam engine shunting cattle cars.

"Jim seems on the mend. What time y' fixin' t' go?" Mathias enquired.

"Soon as w' pack everything."

"Told you before, y' could return with us in a week's time."

"Aa want to get home quicker than that," Tom said.

The trail boss offered Tom an expensive cigar but Tom declined the offer preferring to light his pipe. "What's on your mind, boss? Tom asked.

Mathias turned his head to look at his friend. "You and Jim both got fourteen dollars a head for your cattle and y' wanted cash. That's over four thousand dollars in notes. It's too much of a risk t' carry that amount. You can't deny it!"

"Sure is. But it's safer than a bit of paper from a man Aa don't know."

"That's a dumb thing to say, Tom. He gives you a banker's note to cash in San Antonio, just as he gives me."

"I don't intend going there!" Tom replied.

"So you run the risk of losin' everythin'?" Mathias wailed. "Even Jim's concerned about it."

Tom didn't answer so the two men continued to smoke in silence, until the trail boss decided to end it. "Aa've got a proposition t' make, Tom."

Tom grinned. "Aa guessed as much. Up to now we've been just fakin' to talk, cos everythin' spoke has already been said before! Now, what's on your mind?"

"Aa've got a bank account in Kerrville. If you hand over your cash to me I'll give you a credit note to put into your account there. That way there's no need to carry more money than y' want for the trip."

Tom removed his pipe from his mouth. "Y' don't have t' do that."

"It ain't a risk for me, Tom. It's a favour, that's all." He clapped Tom on the shoulder and they shook hands. Mathias went inside and came outside with banker's notes he had already prepared. Tom signed his name on each and so did Henry Mathias. They conversed a while longer before they stood up and shook hands again for the last time.

"Pleased to have you as a friend, Tom."

"My pleasure," Tom answered. "You've been a good boss and Jim and me are grateful. Look after yourself!" He nodded his appreciation then turned to go back to the camp fire to join Jim and Scott packing their mounts.

After the trail boss had ridden out, Tom and Jim with their own four horses, and Scott with his two from the remuda, called 'Blue Coat' and 'Sagebrush' were set to leave.

They declared farewell to Elias, Mex, Jacob and Reuben, and then set off across the river, splashing through the low water leaving the other four standing on the bank, hooting and waving. Everyone intended meeting up again someday, but it was an easy thing to say when friendships were dividing. Elias's last words to them said as much. "Aa'd be pleased for us to meet you again, fellows, but since it won't be any better than it is now it won't make no difference if we don't."

2

PART 2

SPUR FOR HOME

They rode freely, enjoying the speed of their travel, unrestricted by the tedious slow trailing of longhorns. Tom sat on 'Rusty' with Jim alongside on 'Star', their favourite mounts, while Scott was saddled on his dun-flecked pony called 'Sage Bush'. The heat of the sun was lessened too by the rush of air as they cantered along. They hardly spoke but conveyed their feelings of gladness and satisfaction with cheerful glances.

After about twelve miles they slowed to walk again and their faces shone with sweat. Wiping his forehead dry with his bandana, Jim proved his recovery with a gleam in his eye. "You know Aa'm sure gonna miss that crazy old cook, but not for his bee-stingin' tongue!"

Tom grinned. "Never known a man so happy t' argue!"

"But y-you're T-T-Tileman, like he s-said!" Scott declared.

Tom pulled up and questioned him with his eyes, as if an answer was unimportant.

"G-got to know w-who am r-r-riding with," Scott explained.

Tom nodded slightly. "Aa'm tellin' you, Scott, because you'll keep it t' yourself. Aa killed three men tryin' to ambush a pay wagon and another two later outside a saloon who challenged me. It weren't no more than that. Aa changed my name t' become a family man and t' rid myself of the notoriety which was spreadin'."

"You k-k-killed s-some more on the t-trail." Scott added frankly, meaning the Indians and Jayhawkers.

Jim looked at Tom wondering how he would reply. Tom nodded thoughtfully. "Unlike Hardin, Aa shoot at people Aa need to, not who Aa want."

Scott nodded in accordance. "Me t-too," he admitted with a trace of humour, and after they had swigged more water they urged their horses into another run, aiming to add extra miles before the fiercest sun of the day blazed and when they would rest in shade, water the horses and eat. Without stressing themselves and their mounts they felt they could manage between fifty to sixty miles each day, switching rides. For hardened journeymen, as they had become, it seemed a moderate task. And keeping close to the Chisholm trail, particularly through Indian Territory, added security to their venture. Already to the west of them they had spotted a steam of dust from a large herd and another showed before they stopped past noontime.

While Jim and Scott prepared a fire to brew coffee in a shady nest of small cottonwood trees, Tom was conducting the horses to drink as they circled the one shallow pool of water surfacing in the creek hollow below.

Knowing Tom couldn't hear, Jim was eager to talk. "Couldn't believe it, Scott, the way you just asked him outright and he told you like he'd tell no one else. Sure old Elias suspected him, but Tom never admitted it, even when Hickock recognised him."

Scott shrugged. "Makes no d-d-difference, only now it's n-not you two and m-m-me now. Y-you understand? We're a th-three."

Jim stared at the young, long haired cowboy with his sharp eyed, solid featured face. He nodded. "Sure we are! An' Aa'll tell y' somethin' else; now we're not carrying real money it feels a lot more easier."

"Tom said."

"Aa told him it was crazy but he wouldn't listen until I got Mr Mathias to help out. Sometimes he's as pig headed as me, but don't tell him that, okay?" Jim's eyes twinkled, then he got down on his knees to blow the fire again turning smoke into flame.

Since the horses at the pool were less inclined to barge each other, Tom left them to it and wandered up the other bank and walked along the gully towards the rise where he could see for miles. There, he paused to watch a snake that he had disturbed sunning itself in the open, wriggle off into the grass. The other two saw him on the height drawing on his pipe and thought nothing of it until he returned saying he could see nothing for the haze of wavering heat.

"What were you hopin' t' see, Tom?" Jim asked.

Tom shook his head. "Nothing special, but Aa've a feeling we're being followed."

The other two stared.

"But y' saw nobody, huh?" asked Jim.

"Just a feelin', nothing more," Tom shrugged, squatting down at the fireside where the can was heating.

"I'll t-take a look s-s-soon," Scott said.

Jim nudged Tom. "Thinks - because he's the youngest - he's got better eyes than us."

"Probably has. Beyond ten miles, I sure don't see everythin' the same as Aa once did," Tom quipped.

"Don't worry about it, Tom, y' just need to see as far as that old musket fires," Jim jibed, referring to his old Sharps rifle. Jim had bought himself a new Remington like the ones on the drive and was proud as a panther. Scott had brought his 'Yellow Boy' model Winchester, the same type Hardin had showed Tom.

Tom sniffed as he watched the coffee start to boil. "Aa just hope that sweet lady of yours is gonna be happy about spending money like that."

"If it gets me safe back t' her, she'll say it's worth every cent!" Jim retorted.

Scott pushed another stick into the fire. "Are you s-sure y-you're partners?"

"Partners!" exclaimed Jim. "Cows teeth, no! He's sometimes boss and then it's my turn. Only he cheats!"

Tom and Scott beamed. "That h-hit on the h-head done y-you some good," Scott declared.

Although he still felt fuzzy headed, Jim grinned, then turned and spat away. While Tom unwrapped the meat and cold potatoes which Elias had given them sealed in muslin cloth, Scott poured steaming black coffee into the three mugs. It was a light meal finished off with an apple each, and contented the three lay down in the shade to rest. Within minutes Tom and Jim had dozed off and Scott, who said he would stay on watch, took a stroll up to the point where Tom had viewed the surrounding land. He scanned for a sign of any one but it was impossible to see clearly as Tom had said, so he wandered down again to sit beside the horses watching them. A warm breeze rippled the grasses and leaves, and as he gazed unconsciously at the forms of light and shadow surrounding him, he felt the weightlessness of contentment

Ten minutes later, Tom rose and stretched then came over to hunker down next to him. "Go get yourself some rest," Tom said. "If Aa sleep much longer Aa might never rise!"

"Sure," Scott answered, getting to his feet. "Think w' might get t-t-to Newton before s-sundown?"

Tom squinted up. "We could get to Texas if we wanted, but Newton'll do for one day's ride, Aa reckon."

Scott yawned and wandered off to lie down on his quilt.

He doubted he could sleep, for his mind was too alive and optimistic with the real knowing about Tom's past and Jim's recovery and the expectation of staying overnight in Newton, remembering what the trail boys had said.

Before setting off they had discussed the journey together and agreed to enjoy comforts when they could. The trail north had been arduous and there was no point in sleeping out when a meal and a bed was possible and could be bought cheaply. After all, through Indian Territory there would be no chance of such luxury.

Half an hour later, packed again, they were ready to travel on fresh mounts. Tom rode 'Rock' and Jim took 'Mack' while Scott sat on nimble 'Blue Coat'. With a holler of delight they spurred away again, southwards into the sweltering sun. There was no change in the countryside, just rolling, brown, arid prairie land without any habitation in view, just one more line of cattle a mile or so to their left, creating dust as they headed north towards Abilene.

With long, gentle staggered runs and intermittent walking, the three riders made good progress, eventually reaching the town of Newton early evening. A distance that had taken three days travelling north with cattle, had now taken less than one!

The railhead was not yet completed but newly built stockyards were ready for cattle, while tents and buildings erected on the north side of town had started to provide the usual entertainments for the hoards of railroad workers. Once the line was in operation, the first cowboys would arrive, multiplying numbers to swell the developing scene. As the three riders and their horses came up the dusty street they witnessed girls younger than any they'd seen in Abilene brashly appearing and disappearing in doorways, taunting and tempting customers like little vixens. Two of them even stepped out onto the street to walk alongside the new arrivals.

"Bet y' just dyin' t' have a drink with us, huh?" cooed the dark eyed one looking up at Jim.

"Think of nothin' nicer, honey, but we've been ridin' and sweatin' and it would be nothing but a shame to share your company in this filthy, foul smellin' condition!" he confessed.

The girl giggled. "Mister, we can scrub you cleaner than a new penny, can't we sister?" she cried, turning to the other.

Jim looked hard at her. "Aa bet you can too, little girl!" he scorned, then spurring his horse to a jolt, he startled her off. Left standing in the roadway the two girls cursed them obscenely. The three cowboys laughed and continued along the dusty dirt road into the old part of town where they stabled the horses first before finding a rooming house to stay the night.

By this time Jim's head was throbbing from the day's long ride and all he wanted to do, after washing himself, was to lie down, resting on his bed in the dark. Leaving him in peace, Tom and Scott went out to find a place to eat. In a narrow dining room with six tables down one side, only one table was left unoccupied for them to sit down. Despite the air inside being thick with the smells of cooking, tobacco smoke and burning oil lamps set on each table, the basic room was tidy and friendly. Served from an adjoining kitchen, Tom and Scott tucked in to a large plate of beef pie with vegetables and gravy, talking leisurely about friends and family.

After stewed apricot pie, the two of them sat back drinking coffee and picking their teeth clean with quills. During their meal they had paid little interest to the others present, except for a fellow on an end table who seemed to have a lot to say for himself to his three companions. On his way out this authoritive individual made it his business to speak to the two strangers.

"Trust you two gentleman have enjoyed your meal?" he said.

Tom and Scott raised their eyes. "Good as w' hoped and better than we expected," Tom quipped.

The man smirked. He was portly built with a fine beard rounding off his square jawed face. His hat and clothes were new and costly. Tom's wordy answer took him by surprise. He hesitated. "I own the place so I take that as a compliment, sir," he replied deliberately.

"Then Aa said the right thing to the right man," Tom answered cheerfully.

"Name's McCluskie," he said formally.

Tom put his coffee down. "Mine's Tom Torrance and this here is Scott, Scott McNeil."

McCluskie hung his thumbs on his belt. "If you two are here lookin' for work I might be able to help?"

"No thanks," Tom said. "We drove cattle as far as Abilene and now we're just aimin' t' spur home."

"They say Hickock's doing his best to keep order up there," McCluskie said with an approving nod of his head.

Tom was preparing his pipe to light up. "So they say," he answered, incidentally.

"Well we won't be needing him here when we open up! We aim to discourage wild cowhands from the moment they start pouring in!" he boasted.

Tom met his eyes and grinned. "That's fine, but be careful y' don't stop their free spending all together!"

McCluskie forced a smile. He sensed something about this articulate, older cowboy that made him feel uneasy. He was condescending and challenging at the same time, and yet neither one nor the other was direct enough to offend. Somehow, McCluskie needed to deal with him lightly and show everyone listening he was in charge. "That's true, mister," he chirped airily, "but I'm sure you know what I mean?"

Tom read McCluskie's eyes. He lit his pie and sucked on it. "Aa surely do, and, good luck to y'," he answered – every word uttered precisely.

Unabashed, McCluskie raised one hand. "Good t' talk to you," he said and readily turned away to strut out. At the last table where a lone youth was sitting, McCluskie stopped again to make a final announcement. "Miss Bryson!" he called to the plump woman in the kitchen who had served them food. "Now, you just put young Riley's bill onto my own account. Don't forget!" And patting Riley on the shoulder he made his exit.

"Thank you, Mr McCluskie," the pale boy wheezed after him.

Watching him closely Tom knew by his condition that the youth was consumptive, and knew too, with an uncanny sense, that he was also fearless. Not in the ordinary way in which the young are, believing in their immortality until they're hurt, but in the silent, abiding way he faced the world with a serious illness.

"McCluskie's gonna be a dead man soon," Scott mumbled perfectly, as he leant forward with his elbows on the table.

Tom smiled at his prediction. "You mean he attracts enemies?"

Scott nodded. Tom smiled again, thinking how little he knew about Scott and how in one day, riding side by side he had heard him talk more than on the entire trail. Already, he seemed mature beyond his years.

Tom drew on his pipe and the smoke filtered out with his words. "Aa reckon he may as well. His belly's that full of arrogance he's likely t' burst," he joked.

Scott grinned, then started to chuckle as Tom's humour grew in his thoughts. Tom bit his lower lip to prevent himself laughing with Scott and his shoulders trembled with the strain. Scott buried his face into his hands to suppress his mirth. When he had it under control he looked up and shook his head at Tom and took a long breath. "Hell Tom, you say the funniest th-things!"

Miss Bryson had emerged from the kitchen with the coffee pot in hand and stopped at their table. "More coffee, gentlemen?"

They both declined, then Tom complimented her on the meal.

"Well if you be wantin' breakfast in the morning just you both drop in," she replied brightly at Tom.

Tom looked at her admiringly. She was one of those attractive, slightly older women with plaited hair that isn't appreciated at first glance. Like his wife at home, she had the features of a gentlewoman with sensitive eyes and mouth. She felt his gaze, held it and smiled. "We open at Six."

"Then we'll ride south at Seven, I guess," Tom drawled. "There'll be three of us - if the other's still alive!"

"Oh," she said, her expression changing. "What happened to him?"

"Got a sore head."

"Too much whiskey?" she suggested, lightly.

"Only a bottle!" Tom quipped.

Scott snorted, stemming a snigger.

She shook her head regretfully and moved on to the next table where two customers were waiting for refills.

"Let's p-pay up and get out of h--ere," Scott declared glee-fully. "If Jim's dead wh-en w-we see him yo-u're going to be real s-s-sorry!

Tom looked quizzically Scott and drew on his pipe. "That's an awful thing to say to a friend, Scott!"

Scott dismissed Tom's foolishness with a flick of his hand

and stood up. They left the building, crossing the street to head to their rooms for an early night's sleep, leaving the saloons and the under age girls to others who desired them.

Little did Scott know then, that he would be back in Newton in August, at the time Mr McCluskie got killed, and how a youth named Riley, shot four Texan cowboys in revenge for his murder, before running off, never to be heard of again. It made big news throughout the country and Carlton Brewster, the journalist, would have loved to have known about Tom and Scott meeting McCluskie that evening and what had been said.

After a long sleep, Jim was brighter in the morning and they ate a hearty breakfast at Miss Bryson's place and were on the road riding out of town by Seven-thirty. Tom recounted their evening and told Jim the funny side and he laughed and admitted that he might have been impolite towards McCluskie, so it was a good thing he'd stayed away! All he had needed to regain his health, he confessed, had been a soft bed and pillow, a darkened room and ten hours of undisturbed rest!

Like Tom, Jim found Scott's company more enjoyable than he imagined. On the trail to Abilene, Scott had said little and only entered conversation when drawn into it. His stammer obviously inhibited him in group company, so he was content just to listen and avoid any focus of attention. Now and again, riding alongside Scott on the trail, Tom and Jim had chatted with him and their patience had won his confidence and respect, but he looked out for no one and withheld his feelings from others. Unlike Hardin who was surly and Parker who was objectionable, Scott was sociable without showing any character. Elias had described him as a cloaked figure that revealed little, but he never doubted that he had spine. Scott never complained or cursed about work and seemed tireless. At one time his horse, 'Sagebush', fell and he hit the ground hard and was hurt but staggered up and remounted and, uncomplaining, rode for the rest of the day. Without avoiding his duties he limped for a week and shook his head at anyone's concern. Being resilient, he soon recovered: that was all there was to it and everybody admired him for it.

Now, riding south with just Tom and Jim, Scott was clearly more light minded and increasingly vocal. Their sense of humour appealed to him and their good nature encouraged him to be open and less reserved. He was a good horseman and Tom even let him ride 'Star', his black coated mount. Scott also felt at ease to talk to them about his mother at home in Laredo. His father, a drifter whom she had fallen in love with, had left her when she was pregnant, so Scott never got to know him. The shame on his mother's family and the insults from other children about this, as well as his stammering, had made his growing up a difficult, bitter time.

"But you came through it, Scott!" Tom remarked having heard Scott's story.

"We moved to Lare-do when I was eleven. I was r-raised in Crys-s-stal City," Scott explained.

"Was it easier there?" Jim asked.

Scott grinned. "I learned to fight. An old Mexican sh-hh-owed me how to use my f-fists!"

"Is that how you got that scar mark above your eye?"

"Yeah. He got me and an-nother boy t' practice and some-times it got for r-r-real!"

Tom and Jim smiled and they set the horses into another lengthy run over a stretch of sloping ground before wading across the Arkansas river. There, on the other side of the water they took a short rest then switched horses to continue their journey. Here, Tom exchanged 'Munch' for 'Locust', Jim saddled 'Sugar' in place of 'Tricky' and Scott got a chance to ride Jim's 'Mack'.

Beyond the river basin the yellowing prairie swept before them like a ruffled blanket with slight swells and falls that was monotonous to the eye as they searched the distance for some feature to focus upon.

Stopping at noon to rest, Jim built a fire with wood they had collected on the way and then they sat in shade waiting for the coffee to boil. In a nearby gully, the unloaded horses grazed around a shallow watering hole.

At this point Jim finally spoke to Tom about him turning his head to look back throughout the morning's ride. "So y' still think we're being followed, huh?"

"It's just a habit, Jim. Y' know me."

"But yesterday y' seemed sure."

"Aa did. Aa like t' keep checkin', that's all."

"Seen anythin'?"

"No."

"Then why worry about it?"

"Aa don't."

"But you keep lookin' over your shoulder."

"Habit, I guess."

"Think maybe Wes is comin' after us?"

"It's ain't him."

"How d' you know, Tom, if y' ain't seen anyone?"

"Aa know it. If it's anybody it ain't him, for sure."

"Well who might it be, instead?" Jim insisted.

"Didn't say there was anybody. I just had a feelin' we're bein' followed, that's all."

Jim blew, then turned to Scott who was lying on his back listening, with his hands cupped behind his head. "Hey Scott, if it's not Wes who else might want to follow us?"

"There's no one f-followin' us. Aa've been l-l-looking too."

Bemused, Jim shook his head. He lifted off the pot and stirred the black steaming liquid with a wooden spoon before setting it back over the small fire again. "Well, when you two see someone, tell me about it so Aa can get spooked about it too."

Tom had lit his pipe and sat back resting against the narrow trunk of a bush tree that offered them shade. "Now that you got that tongue of yours rattlin' again, Jim, I guess you're as good as new," he sighed.

Jim stared at him. "Did y' like me better when Aa was dumb?"

Tom took the pipe out of his mouth. "Y' were sweeter, but not as much fun."

Jim chuckled. "Nobody ever called me 'sweet' in my life!"

Scott suddenly sat up. "Listen! Shhh!" he indicated.

They froze, listening. Almost at once the faintest sound of riders approaching from the east made them stand up and reach for their rifles, holding them loosely.

"Whoever it is ain't the one following us," Jim commented, meaning they weren't approaching from that direction.

They watched two horsemen riding towards them and waited for them to walk their horses in. The older of the two was grey bearded. He raised his hat. "Saw your smoke and came by," he said amiably. "We're with a herd a mile or so back."

"We trailed to Abilene only a few days ago. How's it goin'?" Tom said, his hand resting on his pistol.

"We're gettin' there, but we've had our share of trouble. Two men got injured and two rode out on us. Couldn't take no more!"

"They reckon there's thousands of cattle comin' up the trail," Jim said.

"Sure thing. We got held up more than a full day to get across Red River," the man admitted.

Tom invited them to drink coffee and the two riders dismounted to join them and introductions were made. The older one was named Sam, while the other fellow, bearded too, was fidgety and nervous looking. He called himself Billy. They said they were scouting ahead when they spotted fire smoke and came to investigate.

Billy took it upon himself to lead their two horses down to the water while Sam sat down with them, muttering about the heat and the dust and yet how it was better than a trail he'd been on in '69 when they wore slickers more days than they did not, and how the rain swelled the rivers so much every crossing was a risk. Meanwhile, out of sight, Billy, the younger one, sneaked round out of the gully into the brush behind them.

"Now look you there," Sam said, climbing to his feet. He pointed, drawing their attention. "I guess that must be our herd coming. See that cloud of dust?" he asked, distracting the three cowboys to peer in that direction.

At this moment Billy stepped out behind them, pointing his rifle and shouting, "Don't move a hand or I'll shoot you sittin' there!"

Sam drew his revolver. "You heard him! Get you're hands up high!"

They complied, glancing bitterly at each other for being

jumped, and even Tom clicked his tongue with self reproach. The reason for Billy's edginess was obvious now and he hadn't suspected it?

"Keep that rifle aimed at their backs!" Sam instructed the other. "Aa'll take their guns!"

When that was done, dumping them out of reach, he ordered them to thread their fingers behind their heads and cross their legs. Behind them, Billy stayed silent, while Sam positioned himself in front, pointing his revolver at them, ready to talk.

"Two of y' got a stack of money for sellin' beeves. We want it!"

"No we don't," Jim replied, shaking his head.

"Be quiet Jim!" Tom interrupted, fearing Jim's impetuous nature might increase their danger. "Aa'll do the talkin'. It was me that agreed to it, remember!"

Sam spat. "Stand up, you!" he bawled. His face tightening in anger. He stepped nearer Tom, raising his gun to Tom's chin. "Don't lie cowboy or Aa'll blow a hole through your head! Y' got money in bills. That's a fact. Now make it easy and you and me go t' the saddle bags over there and you empty each and every one of them!" he uttered in a strained voice.

Tom knew by now both of them were ordinary cowhands, greedy for money, who had probably overheard gossip about them in Abilene. Neither of them had likely robbed before. Since leaving Abilene they had probably talked themselves into it, over and over, plucking up the courage. Their nervousness made them dangerous. The younger one with the rifle was likely to jerk the trigger in an instant.

Tom lifted each bag separately and tipped out the contents, all their belongings, personal items and food supplies. When he had finished he was instructed again to clasp his hands again behind his head and retire to sit down in his place, leaving Sam to plunder through everything, searching for the money. At last he stood up and stamped the ground in fury and marched towards Tom.

"You better tell me where it is!" he boomed and gave Tom a hard kick in his ribs. Tom reeled over, gasping.

"W' don't have no money!" Jim bawled, angrily. "W' got a banker's note, that's all. Our boss made us change our mind 'bout carryin' real money!"

Sam hesitated, glancing up at his associate. "It's a damn lie!" he bellowed, and let fly with another kick. Tom twisted in time to save himself and took the blow on his arm. Sam was breathing heavily, struggling for control.

"It's no lie!" Jim appealed desperately. "We ain't got the cash!"

"It's the t-truth," Scott added coldly. "The only m-m-money Aa got is wages."

Despite his stammer, Scott's tone, firm and unemotional, seemed to penetrate the man's agitation. Sam blinked, confusion in his eyes.

Tom righted himself again. Boldly, he stared up at his

assailant. "It's the damn truth. Aa've got the evidence in my shirt pocket. See for yourself!" he rasped.

Sam paused, then bent over thrusting his hand inside Tom's breast pocket and withdrew a piece of paper. He opened it up and regarded it blankly, before summoning his partner to read it for him. Billy stepped round, past them where they were sitting on the ground, and took the paper in his hand. His hand was noticeably shaking as he held it up to read aloud, in a slow, tremulous voice.

"I, Henry, Charles Mathias, request a payment in cash of the sum of four thousand, one hundred and sixteen dollars ($ 4,116) to be withdrawn from my account with the San Antonio Cattlemen's Bank and thereby be presented to the accounts of Tom Torrance and Jim Houseman, at the Union Bank, Kerrville. Signed, Henry Mathias, June 21st, 1871."

Billy stared at Sam. "Let's get out o' here!" he protested.

"Give me that paper!" Sam fumed. He snatched it away and immediately set it alight in the fire. "Now," he ordered, "go get our horses! And theirs! Gather their rifles too. We ain't leavin' with them comin' after us!" Billy hesitated. "Do what Aa say, damn it!" Sam cried.

Without replying, Billy turned and scampered away. Still sitting in the same position, hands knitted behind their heads, ankles crossed, Tom, Jim and Scott remained grimly silent as Sam waited, guarding them with his gun, until the other appeared again with all their ten horses roped to their own two. Having collected rifles they quickly mounted up.

Then, without another glance at their victims, the two thieves rushed away.

At once, Tom, Jim and Scott untangled their strained limbs and climbed stiffly to their feet. Tom was last to rise. He grimaced in pain, feeling a cracked rib. Jim spat in anger and he and Scott went immediately to seek their pistols. Returning, Jim's face was livid. "Aa'm goin' after those sons of bitches!"

"Not today you're not! Main thing is we're okay!" Tom mumbled.

"What d' you mean? They burned our bank draft, Tom!" Jim cried.

Tom's eyes flared. "Hell, Jim, the' didn't kill us! It means we're alive, for God's sake! What's a bit of useless paper worth compared to that?"

"He's r-right, Jim. We could've been shh-ot!"

Jim snorted. "It weren't a useless piece of paper! Cow's teeth, w' can't claim our money without it!"

Tom allowed himself a grin. "Now what makes y' so sure they got the real one, huh?" He picked up his hat which had fallen when he'd been kicked, felt inside the rim and produced a folded piece of paper. "Read this here, partner!"

Jim opened it up, glanced at it then let out a whoop of delight. "You old fox! Y' never told me you got two!" he exclaimed.

Jim handed it to Scott to see and then he cheerfully gave it back to Tom to tuck away again. "Did you s-s-ee this coming?" Scott asked cheerfully.

"No," Tom replied, "or we wouldn't have got caught stupid the way we did! An' we wouldn't be stuck here horseless without rifles and -".

A sudden salvo of gun shots in the distance made him halt mid-sentence! At once the three of them stood stock still, hearing just the dry rustle of leaves and grass in the hot wind.

"They better not have killed the horses!" Jim growled.

Tom stepped out and walked forward. "Let's go see. But walk quiet an' keep our eyes skinned!" he commanded, checking his loaded pistol.

They set off cautiously over the ground, heading up the little hill to give themselves a better view of the prairie, northwards, over the ground they had themselves ridden and where Sam and Billy had run off. The high sun beamed down fiercely, blurring the distance in a shiver of heat. They saw no one. They walked on, sweat starting to drip down their faces. Apart from their presence and the whirring sound of insects and the sight of two buzzards circling in the blinding, cloudless sky, the area was lifeless.

Occasionally Tom drew a heavy breath when his ribs stabbed with pain. Jim felt for him, but they continued forward for a mile, concentrated and alert, over the rough, brittle, clumped grass. Following the direction of the two buzzards, they descended into a bare, narrow hollow stretch of ground that had once held water and spotted two bodies sprawled in the dust with the tethered horses clustered together, attempting to pull free. It was Sam and Billy.

Cautiously, with Tom and Scott following him at a distance, Jim approached the dead men. "Dead as can be!" he hollered. "Both hit in the chest, straight through!"

They looked at each other, thinking the same, then they recovered their own rifles. Immediately, Tom set off, struggling up the rise to check the surrounding area. His eyes narrowed as he carefully searched for a movement or trace of another. When he came down to where Jim and Scott had untangled the horses, pain lined his face but he wanted them to look round for tracks.

They separated, checking for places that a sniper might have used. Later, ready to give up the search, Jim shouted. "Someone was hidin' here! The grass is flattened where he hid behind this rock."

Tom and Scott hastened to him. "There!" Jim indicated.

Scott pointed. "And that's where his h-horse shit!"

Tom looked further. "See the marks here," he indicated. "He must have raced off that way." He looked eastwards.

The three of them stared at each other in silence, knowing what was to be said.

"Aa reckon you're right. Someone is followin' us!" Jim acknowledged. "And whoever it is seems t' want to take care of us!" he ended uncertainly.

"Aa don't - get it!" Scott remarked, then wiped his mouth with the back of his hand.

They gathered their horses. Tom and Scott mounted the robbers' saddled pair that were now in their possession, and Jim sat bare back on 'Star'.

"Cow's teeth, ain't w' gonna bury them?" Jim suddenly wondered.

"Hell no," Tom answered. "The only favour they deserve is a kick in the ribs!"

Jim grinned. "Thought you was a decent, religious man, Tom!"

He grimaced. "I am Jim. But not when Aa got pain."

"We'll look at your injury back there, Tom," Jim answered, meaning where they'd camped. They turned the horses round and set off at an easy walk, leaving the dead men to the buzzards.

They made their way back to rekindle their fire, drank another coffee and ate some corn bread with beans, discussing what had happened and the mystery surrounding their follower and his motive. An hour later, after saddling up and loading the bags onto their spare horses, they left the area with bitter misgivings at having been hijacked so easily.

Despite a brave face, Tom was hurting. Jim had earlier examined his ribs and there was a purple swelling showing damage. In order to cushion his ride in the saddle Tom adopted a slightly more forward upright position using his legs for greater support. This method helped his breathing but was tiring, forcing him to stop more regularly. Also, Tom found his big grey horse, 'Rock', the easiest to ride so he stayed on the grey mount all afternoon instead of switching to a fresh one.

As a result of this hinderance they had only gone some fifteen miles beyond the Ninnescah River, which was a mere trickle, when they decided to camp for the night.

Tom was desperate to lie down and made no protest as Jim and Scott saw to the fire and horses letting him rest at ease on the ground. While Jim was preparing food, Scott handed Tom a mug of steaming black coffee. Since his breathing was more relaxed, Tom managed a grin. "Guess you boys deserve a medal for lookin' after me!"

Jim turned his head. "Yeah, just like the one Aa gave y'u for taking care of me so kindly!" he joked, grimacing in a gesture as he stroked the lump above his right ear.

Tom arrested a chuckle. "Don't make me laugh, Jim, it'll hurt like hell."

"Cow's teeth, Tom!" exclaimed Jim. "Ain't got that much sympathy. Still think it was mean not to bury those two back there."

"Nothing s-stopping you going b-ack," Scott quipped.

"An' maybe y' might find whoever killed them returned and done it already," Tom speculated, light heartedly.

Jim lifted the pan from the fire and stirred the stew that was spluttering with the heat. "Chances o' that are slim," he mused. "But what are w' gonna do about him, the rider followin' us?" Jim demanded, fixing his eyes on Tom again.

Tom took off his hat and finger combed his sandy coloured hair to one side before placing it back on. "Let him be, Aa reckon. We've only ridden two days. He'll likely grow tired of it an' give up, or introduce himself!" he added with a smirk.

"Don't unders-tand it," Scott muttered.

"Don't try," Tom advised. "It's kind o' weird, but w' have t' be thankful for him savin' us."

It was simple advice which Tom was good at giving, satisfying both Jim and Scott for the time being. Yet, it was an odd affair. One that words of advice could not erase from the mind. And when darkness fell and they bedded down to sleep beneath the moon and stars, Jim and Scott agreed to take it in turn, an hour at a time, to stay awake, keeping guard, perturbed by the fact of someone's presence, perhaps, somewhere not far away.

The following morning there was no improvement in Tom's condition. A long ride was out of the question.

Jim studied their map. "Caldwell's only two and a half hours ride. W' were aimin' to call there for provisions through the Territory, so let's find someone in town to look at it. At the same time w' can hand over their horses that don't belong to us an' which we don't need."

Tom was still lying on the ground, rested up against his saddle. Unshaved, he looked older with his grey bristles. "Can get all the rest Aa need back home, Jim. W' can make it in about nine days from here."

"Sure w' can, Tom," Jim agreed. "But there ain't no point in you getting crippled for it!" He planted himself firmly and stared down at his friend. "Now, Scott and me have decided for y' t' see a Doc and that's the end of it! Cow's hide, if it takes a few more days to reach home, let it be! Anyways, I bet all he's gonna do is strap y' up an' send y' on your way!"

Tom grinned. "If you know so much what the treatment's going t' be, Jim, why don't y' save me the time an' expense an' just do it!"

Jim sighed. "If y' aim t' get smart about it, Tom, Aa might just have t' give y' another kick in the ribs!" He raised his eyebrows, with a mock, wicked grin and said, "Remember, it was for my own good that y' smacked me over the head!"

After a quick breakfast they mounted up and were on their way. Tom chose 'Rock', while Jim sat 'Tricky' and Scott on 'Sagebrush'. A pale rim of mist in the eastern sky dimmed the early sun and the air was fresh in their faces as they rode south at a gentle lope. At one stop to sip water from their canteens, they gazed towards a line of cattle moving up the trail, remembering what it had been like for them; the sweat and dust and continual daily grind, interspaced by the social gathering at the chuck wagon, where Elias bossed and fussed and cursed and boosted them all, depending on his mood and circumstance. At the time, the trail meant everything, cattle, horses and men bound together in one moving mass.

But now, in reflection, apart from the friendships and the knowing, they felt detached from it, glad once more that the drudgery of its work and duty was over!

Because of the trail, Caldwell had grown from a few buildings into a street. Here, after journeying through Indian Territory, outfits were able to replenish supplies and permit the drovers a little time of distraction. After the rail track passed on through Newton, it would someday reach Caldwell, prospering it into a larger town, but for now, in the eyes of Tom and Jim and Scott, it seemed, as they drew nearer, no more than a sun worn, dull looking, little township.

By chance, there was a medical man to be found. He moved between Newton and Caldwell on a regular basis along the trail, and he was happy to examine Tom's injury and do what he could. The doctor was a young, slim, thinly moustached man who seriously enjoyed his role, meeting and attending to all kinds of characters. When he enquired what had happened, Tom told him he had been kicked by a robber for telling the truth, but that it was better than telling a lie and getting killed.

The young doctor smiled uncertainly. "Well, the rib looks like it's broken and there's not a lot I can do except strap your body and give it time."

Tom's sense of humour was undiminished. "Got no magic cure?"

The doctor frowned at him. "It doesn't work like that." Then he felt Tom's side again, probing his fingers along the division. Tom reacted with a grunt as pain leapt through him.

"It'll heal itself in time. I'll strap it up for now, and God willing, you'll feel easier in about three days time."

Tom blew. "Don't have time, Doc. Aa have t' ride home."

The young doctor studied Tom's expression and knew he was determined. "Okay, but wait at least till tomorrow. The swelling needs to settle down. My advice is that you find a comfortable bed for the night and rest it good and proper. You might be lucky."

Tom grinned. "Aa'll pray for it!"

The other allowed himself another smile. "Didn't take you for a religious man, Mr Torrance!"

"Well Aa am an' not. It's a secret matter between me and God that Aa talk to him sometime t' hold down the badness in me. But Aa think of it more as friendship than religion." Tom eyes sparkled with irony and the young doctor regarded him solemnly as he started to wind the bandage round.

"Mr Torrance, I believe in the Good Lord too, as a Friend and Master. Don't you feel you could be more disposed towards him?"

Tom discerned the zeal of faith inside the young man and answered kindly, "Although Aa don't like t' think of him as Boss, I know who has the most say; else what's the point in prayin' for anythin'?"

The young doctor was reconciled. He nodded approvingly, finishing off his work. "Now, remember what I said, Mr Torrance. Rest well tonight and it might feel easier tomorrow. Though riding, won't help." His eyes brightened. "But I'll pray for it too."

Tom knew it was in earnest. He was tempted to make light of it, but mindful of his gratitude he restrained himself. "Thanks, Doc. Now what do Aa owe you?"

"Four dollars, sir," he said, aiding Tom to put on his shirt.

Tom grimaced as he stood up and tucked in. Then he handed over the money. They shook hands and as he went out of the room another man was waiting to go in. He looked to be in pain with an arm hanging limp at his side. The cowboy glanced up as Tom went out through the door onto the street. He walked across the road and entered the one Saloon in town where Jim and Scott had said they'd wait, and found them leaning against the bar counter. He joined them for one drink and told them what happened and that he needed to stay overnight. They weren't displeased.

"Same thing again that happened in Newton, only the other way round," Jim observed. "One in bed and two out enjoying themselves," he explained.

"Be my t-urn next," Scott said.

"Don't ask for it," Tom warned. "Once heard of a man who always said he wanted t' die with his boots off and when he got injured and was dyin', his boots were too tight to pull off and so he died miserable wearing them. He ought to have kept his mouth shut and he would have died a happy man!"

Scott stared at him. "Didn't s-ay nothing ab-out dyin', Tom."

Tom knocked back his drink then looked straight at Scott. "Yeah, but you're best not sayin' it!"

"Pay him no heed, Scott. He's mad cos he has to go t' bed

an' he wants an argument to sleep on. He'll twist what you say till he's satisfied!" Jim commented, smugly.

Tom rubbed his nose. "Jim, if Scott wants to invite disaster, Aa'm gonna advise him for his own good. And if you-"

Suddenly four men with rifles burst through the door. "Get your hands up!" boomed the leader. Confronted by the weapons pointing at them, Tom, Jim and Scott raised their hands. Tom grimaced at the effort.

"What have w' done wrong?" demanded Jim.

The front man with a pink, scowling face, wearing a black hat, pointed to his policeman's badge. "We've got some questions for you!" he retorted, then ordered one of his men to step forward and disarm the three while he and the other two kept aim. Afterwards, under guard, he commanded them to move outside where they were escorted along the road to a small building and taken inside and locked behind bars in a cage more suitable for one prisoner than three. The small crowd that had gathered at the open door to spectate, had it closed on them.

Inside the room, the pink faced man with a black hat stood before them. "You got horses that don't belong t' you," he said accusingly.

"They don't belong to anyone else," replied Jim, instantly.

"Man in town says they belong t' two friends of his that he was supposed to meet up with here, in Caldwell."

Jim pulled a face. "Well that's interestin'! Somebody shot the two who'd robbed us an' when we found 'em their horses were loose," Jim said. "That's why we brought them in."

The policeman snorted. "Y' think a tale like that is going to get y' off a hanging ceremony?"

Jim glared at him before turning his eyes to Tom who had lain down on the one thin bench in the tiny cage and was staring at the ceiling. Then Jim looked back at their accuser. "Two men robbed us of our horses and ran off. We heard shots and walked t' where they were killed. Nobody was there. We recovered our horses and brought theirs with us here. What else was there t' do?"

In the following silence Jim knew his reply sounded as implausible as it was true.

The pink faced man allowed a little smile to crease his thin lips. "Aa guess y' were lucky t' have somebody shoot them for you," he commented, sarcastically. His three assistants behind him smirked. "An' why would they want to steal your horses and let you live t' go after them?" he added. His scowl returned and hardened. "Answer that cowboy!"

Jim controlled his temper, thinking rationally like Tom would if he was fit to do the talking. "They weren't after our horses they were after money they thought we was carryin'. When they found out it weren't there one of them kicked Tom, him there on the bench, and they stormed off grabbing our horses an' rifles t' stop us chasin' them."

The policeman sneered. "Your made-up story ain't good enough, mister! The only evidence we got is those horses that you took." He turned away and telling two of his men to guard the prisoners he went out with the other man. The two guards sat on chairs and lit cigarettes and started talking quietly to each other. Jim and Scott exchanged glances and squatted down on the floor and remained quiet.

After a little while Tom stirred, groaning a little as he rightened himself to sitting. Jim and Scott stood up and then sat down either side of him on the bench.

"How w' g-gonna get out o' this, Tom?" mumbled Scott.

Tom breathed heavily. "Don't know."

Scott turned his head deliberately towards him. "You better know, Tom, or w-we're likely to get s-strung up." He paused. There was tension in his voice, increasing his stammer. "You h-h-ave to s-peak for us, Tom. You've al-ways known w-what t-t-to say, Tom."

Tom sighed. "I'm tired right now, Scott. Leave it for now," he muttered.

Jim chuckled. "Fine time to give up, Tom, when we're dependin' on you."

"I ain't given up, Jim," he answered hoarsely. "Aa'm weary and sore and Aa can't think of anything t' say right now that might help."

For a while they remained quiet while the two guards sat gazing. Then the door opened and the policeman returned with another man, round shouldered and rough bearded, who came forward alone to the cage and stared at the prisoners. His face twisted in a studied look before he turned away. "Nope. Never seen them before," he admitted.

"But you're sure about those horses?" demanded the policeman.

The other one nodded. "Sure am. They belong to Sam and Billy, alright."

Tom cleared his throat and climbed achingly to his feet and took a step forward to clutch the bars. "Mind if Aa ask you something, mister, about your friends?"

The policeman nodded for the round shouldered cowboy he'd brought in to listen and reply.

"Well," Tom went on, "maybe you knew they were going to rob us an' maybe it was you that killed them to get the money you thought they'd took from us!" The cowboys mouth fell open. "And maybe gettin' us the blame through the horses makes it nice and easy for you to get away with it."

"Aa didn't kill them! I came here to meet them like we'd said!" he exclaimed, turning to the policeman for support. The pink face remained impassive.

Tom snorted. "You had a motive, mister. We didn't. We got plenty horses of our own. Why would we go shootin' for more? It makes no sense. An' if we had would we head straight for the nearest town? Hell, no! We would have run straight into the Territory!"

"He's lyin'!" cried the other and his round shoulders hunched higher in alarm at the accusation.

Tom's voice grew stronger. "Now if it's lyin', why don't someone go right now to see the young doctor that fixed my hurt ribs and ask him what Aa told him about how it happened. Then we'll see who's lyin'!" Tom wasn't going to stop now. He jumped in again, "An' maybe this bill of sale here in my hat should be read too, proving why those two rats were out to rob us in the first place, thinkin' we had cash." He dropped his head to remove his hat and showing the inside removed the note. "Here!" he declared, with assurance, his breathing short and quick.

The policeman's face had reddened by now. He ordered one of his guards to go see the doctor and then he approached Tom and took the piece of paper to read it to himself. Tom explained the story to him about the cattle and how Mr Mathias, his trail boss, had persuaded him to change his mind about carrying the money. Afterwards, the policeman walked with the notice to the table and sat down in the spare chair.

The rough bearded cowboy pivoted, nervously. "Aa done nothing," he called. "Aa knew them a little, that's all, and said Aa'd meet up with them here!"

"Where did they say they were goin', after they left you in Newton?" demanded the policeman.

"They said they wanted to see someone about work later in the year. Aa didn't ask them. It was none of m' business," he muttered, abjectly, now aware more fully of the recriminations directed at him.

Tom sharpened his claws. "You're lyin', mister, and y' know it! You were in on the robbery. Your job was to carry the money on somewhere else letting the other two disappear into the Territory a short while, free of any evidence, and meeting up with y' later in Texas. It's an old trick, t' throw off the scent!" He paused, then went on immediately to confound the protest seething in the man. "You're from down Brownsville, ain't you? What's your name?"

"What's it to you?" the other blurted, his lips quivering.

"Got a feelin' Aa know you," Tom answered assuredly.

"Tell him!" snapped the officer.

"Lochlan. Mike Lochlan."

"Yeah. Y' said y' knew them just a little. You're lyin' again. Sam and Billy were from Brownsville too. Right?"

The cowboy flinched. "But Aa didn't know them," he admitted, feebly.

"Tell me, Lochlan," Tom demanded, "what kind of rifle d' you possess?"

Again Lochlan was mesmerised by the sudden switch of questioning. "Aa got a Henry," he replied, dully.

"A Henry Volcanic repeating rifle with sixteen rounds?"

Lochlan stared dumbly. "Yeah," he said. The door opened and the two who had visited the young doctor walked back in. The grey bearded one confirmed Tom's story. The policeman climbed out of his chair and returned the note to Tom. "Guess we got the wrong men behind bars." He turned his head. "Let 'em out!" he ordered the one nearest the keys on the hook behind the table.

A minute later, a bemused Lochlan was locked up and Tom and Jim and Scott had been given back their arms. The pink faced officer smiled for the first time. "Next time y' see my friend, Henry Mathias, tell him y' bumped into Will Cohen from Caldwell."

Tom nodded with pleasure as they proceeded to go

outside with him. On the mud boards Cohen said he would
hold Lochlan for a week, just to let him sweat, then release
him. "Unless, of course, he confesses to the killin'," Cohen
added.

"He didn't do it," Tom said.

Cohen threw his head up as if to laugh but no sound
came out. "How in hell can y' say that when you've almost
convicted him in there?" he exclaimed in disbelief.

"The shots w' heard came from a Winchester. No Henry
could fire that fast," admitted Tom.

"You sure about that?" the policeman queried.

"Aa sure am," Tom assured him.

Cohen allowed himself to smile. He gave Tom a long,
thoughtful look. "Another thing, how do y' know about them
all coming from Brownsville?"

Both Scott and Jim who had remained tensely silent
throughout Tom's defence, were eager to know.

"They all spoke with the same accent, like a man Aa once
knew who came from down there too," explained Tom,
casually.

Cohen nodded approvingly. Then Tom informed him
they would be going in the morning and said he wanted to
leave the dead men's horses. Cohen thought it was a good
idea and Tom agreed, saying he should have handed the
horses over when they first came into town but with his
injured ribs he hadn't thought straight about it. Cohen
wondered, with amusement, why his two friends hadn't
thought about it either. Tom pulled a face and declared that

neither of them had the brains to consider it and left decisions to him, which was a damn burden. Jim was tempted to argue, but Tom was holding the reins of the situation so he kept his mouth shut, smiling feebly. The conversation ended with Cohen shaking hands with Tom only, wishing him a safe journey and to remind him to Henry Mathias when they met again.

At last when Tom turned and walked away with the other two following behind they heard him groan wearily, in pain. "Right now," he announced, "Aa'm goin' alone t' get myself a room for the night. If one o' you snivellin' jack-asses comes anywhere near, Aa'm gonna shoot your ears off. Understand!"

Jim and Scott halted immediately. "Cow's tits, all w' did was get the best out of him, Scott, an' he thinks we're a burden!" Jim uttered.

Scott laughed. "D-don't think he's g-rateful for it!"

"Don't reckon he is," Jim mused. "But it ain't our fault we depend on him! No sir. We can't help bein' just plain dumb jack-asses!" he mocked, loud enough for Tom's hearing, as he trailed along the street, separating himself from them.

The following morning Jim and Scott were heavy headed from their indulgence in the saloon. Tom was in a better mood and the long rest had revived his spirit. After a cooked breakfast, they bought some extra provisions and loaded up to go.

They spoke about their imprisonment and how Tom had managed to convince Cohen of their innocence. Tom was certain that Cohen knowing Henry Mathias was the crucial factor in changing his mind.

Tom's ribs were still tender and sore but caused him less agony. He rode gingerly on 'Rock' again, but without holding back the pace, and within an hour from Caldwell they crossed into Indian Territory.

The Territory was allotted land for the 'civilised' indian tribes that had been brought to reservation life. Here they were permitted freedom to live their customary ways and through agriculture and hunting maintain their self reliance and an economy which enabled them to trade and purchase provisions from the government agencies which supervised them. It was generally unsafe for white men to venture deep into the Territory other than on the accepted, drover routes, so for security the three riders stayed on line with the cow trail where they would also be able to keep in touch with news from outriders.

As well as a refuge for native people, the wide empty prairie sometimes proved a welcome haven for outlaws on the run. Therefore it was not a regular route home for cowboys returning from Kansas, preferring instead to avoid it.

After a sustained stretch of running, the horses were slowed down to a walk. Tom was still riding 'Rock' the grey one, with Jim riding 'Mack' and Scott again on the dull coloured one named 'Sagebrush'.

"Last y-ear," Scott began, "me and Stilt and M-Mex took the long way r-ound east of the Territory. Took me a m-month t-to get home."

"You walk it?" Jim quipped.

"Hell no," said Scott. "Stilt wanted t-to stop in every damn pl-ace we went near!"

"A long body like his gets tired and thirstier quicker," Jim cracked.

"Aa s-swear, he once fell asleep leaning again-st a tree."

Jim sniffed, amused. "Never seen a man spit tobacco juice as far as Stilt could."

"His height done it," Tom came in. "Same as when he pissed." He heeled his horse ahead and the other two followed.

Coming over a rounded bluff they rode down to a little creek. Here, where the trickle of water filled a clear sparkling pool, they dismounted to splash their sweaty faces and let the horses suck.

Afterwards, refreshed, the three of them left the horses to go and sit in the shade of a batch of willowy aspens, finding on the way a spread of wild sand plums which they picked to suck. The tracks of other creatures that frequented the creek were also imprinted along the water's edge; antelope, deer, coyote, lobo wolf and wild turkey, along with various rodent markings. Scott also found an old hunting knife half buried in caked mud which he spent the next fifteen minutes cleaning and sharpening. He was a natural collector and had patience for it, prepared as he had already shown on more than one occasion, to turn back his horse to check something that caught his eye as he loped past. Tom and Jim were both aware of this obsession, but communicated it only with a glance. Sensing that it was based on curiosity rather than acquisition, it wasn't a habit they wished to belittle.

After the horses had sucked enough water they wandered freely onto the other side of the creek where grass grew in patches of green. After Tom had smoked his pipe in the shade and it was nearing time to set off again, he wandered carefully on foot up onto the bluff and viewed the country. Coming back down he joined Jim and Scott who were saddling fresh mounts.

"He's still followin' us!" Tom announced, slackening the cinch on 'Rock' to transfer his saddle onto 'Munch'.

Jim and Scott halted their actions.

"Whoever it is got a spyglass. He was lookin' out for us and Aa seen it glint in the sun. That's why he don't need to get close and why it's hard for us to spot him."

"Cow's teeth, who in his right mind wants to do this? This ain't funny anymore!" Jim cursed.

"Someone m-must like us a lot t-to go t-to such trouble."

"Or want t' worry us!" Tom added.

Impetuously, Jim grabbed his new Remington rifle and marched up onto the bluff.

"Wh-ats he t-tryin' to do?" Scott asked.

"Trying to show who's followin' that he's unhappy about it," Tom sighed.

Jim paced back and forth a few times and waved his

arms. When he was satisfied he marched down again. "Now he knows we know and he better watch out!" he fumed.

Gritting his teeth, Tom stared at him with despair in his eyes. "Jim," Tom said, "you're the best friend Aa ever had. But when you rush t' do things like that Aa feel like shootin' a toe just to punish myself for even knowin' you."

Jim's expression went blank as it did when he needed to be self controlled and hear Tom out.

"Y' go up there and dance round like you've been drinkin' 'joy juice' so that whoever's followin' us knows we know. Fine! But what about anybody else out there; that way or that way or that way," he gesticulated, irately. "What about some Indians that can't help but notice some crazy cowboy throwing his arms around as if to say, 'See, I got a new rifle, why don't y' come and get it?' An' when the Indians get closer they see three of us and think – maybe those other two got rifles they want to give away as well. And what about their horses. Why not? Maybe they don't need them all!" Tom heaved a breath and spat on the ground. He seemed ready to continue the same line of attack when he paused and his tone softened. "As Aa said, Jim, you're the best friend Aa've got an' Aa want t' see us get home," he appealed. "Scott, too!"

Jim felt tempted to joke about it, to shed the resentment in Tom's sudden outburst, but he noticed the strain in Tom's face. And it struck him then how weary and older he looked. The tireless power of his nerve and wit that everyone on the trail admired about him, was wearing thin. He had grown jaded, and now an air of desperation was overtaking him.

Jim's heart reached out. Perhaps Tom's injury had taken more out of him than he thought. "Sorry, partner. It was a dumb thing t' do, Aa reckon," he admitted.

Tom looked down, sniffed, then raised his eyes to meet Jim's stare. Slowly, the line of his mouth hardened. "But if he's still followin' us tomorrow," he said stiffly, "me and my old gun'll be out t' shoot him!"

Jim's face brightened. "You bet you will!"

"What if he's a f-friend?" Scott demanded.

"Then Aa'll shoot his horse," Tom said with irony.

Jim chuckled to himself at the notion he had of Tom's decline. "Guess you been doin' some serious thinkin' about it!" he said.

Tom nodded. "Too much, Aa reckon."

Shortly, they rode on at a fair speed on fresh mounts. Now on 'Munch', Tom led the way, proving he was fit again to do so. Following at the rear, Jim, riding his white horse, 'Sugar', was glad to see it. As glad as he was of himself for the way he handled Tom's criticism. He remembered vividly how, a few years ago, the two of them nearly came to blows over a similar outburst. He, Jim, had tried alone to 'bronco bust' a wild stallion in the corral. The stallion threw him off and then madly crashed into the fence, injuring its leg so the bone stuck out. Tom arrived on the scene and scolded him for his stupidity and shot the horse. With his pride dented,

Jim told Tom to mind his business and to quit being 'an old women' about danger. Loose words were exchanged with both of them faced squarely at the other, glaring, eye to eye, their tempers rising, until Tom's son, then six year old, came running towards them. For his sake they stepped back and calmed down, but for over a week they remained cross with each other and there was no communication between them.

Scott wondered at Jim's demeanour. "What y' thinkin', Jim?"

Jim lied. "Thinkin' how Indians might like t' scalp off that long hair of yours! You'd be a lot cooler in this heat if y' let me cut it short."

Scott dismissed his idea with a wave of his hand and slapped the long legged 'Locust' up to Tom's side to ride abreast of him. They rode stubbornly for nearly two hours before taking a break to boil up coffee and rest the horses before remounting. From here, they pushed on over flat land until the sun had passed overhead and then they were on the long slope down to the Salt Fork of Arkansas river. There, they found a place to drink and take shade from the burning sun.

Tom was ready for a break and lay down stiffly on his back which was the best position for him to alleviate his pain. Meanwhile, Jim and Scott prepared the fire and a bite to eat; rashers of bacon fried until the fat was running before adding sliced potatoes and onions with herbs and seasoning, covering it and letting it simmer, sometimes turning and adding water to keep it moist and tender. After half an hour it was served out and the three of them tucked in hungrily, thirty-five miles of ground behind them, south of Caldwell.

The day was extraordinarily hot. There was hardly a whisper of wind and the plain shivered with heat vapours. The dry grass was brittle and baked, seething with sounds of beetles and insects and where the cowboys rested in a tree's shadow, flies were crazy and aggressive, giving them little peace.

Restless, Scott walked away to find another spot to relax. Here, on a small knoll above the river bank he had just sat down when he saw a bunch of Indians on the other side of the river, over a mile away, riding in their direction. He ran back down to Tom and Jim, waking them from their slumber, and they reined in the team of horses and fastened them to a clump of willows out of view, before sneaking off clutching their rifles onto the rise where Scott had spotted the Indians and kneeled down behind the bulk of an uprooted tree.

There were about twenty Indians on ponies heading for trees beside the river quarter of a mile upstream from them. Reaching the water the band dismounted and for a minute, obscured by the dust of their gathering, it was unclear what was going on. Cautiously, Tom, Jim and Scott watched in silence, peering out from their hiding place. And then, as one of the ponies was led away to the tallest tree, it became apparent that it was carrying a dead body wrapped and tied in a blanket. Out of the crowd, two braves now started to climb up the tree into the highest branches where a rope was thrown up for them to fling over a limb. The wrapped body on the ground was secured to the rope and then the two up the tree began hauling up the corpse, slowly hoisting it towards them.

At last, when they had tied it carefully to a branch, the two Indians climbed down to join the others below. Meanwhile, some others had collected wood and made a pile on the ground beneath the corpse and set fire to it. To cause smoke, they threw grass and green wood onto the flames and the grey, murky clouds billowed upwards, engulfing the body in the branches so that it became briefly invisible. In time, as the fire subsided, a trail of white smoke above the tree thinned into the glaring, scorched, pale sky.

The ritual continued with the Indians starting to chant, developing it with a slow, stepping sway. An antelope which had been killed and carried with them, was then hurriedly cut up and the skewered meat was cooked over the large fire as the movement and voices started up again, with what looked like a medicine man, heavily decorated, pacing round the fire, raising and lowering his arms in a looping gesture.

"That's one hell of a send off," Jim whispered.

"Right up to heaven," Tom muttered.

Scott, with a wad of tobacco in his mouth, snorted in the notion.

Gradually, the motions of the ritual ceased and the gathering of natives sat down to share the cooked meat, passing the sticks round between them, and only to stoke or add wood to the flames did an individual stand up.

Nearly an other hour passed before the band of Indians

eventually got their feet and prepared to leave. The final act was to rekindle the fire with wood and smoke it again before they climbed onto their ponies and trailed away in the direction they had come, leaving the wrapped corpse tied to the high branch of the tree.

When the tribesmen had left, the three cowboys came stiffly down the bank to their camping place and splashed themselves in the shallow water, soaking themselves cool with pleasure and relief. Scott set the horses free then squatted in between Tom and Jim who were sitting at the edge, giving Tom a friendly clip on his shoulder.

"You be careful, Scott, Aa ain't fit yet for horseplay," Tom informed him.

"No, but y-our sure in a b-better mood than before," said Scott.

"It ain't hurtin" as much, that's why," Tom admitted, stroking back his wet hair.

Scott spat out the residue of tobacco juice left in his gums and rinsed out his mouth with a handful of river water. "What about the Indians?" he said.

"They won't be back. The ceremony's over and they've left the body for bird bait," Jim replied, then rose to his feet. "Aa reckon we ought t' boil some coffee before w' go. Another half hour delay'll make no difference." He went to the ashes of the fire which were still warm and stacked some dry twigs to set fire to them.

"Why'd you need to l-light a fire?" asked Scott.

Puzzled, Jim stared at him. "Are you dumb or somethin',

Scott? No fire, no coffee," he explained, then bent over to blow an ember.

"Jumping f-fish, Jim, don't y' know there's a f-f-fire b-urning up stream w' can use!" Scott grinned.

Jim frowned. "Scott, if you're gonna be as smart as Tom there, Aa ain't gonna like y' either. Anyways, interferin' with a funeral fire is bad medicine an' could bring bad luck."

"Cow's belly!" Scott mimicked, laughter in his face, "Aa never t-took you f-f-for a spook!"

"Boys!" Tom interrupted, raising his voice with his eyes fixed beyond them. "If y' both want t' be spooked some more, I suggest you be real slow an' turn your eyes up the slope there!"

Standing openly above them on the high ground that they had observed the ceremony, two Indians sat on horse-back. Tom slowly stood up and stepped forward with Scott following him. Tom raised an open hand and waited for a response.

One of the Indians called for tobacco.

"Sure," Tom called back. "Aa'll bring it to y', okay?"

There was no objection so Tom stepped towards his saddle bags and took out a packet. Scott approached him. "Let me take it," he said. Tom looked at him and saw in his eyes that he would not be denied and handed over the packet.

"Scott," Tom whispered, "if there's more of them than the two we can see, take your hat off an' scratch your neck. Also, keep your eyes fixed on them and if they make a move t' harm you leap out the way 'cause Aa'll be shooting."

Scott grinned and turned to go. At the same time Tom picked up his rifle and he and Jim watched closely as Scott scaled the slope and approached the two Indians. What seemed like the older of the two, took the tobacco from Scott, then continued to talk. Scott raised a hand to remove his hat. He scratched his neck and seemed though he was talking back. The two Indians glanced at each other then turned their horses and rode away.

When Scott came back down he told them there were three more of them on ponies a little distance away. He said they had also wanted a horse but he refused them. Then they left.

"Cherokee?" asked Jim.

"Looked like it," Scott replied.

"Which way did the' go?" Jim asked.

"Up r-river."

Jim looked at Tom. "All the others went off, didn't they?"

"Sure. Could be they were late for the funeral," Tom explained.

"Let's check, huh?" Jim suggested, asking first, to avoid any rashness on his part. Tom nodded and the three of them climbed up the slope to see where the riders had gone. Right enough, the five Indians had found the big tree where the body was strung. They dismounted and sat down in a circle round the smouldering fire, nudging it alive. A few minutes later, having paid their respects, they mounted their ponies and set off after the main batch of Indians.

Tom stroked his moustache and stared down at the ground. Ants had crawled onto one of his boots. He stubbed the toe against the ground to knock them off. "Tell y' what, boys," he said, looking up, determinedly. "Let's get the horses ready, fill up on water, an' then ride as far as breath'll take us."

"Why Tom? You r-reckon they'll be comin' after us?"

"No, but we've wasted nearly three hours here and Aa'm just itchin' t' go!"

"Me too!" insisted Jim, enthusiastically. He looked away, northwards, over the ground they had come. He smiled. "An' if our shadow rider wants t' keep up he's going to have work some. Y' never know, he might even meet some Indians that want a horse!"

His comment amused Tom and Scott and they grinned as they dropped down the bank to rig up the horses.

Seated on their fresh mounts, 'Rusty', 'Star' and 'Blue Coat', they chewed jerky meat, waiting for Tom to fold the map away. "If we're good riders," he drawled, "w' could almost make it to the Cimmaron River by nightfall. Anybody got doubts?"

"W-What if your r-ribs start hurtin', Tom?" Scott asked.

Tom wiped his moustache, throwing him a scornful look. "Just weep for me, boy!" he jested, starting off. And with a chortle and a holler they spurred off after him, hats pulled flat against the sun's glare, upper right.

They rapidly fell into a constant, pacey rhythm. The spare horses, sharing the baggage, needed no towing, fitting neatly into the loping stride set for them to follow. The flow of air that was created by motion was cooling, and they proceeded with an ease of relaxation only journey hardened riders may enjoy. Throughout the venture, with the horses' drumming hooves ringing in their ears, the three calmly sat their horses, rocking easily, absorbed by the repetition of sound and in the purpose of progress and distance.

Even before their first interval stop along the way, they spotted two trail herds three mile to the east of their position, bound for Abilene. And on the second stage, they spied another one. After walking the horses for half a mile to regain their breath, they hardly got going again when they ran into a huge herd of grazing buffalo which scattered in all directions as they rushed through them.

If Tom felt discomfort there was no indication. He appeared to hold his carriage comfortably with the other two riding alongside. From time to time a glance of acknowledgment was exchanged between them, and adopting teamwork, they took turns edging to the front to maintain the pace. Consequently, in a natural, focussed manner, they felt the inspiration of a speed that was enjoyable as a challenge, without any thoughts of failure.

When they had covered about thirty miles, they took another short break to drink water from their canteens and for Tom to check the map sketched out for him. "Reckon soon we aught to veer to the right a bit and come onto Turkey creek. It runs south into the Cimmaron, so we can follow it down."

"How much further?" asked Jim, wiping sweat from his brow.

"Another twenty, I'd say, maybe more."

Jim blew. "Two hours an' it'll be growin' dark."

Tom patted 'Rusty' on the neck before dismounting to switch his saddle onto 'Rock'. "Guess it won't matter if w' don't make it, but we'll see how it goes. What d' y' think, Scott?"

Scott shrugged. "Don't m-mind either way."

Tom paused. "Meaning what?"

"Meaning Aa d-don't m-mind," he echoed, dismounting to change rides onto 'Sagebrush'.

"Warned you," Jim said to Tom "He's learnin' t' be smart as you are. An' he's got years on his side to improve it!"

"It's a good thing you've got admiration for him, Jim," Tom insisted, adjusting the cinch. "Means if Aa don't make it back home you got someone else t' take care of you!"

Jim puffed. "Aa got you the job, Tom, so don't y' dare let me down!"

Tom lifted down his saddle and steam rose from the horse's back. He shook the damp blanket and laid it over 'Rock'. "You got me the job, alright, Jim, and the only time Aa regret it is when y' try t' have the last word."

Jim quickly tightened his saddle onto 'Tricky'. "Don't

know what it is about you, Tom, but every time we get to jawing at each other Aa need t' go and lay an egg!" Without waiting for a reply he scurried off a little way to drop his trousers and perform, leaving Scott and Tom to rig the other horses to leave.

"You okay, Tom?" Scott enquired.

Tom understood. "Sure Scott. It still hurts some but Aa want us out of the Territory day after tomorrow."

"What about the rider f-following us?"

Tom remembered what he had promised. "Let's see if he's still there then, huh?"

Scott agreed and he and Tom mounted up. When Jim, returned, tucking in his shirt, he also climbed into his saddle and the three cowboys set off once more, quickly settling into a fair pace as the late afternoon sun was burning lower in the sky, dazzling their eyes when they raised their chins.

After seven miles they came onto Turkey creek which was almost dried out and followed its course, southwards, pressing the horses on in their desire to reach their destination. By now, signs of weariness were starting to show. With mouths open the riders breathed more deeply, and as their bodies began to tire they slouched forward, smaller in the saddle. Like them, the panting horses grew heavier in step and their stride gradually shortened, losing its thrust and flow. Yet still they persevered, plugging on relentlessly, until, in the angled sun, a look of strain started to glaze over the stare of both animals and riders.

Eventually, in the first red glow of sundown they

reached the river. Hot and aching they glanced proudly at each other for achieving their goal, and as their loosened horses stood knee deep in the water, the three cowboys splashed themselves to cool down, before hurrying to build a fire before darkness fell. Already, Scott had walked off with his rifle hunting for meat and spying a wild turkey settling down to roost in a bank side tree, he shot it and dragged it back to pluck and clean and make ready to roast on the fire which was now burning avidly, the flames licking up the dry wood.

As night closed around them they drank coffee and chewed some bread whilst waiting for their meal. Jim took charge again. After adding cooked turkey meat into a pan of chopped onions, red beans and tomatoes, he used a little wild garlic and oil to stew gently for fifteen minutes. Absorbed by his task, Jim reflected gladly that Elias might have been pleased to see his endeavour and pictured the cook hovering with advice.

It had been a long day. They had left Caldwell in the morning and ridden over seventy miles, deep into Indian Territory. About two miles to the east of them, downstream, lay the Chisholm trail where herds would be bedded down for the night. But that didn't matter. They felt separate and liked it, and though worn out, they valued their achievement, as if, after all the interruptions, they had covered an appreciable distance and taken a big step towards reaching home.

They ate their food ravenously. It tasted wonderful and Jim was praised for it. A mutual spirit of wellbeing existed between them as they chatted willingly about another long run the following day.

Tom examined the map. "We sure made up ground today. Okay, we're worn out an' longin' for sleep but Aa feel more alive 'cause of it. The ribs hurt some, but what the heck! Aa can't run round a horse but Aa damn well proved Aa can ride one!"

"Cow's belly, Tom, y' were pushing t' go faster all the time," Jim complimented him. "The good thing is we know w' can go further too, if we don't get held up by burials or robberies or jail, or even lookin' over our shoulders all the time for some 'sourbug' that wants to chase after us!"

"Hope his h-horse b-broke a leg in a gopher h-h-ole and he landed in a pile of a-ants!" Scott cursed merrily.

Tom sniggered. "Yeah, and the' crawled up his nose and farted!"

Jim smirked. "Never mind him. What about tomorrow, Tom?"

"Well," Tom commenced, studying the sketched map, "if we can get in about eight or nine hours riding, outside of stopping time, we should land up somewhere between the Arkansas and Red river, nearly a hundred miles south of here!"

Jim whistled. "Cow's teeth, back there Aa thought y' were done for, all sad eyed and grey faced, an' now y' got energy to think of dragging me and Scott over a distance like that!"

Tom paused. "W' have the horses t' do it!" he chirped. "An' another thing, boys, w' want t' get into Texas as quick as we can. This ain't a region to dally through, with Indians and desperadoes hiding from the law."

"You ain't s-scared, Tom?" Scott posed lightly.

"More sensible than scared, Scott," he corrected him, then yawned.

Infected by it, Jim yawned as well before speaking. "Now, if you two want to get some shut eye I'll take first watch. Okay?" They nodded their approval and got to their feet to prepare their bed. While Tom and Scott settled down Jim saw to the horses and then the fire, before moving off with his Remington towards a tree where he squatted down alone to begin to watch and listen to the night; his mind and senses acutely aware of the purring, moonlit river, and the chirping crickets among the leaves. Then he burped loudly and smiled to himself as he tasted in his mouth again the juices of his stew. The smile was lingering still as he checked the sky to know what time was his, and it occurred to him then that he might stretch it out, taking in Tom's first watch as well. After all, he reckoned, the 'old boy' deserved it!

Early the following day, dawn stretched over the sky like an eerie shadow.

"When you're tired out you sleep! Aa heard Elias say," replied Jim to Tom's protest about letting him sleep through the entire night.

"Course Aa was tired. But it was your job t' wake me," he

complained, then sipped his coffee. It was not yet sun-up but the fire was already stoked brightly and breakfast was cooking.

Later, fed and coffee happy, they were packed and ready to go. The air was cool with grey cloud blocking off the emerging sun, and there was a charge of determination in their veins as they moved off, dauntless, riding south on horses eager to run.

Being less warm than usual, it was a perfect morning for riding. In under two and a half hours they reached the North Canadian river where they took a brief rest before setting off again on second mounts. Over an hour later they were crossing the South Canadian when they were held up a little time by Scott's borrowed horse, 'Sugar', getting bogged in sand. With a rope they were able to pull her free without damage and continued on their way.

In a business like way, without urgency, they made it their target to reach the Washita River before stopping again to eat and rest. Tom on 'Rusty' and Jim sitting 'Star' let Scott lead them on the now, mud-stained, white horse. With his big brown hat and long flowing hair, Scott's head seemed a size too large for his body. Secretly, this amused Tom and Jim.

Coming up onto a slight hill, Scott slowed down for them to ride alongside and all three fell into a walk that stopped at the top to let their mounts catch their breaths. Looking round they had an outstanding view of the vast, undulating, brown, prairie landscape that stretched into the distance in every direction. By now the sun had past overhead and the morning's cloud had broken up so that huge ponds of shadow were seen floating over the sunlit grass. It was a sight for them to admire and enjoy silently, in wonder.

About five miles to the east of them they could spot another long, thin, dark line of cattle plodding slowly north. And then, almost simultaneously, they wheeled their horses round to look back for any sign of the phantom rider. Jim slugged water from his canteen. "Reckon he won't like the pace," he grinned.

Tom climbed down and used his hat to hold water for 'Rusty' to sip. He stared northwards, scanning the landscape. Hopping down to stretch his legs, Scott spat out tobacco juice then transferred the bulge from one cheek to the other. "Maybe he q-quit," he drawled.

Tom didn't answer and mounted again, grimacing slightly as his leg lifted over the saddle. Jim observed his pinched expression. "You okay, partner?"

"Damn right I am," Tom replied, finger combing back his wispy hair before replacing his hat. "Tell y' both, we've got plenty ridin' t' do without keep thinkin' about him trailin' us. Let's go!"

Scott sprang up and with a shout of glee they set off again at a lope, into the rhythm of speed that their bodies were familiar with, running into and out of sunshine as the sound of the breeze and hoofbeats dominated their hearing. At the thought of having covered at least forty miles already and the Washita about an hour away, they felt good in themselves facing up to the challenge of the day.

Six miles on, they spied a distant bunch of Indians turning to tail them. Tom ordered they should keep on riding and up the pace a little to see how they would do. The Indians numbered no more than ten. Fortunately, they never made up ground and after two miles pulled out of the chase and circled away. Relieved of it, the three cowboys whooped and hollered and laughed aloud as they pressed on, keeping the race going for another mile before slowing to a reasonable speed. "Nothing's gonna stop us, boys!" Jim hooted. "Tom's right. W' got the horses!"

"If that c-crazy rider's still c-c-comin' after us he's gonna need w-wings!" Scott shouted triumphantly.

"If he's comin' at all, he'll be right on the trail line. Or maybe travelling at night!" Tom called. "Believe me, whoever it is, he ain't no fool!"

Jim glanced at Tom, knowingly. He knew Tom was still agitated by the thought of the rider. Despite his composure and logic, it irked him. "Well," Jim voiced, "Aa see no point in us talkin' about him when it was Indians that came after us! Damn him!" he cried, slapping his sleek black horse into the lead.

A mile further on, when the ground began to slope away before them, they could see the trees ahead where the Washita River ran. They remembered crossing it on their way north with the cattle, someplace else, upriver. By then, they recalled, both Fletcher and Selby were dead. They glanced west across the country, thinking of the two men and picturing the ground where they lay buried.

At the water's edge the horses were relieved of their saddles and bags and set free to drink and graze. Having washed off the dust and sweat sticking to their faces and necks, the three cowboys quickly built a fire and in no time coffee was boiled and food was cooking. It was Scott, wandering away to loosen his belt and squat down in some bushes, that noticed storm clouds in the far western sky. Returning, he informed Jim and Tom and they both stepped up the bank to see for themselves. Beyond the distant horizon a thick wall of purple blackness was visible with occasional flashes of lightning shuddering above. It was far, far away but they guessed it was a big one. However, judging by the direction the clouds were drifting overhead, it seemed unlikely it would sweep their way. Though the land was desperate for water, there could be a problem if rivers swelled.

After they had eaten they took a shorter rest than customary before preparing to ride again. Despite being tired, not one of them dozed off, the distant storm and the many miles ahead occupying their minds, nibbling at their thoughts like a two headed monster. And so, it was with some relief that they actually mounted up and set off once more.

Now on 'Rock', Tom took the lead. The big grey horse carried him with pride. To the rear right Scott followed on 'Sagebrush' and on his left Jim sat on 'Tricky'. The free horses, 'Rusty', 'Star' and 'Sugar' ran bareback, relieved of any weight, while the remaining four, 'Munch', 'Locust', 'Blue Coat' and 'Mack', lightly shared the baggage load.

Mid afternoon, twelve miles beyond the Washita, 'Tricky' stumbled but Jim stayed on. Stopping to check the horse, there was no visible injury but there was damage in the joint causing a faint limp. With Jim switching onto 'Mack', the group continued their journey.

Facing a rising wind their progress slowed. Also, ahead, a large dark cloud had formed and was rolling towards them. Tom shouted for them to look for cover and they knew what it meant. They pushed on, eyes scanning the high plain until Scott spotted a meagre stance of low trees to the west of them about a mile and a half away.

Arriving at the dry creek bed they hurriedly jumped down and roped the horses together beneath the canopy of branches of the widest oak tree and they themselves pulled on their slickers and leant up against the squat trunk under the limbs. Soon, the noise of the wind increased, rushing through the leaves, as the dark, turbulent cloud cast its shadow over them and the first hailstones thudded down. As large as fists, the white balls crashed into the tree and bounced off the hard ground as high as jumping grasshoppers. The horses snickered in panic, but the blows that struck them were fewer than would have been out in the open.

It lasted no longer than five minutes before the fearful noise ended abruptly and the wind dropped. Stepping out, Jim untied the tether rope and the horses, apart from 'Tricky', danced from beneath the tree, all frisky and agitated with their ears pointed high. The three cowboys removed their slickers and laid them down.

"We'll give the horses a little time to calm down then we'll be on our way," said Tom, taking out his pipe to light up.

"Lucky w' found cover!" Jim insisted. "Damn well kill a man them stones. Got caught out once and had to sit holding a saddle over me for protection! Cow's teeth, it saved me it did!" he vouched.

The sun suddenly emerged and they felt the heat immediately. The wind had gone completely and there was an unreal sense of stillness in the air.

"Sure Aa'm h-h-happy w-we're not t-trailin' beeves any-m-more!" said Scott. "S-s-storm like th-at s-sends th-em s-stampedin'!"

Tom and Jim glanced at each other. Since riding with them his stammer had never sounded as bad. The only possible cause, they thought later, was the storm and shake of the air? Tom had often maintained to Jim that the weather in which a child enters the world could partly shape its character. He remembered them one time, with Brewster there too, talking about it! Wes, it was proposed, must have been delivered during a violent storm! And Elias suited a windy, dusty, unsettled day! Tom often mused about people's behaviour and how it was.

Tom drew on his pipe and exhaled smoke. "If a herd's spooky it don't take more than a sneeze to set 'em off. Guess we were lucky in many ways. Travis couldn't remember trailin' a more docile bunch!"

Jim took off his hat and pondered. "We sure didn't have any storms out of the sky but we had them on the ground alright. With Hardin and Parker there, trouble was always round the corner. At first, Scott, Aa thought you was in their team."

Scott had picked up a coloured stone and was examining it in his hand. "Tom t-talked to Wes more than Aa did," he answered.

"But y' were friendly enough with him," Jim insisted.

Scott stared at him. "Elias asked me t-t' be. He and Wes were k-kin!"

"You knew about it?"

"Sure. But he s-said not t-to tell anyone!"

Jim and Tom looked at each other and laughed out loud. "That old snake must have told everybody the same!" Jim declared.

Tom shook his head in amusement, walking away to fetch the horses that were grazing round bunches of buffalo grass. Spotting him, some prairie dogs sitting on a sand bank scampered underground and a hawk sailed out of a dead tree. Tom was concerned to see that 'Tricky's' leg was worse, but Jim decided it wouldn't hold them up, and a few minutes later they rode on.

At first they jogged a while until the horses showed a willingness, then they moved into an easy lope. Hats low against the sun's glare they headed towards hillier country, knowing every mile would be harder but one more to add to the long day's haul. Later, walking up a long slope they reck-

237

oned they had travelled over seventy miles that morning, from the Cimarron, and they figured that on fresh mounts, they still had almost two hours left in them. At the top of the rise they paused to look back more than a hundred miles. The storm cloud had vanished and now the pale sky held only bubbles of silvery cloud. To the east they could make out at least four lines of trailing cattle, and westwards towards the mountains, the blackness on the horizon had turned a misty grey. With only the sound of the breeze and horses shuffling they felt as if they were destined to be there, present witnesses to a world they were privileged to observe.

"It's a fine picture, boys. One t' store an' pull out from time to time just t' remember how y' helped an older cowboy home to his family!" stated Tom, impishly. "Come on!" he urged turning 'Rock' about and spurring him lightly into a downhill run.

An hour passed with the sun burning lower against the right side of their faces. Their run over hilly ground had become choppy and fatigue compelled them to change mounts for a final push. With Tom on 'Munch', Jim on 'Star' and Scott on 'Blue Coat' they continued staunchly, bearing in mind what they had set out to do.

Twelve miles on and blowing with effort, they trooped forward, hardly able to speak, eyes searching ahead for what could be a good camp site. They needed water, but every hollow and cutting was dry. Eventually, they halted and Tom pulled out the map. The other two squeezed alongside and leaned across, peering at it as well. They supposed Cow Creek was probably another seven or eight miles.

"Might even be ten," warned Jim, "an' then it could be dry!"

Tom looked to hear what Scott had to say. He took off his hat and wiped sweat from his brow. "W' can always go into a c-cow camp for water if we d-don't find none," he said.

Tom nodded. "Don't like the idea of it, but it's a way out."

Jim's eyes were screwed, looking skywards for birds flying for water, but nothing showed. Despite his lame horse he agreed they should continue, even unto darkness. So they took a little swig of water from their canteens then kicked off again, veering left to take a line closer to the trail.

It was four miles further when Scott's young eyes spotted cranes, six of them, sailing ahead across the sky, descending beyond hill to the right of them. They steered the horses in that direction and the animals began snickering and shaking their heads, nostrils wide. Reaching a low divide between two bluffs, they picked up on a gravely hollow that surfaced several small pools of water dotted with scrub oak. Their arrival caused a disturbance as the cranes and other birds flew off, and a little distance away three prong horn antelope paused long enough for Tom on horseback to pull out his Sharps, unclip and take aim while they raced up the bank. He fired only once and the last one stumbled and toppled backwards as it leapt, rolling back down.

"F-fine shot!" Scott enthused, controlling his horse.

Tom snorted. "Not if a party of Indians arrive, uninvited!"

239

"Th-en why shoot?"

"Hunger! We've ridden all day about ninety miles and my belly wants more than a jack rabbit or a bird. Now you go, Scott, and see to it. Aa'll look to the horses and gather sticks. Jim, take a look around and check where we are and nobody's comin'. It's not that I'm bossin' anyone but w' don't have time t' discuss it, alright?"

Jim had tilted back his hat. "Whatever y' say, boss!" He laughed and after permitting 'Star' a taste of water, he rode off to patrol the area.

It wasn't long before the day's sun seemed to suddenly dip letting in darkness and they sat down in the fire light waiting for coffee to boil. To the side of the flames, strips of deer meat pierced on sticks were slowly roasting. Nearby, already watered, the horses were now grazing. Being ranch steeds they knew who they belonged to and there was no need to hobble them. Anyhow, Jim commented, at the end of a long day's ride they were as weary as their riders and in no mood to wander.

There was no more to add to it. Conversation trickled to a bare minimum. Only the thought of first watch provoked their minds, but that was reconciled by Tom's volunteering. To make it less of a burden, he suggested that they do an hour at a time and the other two nodded.

Next day, early dawn, they folded their quilts inside their tarps and rolled them up and fastened them tight. Heavy with weariness, they lumbered stiffly to the water and splashed their faces, then they built up the remains of the fire and cooked breakfast. Coffee and food stimulated their bodies and the happy thought of leaving Indian Territory later that day roused their mood. Unfortunately, it was soon upset when Jim discovered that his horse, 'Tricky', was in no condition to run. Through the night the injury had swollen more and the creature was crippled. Tom and Scott said nothing, leaving Jim to make up his own mind. His look was sombre. "I can't leave him here like this!" he announced. "Sure, he can hobble around for a few days and eat and drink water but it ain't likely he'll recover." He looked helplessly at Tom and Tom understood and gave Jim a nod of assent.

While preparing to leave, and before he climbed onto his saddle, Jim spoke fondly to his speckled horse before finally taking out his gun. He watched his horse go down then, sad eyed, he mounted 'Sugar' and spurred away.

The three cowboys rode in silence from the scene and never looked back. The rising sun warmed the air but would soon move behind a blanket of dismal cloud which stretched across the eastern sky. To rid himself of misgiving, Jim led the way. Behind him, Tom and Scott loped side by side on 'Rusty' and 'Locust' with the other six horses trailing them. Tom reckoned it was near enough fifty miles to the Red River so it would be a shorter ride than the previous days. Since his ribs were on the mend, he'd lost the grimness of face that showed his torment. Riding with Scott, he was pleased to tell the younger man some more about his family. Scott remembered how Tom had described Johnny and now Tom told him about his daughter, Amelia, saying she was like her mother, both bossy and pretty. Scott smiled but Tom insisted he wasn't joking. He said it had been Amelia who had equipped the horses for the cattle trail, and she would be mightily upset about losing 'Tricky'.

The rolling hills levelled out and they found their rhythm again and made good progress, linking up with Beaver creek where they climbed down to stretch their legs and let the horses water.

The cloud had spread overhead and the ball of the sun was visible from time to time but was weak. Elsewhere, in darker areas of the sky, it looked like it was raining. They knew how desperately the land needed a soak and they joked that they wouldn't mind getting wet themselves. "Not storm wet!" Tom insisted. "Just rain wet will do!"

"Cow's belly, if y' want real wet go an' jump into the river!" Jim replied, eyes shining.

"We're going t' get wet alright, just crossing over. That storm out west, yesterday, must have swelled the rivers by now!" Tom argued.

"Take more than a day's storm to fill those rivers, Tom!" Jim retorted. "The drought's turned them into streams!"

"We'll see," Tom muttered sucking on his pipe, watching Scott as he toed the ground near a group of rocks.

Scott hunkered down and sifted the dusty soil with his

hands, picking up an old arrow head. He also found a brittle string of bone beads and stood up to examine them. "Seems we're not the only ones t-to rest here."

Tired of waiting, Jim glanced knowingly at Tom and they both went to their horses and mounted up. Scott, however, paid no attention and prolonged his searching. Jim muttered to Tom that they ought to teach him a lesson and set off immediately. For amusement, they pressed their horses faster so that Scott, in pursuit, was only able to catch them up further on.

He was breathing deeply from the chase. "Tried h-h-hollerin' but yous rode off in such a h-hur-ry! One of y-you must have left a c-c-canteen where we stopped!"

Jim realised immediately that it was his, and pulled up to a halt, with Tom and Scott riding on, chuckling. "Cow's teeth! It wouldn't have hurt none to fetch it for me, Scott?" Jim bawled after him.

"No sir!" Scott declared, and laughing aloud he hastened forward, leaving Jim to bellow a curse before tracking back alone to where they had been.

Scott slowed for Tom to draw alongside and together they walked the horses to let Jim catch up later. Scott chortled again over Jim's misfortune. "He was in s-s-uch a hurry to l-leave me b-ehind, he got what he d-deserved!"

"Aa went with him," Tom confessed.

"Sure, but it w-wasn't your idea. It w-as his!"

"How d' you know that?"

Scott stared at him lightly. "Cos Aa know y-you wouldn't."

243

"But Aa agreed to it," Tom mused.

"Aa w-would have too!"

When Jim eventually caught them up he merrily criticised Scott for leaving the canteen where it lay. Scott was unrepentant, and Jim, at last, conceded that the last laugh was on himself.

Despite their fatigue from yesterday's long, exhausting ride, their spirits rose. Invigorated, they broke again into an easy run, following the creek bed as it coursed its way south towards Red River. Under a dull sky and cooler air, they felt relaxed and comfortable as they crossed the yellow prairie land, knowing they could be in Texas before the day was through.

In the afternoon, after a long midday rest, they changed horses and continued on their way, staying close to the creek, still a few miles west of the trail. Riding 'Mack', Jim's anguish about shooting 'Tricky' was behind him now and the three riders rode together in a line with him in centre position. They saw no one else, disturbing only a few buffalo and their young calves grazing alongside elk. The day's sun emerged sporadically between breaking cloud but not once did they feel a spot of rain, somehow managing to miss the small showers that dampened the brown grass.

Two hours later as they descended into the river basin they witnessed the river's flood and Tom took no pleasure in being proved right. The violent storm in the west had sent a huge volume of water crashing downstream, overspilling at bends and low banks. They halted their run to stare at it.

"Cow's arse!" Jim blasted. "How in hell are w' gonna get across

that?"

"We're not gonna jump it, for sure," Tom said grimly. "And we're sure not swimmin' it either!"

Jim spat. "We rode as fast as devils to get out of the Territory an' w' get held up here, of all places!"

They fell silent, sitting on their horses, gazing down at the muddy, swirling, wave splashing water, charging down-river like a buffalo stampede.

"Nowhere near here to even think of crossin'!" Jim bemoaned.

"Full as any r-river Aa've ever s-een," Scott said, scratching his unshaven, feathery chin.

"Maybe w' ought t' head downstream and see what the situation is at the trail crossin'. If there's a chance of goin' over it'll be there," Tom advised.

They moved on down slope and swung left. Dark clouds from the west were edging closer and they spurted forward as if they could outrun them. On a huge bend where the river turned south they put on their slickers then cut away from it to head for the cow trail three miles to the east where they would meet the river again at the crossing. At the thought of being held up any length of time, a sense of frustration clamped their minds. The feeling was not eased when the rain caught them, teeming down with the force of a blizzard. In desperation they ignored it, galloping on towards the low trees ahead at the edge of the trail route that angled off down through sparse woodland to Red River Station.

Near the swollen river they found shelter from the downpour beneath a huge cottonwood. Gloomily, they stared at the fast flowing water that was impossible to swim, and even through the rain they could discern the figures of cowboys, horses and cattle that were held up on the far side.

They waited for half an hour before the rain slowed and clouds brightened. Emerging out of shelter they walked the horses to the river's edge. The late afternoon sun sneaked through, silvering the drizzle as it drifted away. A cowboy on the far bank saw them and shouted a greeting. With a booming voice to overcome the river's din, he informed them that there were four herds waiting to cross and another approaching.

"How long have you been here?" Jim hollered.

"W' got here yesterday, about this time. The herd in front of us got over in time, about two hours earlier, but we were too late. Boss saw it comin' upstream, said it was just like walls of water, leaping up the banks!" The cowboy removed his hat to shake away the drips.

"Hope it dies down soon!" Jim shouted. "We don't want t' be stranded on this side too long, either! We're heading home!"

"Guess you ain't got much t' worry about then, wi' no cattle t' get across!" the other hooted.

Tom snorted, knowing their own dilemma was nothing compared to those on the other side; what with cattle crowding and the threat of one bunch stampeding the rest. They waved the rider farewell and turned their horses to find a spot to make camp. The air was already warmer and Tom feared the rain and the sun would bring out the mosquitoes and warned that unless they wanted to be eaten alive they should move away from the river and trees to spend the night. Jim glanced at Scott. They could have made the same decision but Tom always seemed to have the knack of thinking and saying it first. Jim knew his friend didn't do it to be smart or to assume authority. It was simply in his nature to be alert and consider consequences. Jim heaved a sigh, not because it aggravated him, but out of admiration for Tom's shrewdness.

In a low sun they walked the horses up slope to higher ground and finding a gully with a few mesquite trees offering wood, they made camp beside a small trickle of water springing from the ground. Skilled at fire making, Jim, on the way, had already collected a small bundle of dry sticks to feed a flame, so he soon had a hot base on which to build a solid fire for cooking. The dark afternoon clouds had moved away completely and the clear evening sky darkened towards night with the moon and stars showing faintly. Somehow, with food inside them, the taste of coffee, a warm fire and the chance of a dry night to lower the flood's level, their despondency at the delay lessened, leaving them to the prospect of a good night's rest.

Tom was lighting his pipe when Scott asked him how his ribs felt. Tom joked that they hadn't bothered him, but now that someone had asked he could feel them hurting again. Jim stated that sometimes pain was just a thing of the mind! He once had a stiff shoulder for nearly a year after a fall and it was due to him keep thinking about it that it never got loose. And that was why he believed that thinking too much sort of interferes with what is natural. He went on to say that Brewster was one of those who had to try and work out everything and explain it.

"That's why the boys were w-w-wary of him. All except T-Tom," Scott remarked.

Tom rubbed his nose. "Me an' him liked to put thoughts into words. Nothing wrong with it. Makes living more interesting if y' think about it!" he insisted.

"Tom, y' once told me you spent too much time wonderin' and got yourself vexed too often about things that weren't worth the trouble," Jim reminded him.

Tom puffed his pipe considering an answer. "Don't recall sayin' that to y', Jim," he began. "An' if Aa did, Aa more than likely said it t' keep y' happy. Sometimes when we argue, Aa do it t' keep the peace." Tom kept a straight face.

Jim raised his eyebrows. "Cow's teeth, you've never backed out of any argument with me. You like to rile me, Tom. It gives y' pleasure an' Aa know it!"

Tom yawned. "Aa don't rile you, Jim, you rile yourself."

"Y' sure in hell do, Tom. Remember when I lost your knife and how you kept asking if I'd found it. You just wouldn't let it go!"

"Why should Aa let it go, Jim? It was a damn good knife you borrowed."

Jim spat towards the fire. "Loosin' it was an accident, Tom, but y' kept askin' about it as if it weren't and Aa started to feel that you weren't happy with how I lost it cos you kept going on about it, asking if I'd found it!"

Tom blew smoke calmly in a fine stream. "I reckon y' wondered too much about it at the time, Jim. Didn't know until now how much it irritated you. Y' should be like Brewster and me and talk about things, then y' wouldn't get riled so much!"

Jim spat again more vehemently then drew a deep breath to console himself. "If y' weren't my best friend, Tom, Aa'd curse and loathe you all the way to hell!"

Scott shook his head. "Never known anybody like y-ou both!"

Tom's and Jim's faces lightened and they finished their coffee. Scott gathered the mugs and went to rinse them out. On his return, he laid out his bedding as they had done, and then announced that he'd take first watch. With coyotes calling down by the river, Scott left Tom and Jim, and then taking his rifle went clambering up the side of the gully to squat against a mesquite tree. Chewing tobacco, he peered towards the flooded Red River, and on the other side of it was able to observe the numerous camp fires of stranded outfits.

By dawn they had eaten breakfast, and by sun-up they had the horses ready to travel down to the water's edge. From the north bank of the river they could see the mass of waiting herds stretching into the distance, and they could hear the sound of bawling, impatient cattle.

They discovered that the level of water had lowered, but the river was still in spate and looking dangerous. They were not alone. Four riders on the opposite bank were assessing it too before they travelled upstream a little way, stopping again to deliberate upon the risk of crossing. Deciding against it they gave a cursory wave and turned to ride away. Tom, Jim and Scott realised too that their delay would continue for two or three hours at least, and they stared grimly at the torrent and reconciled themselves to this fact. With a sigh, they turned their horses and wandered back into the trees.

While Jim made a fire and boiled coffee, Tom and Scott dozed on the ground. Free to roam, the horses nibbled the grass and then lifted their heads to pause, motionless, as if transfixed by the uncertainty of delay. Casting misty rays of light, the morning sun climbed warmly through the leaves.

With a look of resignation, they were't prepared to squander time, accomplishing small tasks such as airing their bed rolls, cleaning equipment and shaving and trimming hair. Even Scott was persuaded to lose an inch at the back. And it was him, later, that spotted the same four trail riders returning to the far riverbank. Curious to watch what they intended, the three of them mounted and trailed down to the river. It was late morning now and the flood water had clearly dropped but it still appeared hazardous and wide.

The trail riders moved upstream to the same spot they'd visited earlier, talking and gazing at the river. Then, suddenly, one of them charged down the bank side into the water and swimming frantically, the horse and cowboy ploughed their way across at an angle towards them. They watched anxiously, in excitement, as the horse with its nose high and the man clutching the horn of his saddle with one hand and thrashing with the other reached beyond half way. Jim yelled encouragement and he and Scott advanced into the river to meet him, both their horses knee deep in the thick red water.

They both saw it. A submerged log rolled up to the surface and before they could holler it had struck the horse, toppling it over, and at once horse and rider went under. For a few seconds they vanished, then the rider came up, arms splashing as he spluttered for air. Scott reacted first. Grabbing his rope he advanced 'Blue Coat' down river up to its chest and standing in the stirrups swiftly swung the loop above his head and tossed it accurately in front of the man as he flailed downstream. It almost landed in his hand and snatching it he held on for life as Scott turned 'Blue Coat' and retreated out of the river, dragging the man towards the water's edge where Tom was wading in to help him out.

Meanwhile, Jim on 'Star' had gone after the horse which had surfaced once further down only to disappear again.

"We got y', don't worry!" Tom reassured the cowboy as he

supported him onto dry ground, sitting him down. The bearded man coughed and gasped until his lungs cleared, then he breathed quickly for a short time until he had recovered enough to speak.

"Thought Aa was gone," he rasped.

Scott had dismounted and was beside them gathering his rope. Tom grinned at him. "You moved fast, Scott."

The man looked up at him. "Thanks."

"P-pleased t' help," he replied modestly. They aided the man to his feet and he waved at his three friends on the other side as Jim was returning with the missing horse.

"Cow's ears, this pony got fish's lungs in him! He goes under water for over a hundred yards, coming up only once, and then walks out like he does it every day, no spluttering or choking or nothing 'cept a cough!" Jim exclaimed.

The man stood up. He had black pebble eyes that gleamed. "He's the best swimmin' horse I know." He turned his head, looking back across river. His friends waved. "Would have made it alright if that log hadn't turned us over."

"Why'd y' risk it now when in two hours it'll be safe enough to cross?" Jim queried, in light reproof.

The cowboy's eyes glistened on Jim. A drip on the tip of his beard was ready to drop off. "Wanted to test it. It's hell over there on the other side. None of us slept all night, holdin' the cattle back from runnin'. W' want t' get ahead as soon as it's possible. Twenty thousand cattle ready to go berserk ain't something you want t' sit waiting for."

Jim nodded then introduced himself and Tom and Scott.

The cowboy's name was Warren Dalz. He repeated it for them. His clothes were soaked so they invited him to their camp fire for coffee, where he could wring them out and dry in the strong morning sun. He told them he was the second man on his drive under a boss called Mitchell, and the outfit behind was led by the well known Shanghi Pierce who would cross before them if they dallied any longer than necessary. Dalz added that Pierce and his boss Mitchell were not exactly friends.

Sitting in his underwear with his hat on, Dalz drank coffee at the fire while his clothes spreadeagled over bushes quickly dried. His round shining eyes showed gratitude and humour. "Good thing 'bout being here is Aa ain't over there working like a dog!"

Tom, who for a change had not said a great deal, came in. "Dog's only got one life, though."

The bright eyes settled on him. "That's true, Tom. He scratched his black beard, yawning.

"And a dog needs its sleep," Tom smiled. "You grab some when you got the chance."

Dalz nodded and going into shade lay down with a blanket that Tom gave him. Scott and Jim had gone back to watch the river so Tom took went alone on 'Munch' back up the slope to where they had camped the night. Looking south over the broad river basin, the sight of stranded herds stretching for miles was incredible, making its mark on him. He took in a deep breath. Once more, facing homeward, he thought of his family and the events of his journey worth describing to them, and this here had to be one. He imagined their faces and their eyes gazing into his as he described it and he felt the sensation of his love for them rising in his chest. Acutely aware, Tom understood that this was one of those moments in his life that would be unforgettable.

He day-dreamed about them a little while longer until instinct made him turn his horse and head up to the top of the rise to scan the prairie to the north. He spotted no other rider in the yellow ocean of grass but patiently sat his horse as if in anticipation of a sighting, sensing it almost with a will. Throughout his life, on certain matters, he knew he carried an obsessive urge. Despite no good reason, he suspected, subconsciously, that they were still being followed. He loaded his rifle and with a stern face set off up the trail for another mile to check it out.

Tom returned downhill towards noontime. The other three were seated round the fire ready to eat. 'Munch' was glistening with sweat as Tom unsaddled him and by the time he joined them his plate was waiting. While they tucked in to their grub, Tom admitted that his inkling had been justified. He had made out a solo rider in the distance but was unable to identify who it was. He'd waited in hiding but no one approached. "Maybe he saw me earlier with his spyglass," Tom said. Then he twisted his mouth. "Anyways, we got somethin' bigger on our minds to discuss. Back there, on a rise, I got a good look at the sky and there's a chance more rain's gonna fall. Maybe not here, but up river."

They chatted of how the water level was dropping and that they should attempt to cross over in the next hour, before any herd came forward. Also, if they were going to be soaked they'd want the afternoon's sun to dry them off.

"Know nothin' 'bout the man trailin' you, but reckon w' can get over now since the river's dropped a bit since Aa tried swimmin' it," Dalz said.

"Sure has," Jim vouched, staring at it. "An' y' would've made it, hadn't been for that branch spillin' you!"

It was decided. They drank coffee then started to pack up and gather their belongings in readiness for the crossing. Each man wore a look of purpose. After their rush through the Territory their forced delay had depressed them, and they longed to stand again on Texas ground. Though patient in their preparations, the urge to leave was overpowering.

At last, when it was time to go, Scott, volunteering to go first, moved forward to the water's edge. One by one, they lined up behind him, ready to follow.

It was at that point that the sound of someone whistling a tune prompted them to turn. They twisted in their saddles to see a horseman approaching from behind a thicket of bushes. At first they did not recognise him, but when he tilted his hat back from his face, they saw it was Jacob, the black cowboy who'd ridden with them. He ceased whistling his tune and they heard his deep gravelly chuckle as he urged his horse, with a spare one following, down the bank towards them.

He laughed and beamed all the way towards them sitting their mounts at the river's edge. Tom and Scott were pleased to see him but Jim was less inclined. "You son of a gun! You've been on our tails like a ghost, givin' us the shakes and now you - laugh! If you weren't a friend I'd kick your balls all the way to Montana!

Jacob guffawed. "If it weren't for me rescuin' your horses you'd have no feet to kick sand, Jim. Lord knows the trouble you'd be in."

"What in hell's name were you following us for?" Jim demanded. "Y' could have easily joined us."

"Well, maybe I could and maybe I couldn't," Jacob replied lazily. "Aa never gave it a thought till you was gone. Then I thought, maybe Aa' should so Aa' did, only you was way ahead an' Aa' couldn't catch up an' that's when I just got the idea t' tail you."

"What about the spyglass?" Tom added.

"Elias lent it t' me. Said it might be useful." Jacob climbed down from his saddle and Tom dismounted and shook him by the hand, with Scott and Jim doing the same. "Hope you ain't too sore about it. Aa kind o' enjoyed the game, trackin' you like a sheriff after outlaws," Jacob said gleefully.

"Well we was, but seein' it's you, Jacob, and y' sure did us a favour with those two horse thieves, Aa' reckon w' can let you keep your balls!" Tom explained, grinning.

"Y' might have got yourself killed doin' it, Jacob. We

weren't too happy an' was on the lookout ready to shoot," Jim said.

"Lord, you only left Abilene six days ago. Aa' could hardly keep up." He released his horses to drink and splashed his face in the water.

"We got lots to talk over, Jacob, but it'll have to wait. We're about to go across,"Tom told him.

Jacob viewed the prospect. "Good job A'm here to advise you." He laughed again. Meanwhile, Dalz still in the saddle and seemingly wary of the black man, said they ought to go now as they'd planned.

"You gonna j-oin us or come later, like you been doin'?" Scott teased Jacob.

Jacob stared. "Never heard you speak a sentence that long all trail, Scott. Been teachin' him, Tom?"

Tom paused. "No, Jacob, he just taught us t' listen."

Jacob laughed again and they shared his amusement.

Scott went first, angling his horse slightly up river. At the middle and deepest section, the water covered the animal's legs but the torrent had subsided. Quietly, they watched his progress and cheered when he reached the far bank without a hitch. In turn, Dalz followed, then Jacob, then Jim on 'Mack' and finally Tom on 'Rock'. The loose, spare horses had other ideas, floating away into deeper water where they had to swim, climbing out fifty yards downstream.

Relatively dry, the riders gathered happily on the Texas side. Leaving the Territory made it feel more of a triumph. Wishing Dalz farewell, the group wanted to make up for lost time. Collecting their spare horses, they set off, determined to cover as many miles as they could before their first stop. Rested by the delay, the horses were fresh and bound easily over the ground peeling away from the line of herds waiting to cross Red River. The mass was a spectacle to behold. At a guess, there was up to ten thousand cattle.

The dark clouds in the west thinned and the afternoon sun grew bolder, fiercely beating down. After an hour's ride, finding a shallow creek with a thin stream of water, the four stopped to slug water from their canteens and let the horses drink. Moving off, they walked the horses for quarter of a mile which gave them a chance to talk. They had lots to ask Jacob about; his shooting of the two robbers and how he had managed to keep track of them and had he seen the Indians. Jacob laughed again. The closest he had gotten to them was when he killed the horse thieves. He had spied them through the eyeglass setting off and had ambushed them as they came near the rock he was hiding behind. He gleefully told them that the shots from his Spencer Rifle did the trick.

"So why didn't y'u bring the horses to us?" Jim protested.

"Saw y' comin' an' wanted to keep y' guessin' a while longer, I guess," Jacob answered with a shrug.

Jim told him about their visiting Caldwell and how they'd been arrested, but Jacob said that he knew nothing of it. He added that he'd spotted them a day later and that was about it. "Never saw you again for a couple o' days but knew where you was aimin' for an' Aa just kept comin'."

Shortly, they broke into a run. It was hoped that they would reach the West Fork Of The Trinity River before making camp for the night. Gladly, once again they found their rhythm and glided over the rolling prairie where loamy strips held cacti and scrub brush and small mesquite trees.

At another brief stop to change horses, they rested down from their saddles to stretch their limbs and ease their backs. Jacob said that he intended going to Kerrville hoping to join another outfit, but before that he wanted to call in to see relatives that homesteaded on the upper reaches of the Leon River. Scott was undecided about his future plans but wanted work, someplace. Tom and Jim admitted that their ambitions were straightforward - to return home, to see their families again and to continue farming their land and breeding cattle.

On fresh mounts they set off again; this time Tom sat on 'Locust', Jim on his white 'Sugar' and Scott on 'Blue Coat'. Jacob's second horse, 'Milton' was tan coated and blind in one milky-coloured eye. "Born that way," he told them, blandly.

They journeyed southwards at an easy lope, kicking up dust. The sun to their right threw shadows that grew longer as the afternoon receded into early evening. They kept a look out for trees in the distance where the Fork River ran and drifted towards lower land, closer to the Chisholm Trail.

To check the way ahead Jacob pulled up and, using his spyglass, shouted to the others informing them of a herd of cattle heading north less than two miles away and of two riders in advance. Tom decided that they should seek information from these drovers and took the lead veering left towards them.

It turned out that they were scouts, forging ahead, on the look out for suitable ground where they could bed the cattle overnight. Introductions were made and Tom lit his pipe. The smaller of the two was called Jeff Logan and the other man was called Brett Guthrie. To flex their limbs the six riders climbed down off their mounts and Tom showed them his map asking for advice. Guthrie, an assistant boss, pinpointed a spot near the Fork River that was good place to camp. "There's shelter, some grazing and clear spring water among some rocks."

Guthrie, a narrow faced, intense man, spoke glumly of the drought and how desperate things were becoming throughout Texas, saying cattlemen were worried sick and eager to sell their stock at any price rather than see them wither and die.

"It's been talked down the line from Abilene that beeves are selling as low as eleven an' ten dollars a head. Is that right?" Logan asked outright.

"Our boss managed to average about thirteen. But we had first rate cattle," Tom added carefully.

"An' if y' don't mind the askin', what was the name o' your boss?" Guthrie enquired.

"Mathias. Henry Mathias," Tom answered.

Logan and Guthrie nodded lightly at each other.

"There'll be nobody else get a higher price all summer than what he got," Guthrie surmised. "Only man capable o' gettin' the better of Mathias is the top man, himself - Joe McCoy!"

"You know of Mr Mathias?" Tom stated.

"Sure do," Logan came in. "One of his hands, Selby Logan, is my youngest brother. He's ridden with Mathias for the past three seasons."

Tom hesitated and lowering his pipe glanced sideways at Jim, then Scott and Jacob. "Aa'm sorry t' tell you, Jeff," he continued, "but your brother got killed on the way up. His pony fell in the one stampede we had."

Jeff Logan twisted his mouth as the news registered in him. "Where's he buried?" he demanded.

"Indian Territory. But we weren't on the Chisholm trail, we were west of it before we cut across. Jacob, here, helped to bury him. They were friends."

"Selby was a good cowboy and a good man," Jacob said solemnly. "Though he never talked about family, excep' for a sister."

"Mm," the little man uttered. "He an' me weren't close, but he was my brother."

"He was a g-good man. Worked hard and was r-rel-iable. If he said he'd do s-somethin' he always did it," Scott declared.

Jeff nodded his appreciation of their compliments.

Guthrie cleared his throat. "Best get goin' back t' the line," he said to Logan. "An' you men too, Aa reckon, if y' aim to reach the river before nightfall."

They mounted their horses and bidding farewell they parted company, breaking into a run. "Cow's teeth, fancy us bumpin' into Selby's brother!" Jim shouted above the noise of hooves. "Small world, huh?"

They rode at speed, each of them still thinking about Selby and the time he was buried, and although it was less than a month since, so much else had happened afterwards, making his death seem like it was longer ago. Trailing cattle was a drawn out, tedious affair, that every yesterday felt as if it were a week before. Moments filling minutes distorted time and happenings were swiftly overtaken by new ones. Between Selby's death and their chance meeting with Jeff, his brother, a succession of other experiences crammed their memories.

They made good time and reached the designated place at the riverside before sunset, enabling them to make camp, light a fire and cook food while drinking coffee. A sense of satisfaction boosted their chattering. From crossing Red River after midday, they had covered something like fifty miles. "Our clothes might be stinkin' of sweat and dirt, but we're as happy as kids at a birthday party," Jim averred.

"Amen to that!" Jacob guffawed, grinning ear to ear.

Scott yawned then addressed Tom without a fault. "How's the ribs, boss?"

"Gettin' better by the day, Scott. Thanks. But sure ready for sleep." He gave a yawn too and then stood up to unroll his tarp.

Jacob volunteered to do first watch. The fact that there

was now four of them to share the role was considered a bonus and the other three went to lie down with an air of contentment.

Next morning, as the early sun loomed low over the plains, the four horsemen were on their way again. They rode easy, hoping to cross the Brazos River before noon. Depending on their progress, they aimed to rest at midday near the Bosque River.

About four miles to their left they saw dust rising from an approaching herd. The prairie grass was parched and yellow, shrivelling with the heat. In other areas, cracked and wrinkled bare ground yielded to a merciless sun.

Mid morning, they paused to switch horses in the shade of two live oak trees straggling a small, dry creek. Here, Scott spotted a cloud of wild pigeons advancing their way. He and Jim ran hurriedly across to a small bank and lay on their backs with rifles raised and as the birds flew by them, they fired bringing down some. Gathering them into a sack, they tied it onto one of the spare horses carrying light provisions.

"Make a change from the p-rairie chicken we been eatin' the past two days," Scott remarked.

Jacob sniggered. He couldn't get over the improvement in Scott's speech.

"Where'd you say some o' your family settled, Jacob? Them you want to visit?" Jim wondered.

"Up on the Leon River, 'bout two miles from a small place named Hamilton."

Tom pulled out his sketched map and unfolded it. "Look here, Jacob."

Jacob stared at a scrawled word. "Can't read, Tom. What you thinkin'?"

Tom traced their route. "We'll be passin' that way. Maybe even get close to there by nightfall if we want to."

Back on their saddles they started again and seeing three duck take off some distance away, they found water there bubbling up into a small pool. They let the horses take a short drink and topped up their canteens. Riding away, they appreciated the breeze, though warm, airing them as they continued southwards.

An hour later, pausing for breath, Jacob's spyglass told him of signs indicating one more hour's ride to reach the Brazos. Despite an increasing weariness, the very notion of it willed them to make another surge. After changing mounts, they slurped water into their dry mouths, then set off heartily; Tom on 'Rusty', Jim on 'Star', Scott on 'Sagebrush' and Jacob riding the one eyed tan, called 'Milton'. "When Aa got him that was his name. Told it was after a blind writer or somethin'," Jacob explained. None of them had knowledge of it.

The horses must have smelled water. They ran eagerly, wanting to go faster but were held in check, in case of a fall and needless injury. After a long, gentle decline the four cowboys arrived at the Brazos.

Tom was the driving force. After a brief rest, he insisted upon a change of horses with the intention of continuing, targeting the Bosque River for their noon-day stop. The others couldn't argue. He was the oldest and the one carrying an injury, but yet he had the staunchness and stamina to persevere. Nevertheless, Jim couldn't resist expressing a mild protest. "Don't y' just want t' spend a bit longer sitting and listenin' to all the interestin talk the three of us are eager to share with y', Tom?"

"Aa've heard enough tales, true and made-up, to last a lifetime, Jim. Much as Aa appreciate and like all three of you, the comforts of home are a lot more attractive than what your conversation offers."

Jacob gave a chuckle. Tom's snappy talk delighted him. "Sure thing, Tom. Livin' in a saddle ain't easy. Your right, let's get goin'. If we can make Hamilton country before sundown we'll get ourselves the best fried sourdough bread you ever tasted afore."

"Y'u mean at y-your folks?" Scott asked.

"Sure thing, Scott. Aunt Mae's jack-rabbit stew is way tastier than what Elias made us. The sooner we get there, you'll find out. Tom's right. Let's ride," he urged.

They mounted up and bound away with renewed zest, kicking up dust. The terrain between the rivers was rockier than before with swathes of brush and cactus crammed into dry beds and hollows which they rounded, staying on higher ground. The warm wind was constant, but refreshing the way it brushed their faces. Though the dread of it strengthening, creating a dust storm, was ever lurking in their thoughts as they soldiered on, picking their route over small rounded hills. Tom's horse, 'Rock', led the way, striding effortlessly, and the others stayed close behind.

About an hour's ride, south of the Brazos, they came upon the Bosque River and gladly climbed down. Since they'd covered beyond fifteen miles since their last, brief stop, they felt desperate for coffee, grub and rest - in that order. There was plenty dried wood to build a fire and they settled down letting the horses wander, grazing along the river's bank.

Later, in the shade of a cottonwood tree they sat on the ground and savoured everything that passed their lips. A sense of euphoria floated over them like a draught of sweet scented air; though weary and ready to nap they remained awake, desiring to relish the experience, the thrill of the occasion, the setting, and overwhelmingly, their journey's progress.

"There's times in life when things seem t' stand still, like us here now," Tom uttered, expressing deep satisfaction.

Scott and Jim lay back to relax and, feeling drowsy, stayed silent. Faintly nodding to himself, Jacob considered Tom's statement, his brown eyes gazing afar.

Tom stared at the rippling surface of the river. His viewing wandered and he suddenly spotted movement downstream on an opposite sandy bend. Pointing finger, he quietly alerted Jacob to it.

A fox had emerged from brush, sniffing the ground.

Shortly, another appeared and approached the first in a confrontational manner. They circled each other, uncertainly, before the intruder swiftly lunged forward in attack. Both reared onto their hind legs, jaws snapping. They fell and rolled, fighting like wrestlers, grappling, twisting and gnashing in a sustained frenzy until the first one broke free and scurried away, escaping out of sight. The victor stood panting, fixed, waiting to resume battle if necessary. But the other fox had fled. The winner turned and stepped gingerly into the shallow edge of the river. After slurping water it flopped down to cool off, before rising again, gleaming wet, and slowly trailed away into the brush.

"What was all that about?" queried Jacob.

Tom shrugged and his smile lingered as he answered. "Aa reckon he had a grudge an' wanted it settled." He held out his mug for more coffee and Jacob obliged, lifting the hot can from the fireside stone with a thick cloth.

After tidying up and saddling fresh horses, they stepped into the river and splashed water over themselves to shake off their lethargy and then mounted and trotted off, abandoning the place and its charm for the arid prairie land south of the Bosque.

Keeping a steady pace, they crossed undulating prairie land leading to hillier country. The wind continued to blow, sometimes swirling, humming through the dry, yellow grass and clumps of brush, but failed to strengthen. They saw a small herd of buffalo which scattered at their coming and it reminded them of Brewster and the two skinners that were killed. Other than these animals nothing else moved or caught their attention; the sun's furnace dominating the sky and earth, disabling most living creatures - so it seemed.

Mid afternoon, they took a break, quenching their thirst, and after changing horses, set off again, resolved to reach the Leon River, near Hamilton, by early evening. Over a long rise, Jim, in the lead on 'Mack' gave a sudden holler. Alerted, the others hurriedly pulled up at his side, and were immediately confounded by what they witnessed.

A mile ahead, a train of at least three thousand wild animals were moving eastwards, as if in a spectacular, biblical exodus. Open mouthed in awe, the four cowboys stared in wonderment

"Lordy Lordy! God on High!" Jacob exclaimed. He grabbed his telescope and raised it to his left eye. He blew in amazement. "Ain't seen nothin' like it. No sir." He paused as he scanned the line. "There's buffalo, wild horses, elk, antelope, deer, wolves - you name it!"

"Let me see?" Jim said. He raised the glass and was silent, then passed it on to Scott who, in turn, handed it to Tom. Tom whistled softly. "Heard of this kind of migration, but never believed it."

Scott shook his head. "Somethin' gonna happen, m-aybe?"

His question remained unanswered. The horses grew

agitated, shaking their heads and tails and snickering. "They got the urge t' go with 'em, Aa reckon," Jim commented.

They spurred their mounts forwards, directing them to the right, rounding the rear line of beasts. Fortunately, the dust the animals stirred was blowing southeastwards when the riders passed, but what they envisaged, plus the omens it presented, engulfed their minds for the remainder of the ride. "Tellin' you, it was somethin' to behold - somethin' a man gets t' see maybe once in a lifetime!" Jacob exclaimed on the gallop.

Doggedly, they pursued their aim to reach the Leon River before nightfall. It promised to be a hard slog but the monotony of the prairie was secondary to the stored image of the mixed herd of wild animals traversing the land. Nothing in nature would ever surprise them more than it.

They journeyed and rested and journeyed and rested, swopping horses three other times before they saw the hills where the river coursed. They whooped for joy and Jacob laughed louder than the other three as they charged forward. "Aa can taste that fried sourdough bread from here!" he shouted.

"Same here," Jim echoed gleefully.

"Me as w-ell!" Scott cried cheerfully.

"It better be as good as y' said, Jacob!" Tom shouted above the beat of hooves.

"Smart as you are, Tom, y' wouldn't bet against it!" he shrieked and chortled again.

At the river side they halted and rested briefly, letting the horses drink while they stretched their legs down off their saddles. Tom opened his map and he and Jacob examined it carefully.

Hamilton wasn't marked but Jacob guessed where it lay. "My folks have a place upriver, Tom. Two miles, maybe. Aa'd know it when we was there."

Tom frowned at him. "Hope so, Jacob."

"They live below a hill, two miles from the river where it bends back on its self. Aa know that for sure," he claimed.

Tom nodded. He viewed the lowering sun. "Then let's cross the river here and travel upstream. Yeah?"

"Sure thing, Tom," Jacob replied, eyes beaming, then he nudged 'Milton' into the water.

Pressing forwards, they reached the big bend of the river and Jacob led them excitedly through trees onto open ground. He pointed the way and they followed him at pace. The hill stood out before them. To confirm it, Jacob made a fist and they rode gladly alongside a nearly-dry, narrow creek, before turning off along a track leading towards two sod house dwellings with another wooden one under construction

They had already been seen. A group of three black men, two holding rifles, had gathered to meet them. The third, a youth, held two dogs on a leash. Jacob removed his hat and waved. "It's me, cousin Jacob!" he hollered.

One of the men beckoned the families and in an instant, three women and eleven children swarmed outside. Jacob leapt down off 'Milton' and was immersed by the crowd, hugging and kissing and shaking hands.

"Praise the Lord. Praise the Lord!" a woman shrieked;

"Amen. Amen," came a united response.

Jacob introduced his friends and they dismounted and shook hands with the adults. Tom addressed Aunt Mae, the eldest of the women who had white hair, beaming eyes and a joyous, kind looking face. "Jacob made us ride all day so we could meet you an' it's a pleasure, Mam," he said cordially.

Jacob laughed. "Told 'em about your cookin', Aunt Mae, and they came a runnin'!" he added.

She giggled. "Get yourselves settled an' Aa shall treat you to somethin' special. My, it's real good to see you again, Jacob," she declared with affection, then suddenly chirped out orders and there was an immediate buzz of movement and excitement, as if she'd cracked a whip.

Jim handed over the pigeons he and Scott had shot earlier in the day, then they were led to a dugout in a slope behind the homes where they could stay the night. Three of the older children led the visitors' horses away to give them water drawn from a well and tossed out some hay from a pile heaped inside a rough-made shelter. Jacob's cousin, named Peyton, a lean, earnest looking man shouted that there was coffee waiting and they all trooped towards the houses and sat outside on a ring of logs with a fire glowing in the centre.

Hanging from a rack, two pots were simmering. Tom lit his pipe and gazed at the setting sun and the blood red of the western sky. He turned his head to look over a sizeable field with crops of potatoes and cowpeas and corn. Despite the drought conditions, they seemed healthy. He mused that whoever had first claimed this ground - benefitting from the shelter of the hill against southern winds and, crucially, its hidden source of water - had chosen well. Close by, within a roped enclosure near three leafy trees, two cows and a mule lay at rest. Free to roam elsewhere, there were hens scratching and pecking the ground. Tom reflected on his own land and how he had, in twenty years, cultivated it and reared cattle. Thus, he was curious to know who had been responsible for selecting and developing this plot.

Jacob supplied the answer. "It was Uncle Marcus, husband to Aunt Mae. We was all slaves on a plantation near Brookhaven, Mississippi. Since he was a boy, Uncle Marcus had a special talent for readin' the land, knowin' good soil an' finding water. On the plantation he was in charge of what's called irrigation. Because of his skills our family was sort of privileged." Jacob paused to toss out the remains of his mug's coffee. "Anyways, after w' was freed, Mr Randolph, who'd owned us and was a decent man, encouraged Uncle Marcus to take his family west and seek out homesteader's land. Even gave money to help out. After months of wanderin' Uncle Marcus finally came here. He studied the land hereabouts south of the river and chose this patch 'cause of the workable ground, an' put in a claim." Jacob stood up stretching his back and sighed. "He and his boys, cousins Peyton and Joe, an' the women as well, worked long days an' prayed an' laboured to make it prosper. Before he died two years ago from illness, an' worn out, Uncle Marcus had the satisfaction of seein' what he'd dreamed; his family free, ownin' some land an' able to survive."

Tom, Jim and Scott remained silent in respect of Jacob's words and knowing nothing finer could be said.

Peyton's eldest daughter, Mary Jo, a lanky girl, approached the fire and placed a skillet pan on a flat stone beside the fire then stirred the contents of both hanging pans.

What's your Grandma cookin', Mary Jo?" Jacob wondered.

"She makin' a pot roast wi' chicken in this one an' red bean soup in the other." She pointed to the skillet, "Here, we got beef ribs with steak sauce."

"Is that all?" Jacob teased her.

"Nope," she replied without a smile. "Grandma got you some fried sourdough bread just waitin' t' bring out. Said it was your favourite."

Jacob chuckled. "Told you boys it was worth comin' for, didn't Aa?"

"We just might have to stay another day," Jim said light-heartedly.

Mary Jo looked gravely at him. "Aa'll go tell Grandma," she said.

Jacob laughed and put a comforting hand on her shoulder. "He's teasin' you, girl. Don't believe everything a cowboy says, 'specially when his belly's empty."

Later, round the fire, before night closed in, they and all the family ate sumptuously. There was loud chattering and some laughter. After clearing their plates, the guests sat back with fresh, steaming coffee. The children had gone inside to their beds, before Tom, Jim and Scott, like the children, drowsily dragged themselves off to spend the night in the half shelter of the dugout. Staying to talk with his cousins, it was a while before Jacob joined his three friends that were already asleep, happily snoring.

Rising early morning, they could discern something was troubling Jacob. While they packed up their belongings ready to ride after a promised breakfast, Jacob went and joined his family inside one of the houses.

Though curious, they waited for Jacob to summon them outside where he decided to explain his concern, and his reason for staying another day, or even longer.

"Day before yesterday six horsemen rode in. Said they were Texas Rangers, warning folks in the region 'bout renegade Indians an' how they aimed to protect places by scarin' off the hostiles. For that they said some payment would be appreciated. Aunt Mae suspected them and refused their offer. They said she should reconsider their proposal. Said they'd come back this mornin', hopin' she'd change her mind, thinkin' of her family and their safety." Jacob paused. "Aa want t' be here an' see what they have to say!" he concluded with ire in his voice.

Jim bristled. "Reckon Aa might stay too, just t' hear them out."

"Yeah. Count m-e in," Scott said.

Tom nodded. "Guess it makes numbers equal. Six of them - six of us." He paused at the thought of it. "Only payment we require, Jacob, is Aunt Mae's cookin'," he added.

Jacob grinned. "Grateful to y' all. Sure am."

Aunt Mae's reaction to the news was alarm. She feared trouble. Their nearest neighbours were two miles away. Hamilton was eight miles. "Don't want anyone gettin' hurt," she pleaded.

They unloaded the horses and ate breakfast slowly. Afterwards Tom advised his group they should stay out of sight, waiting in the dugout. "Seein' us they may decide to postpone their visit," he reasoned.

The sun reached mid morning when one of the children on look-out came running back to announce the riders approach.

Aunt Mae and her two sons came out to meet them. Talking had begun when Jacob walked out with his three friends to join the assembly. The riders looked surprised and uncertain.

"An' what have we got here, huh?" the lead horseman demanded. He was unshaven and looked as young as Scott.

"Family an' friends," Jacob said coldly.

"We can tell who's family," mocked a bristled, older man.

Jacob stared hard at the individual. Despite the rider's confidence and the scar down his cheek, he was small and puny looking. "Let's hear about this protection your offerin' and how much it's gonna cost?" Jacob demanded.

Their spokesman hesitated. "The's a bunch of Comanche Indians on the loose, stealin' an' settin' fire t' settlers' places. We're watchin' out for them, t' keep them away, stoppin' them doin' harm to decent folk, like we got here. We only get paid what folk care t' give us."

"For your service, eh?" Jacob interrupted.

The rider with the scar nudged his mount forward alongside the leader. A scowl pinched his face. "Listen good, we came t' talk business not for a black cowhand to set himself up as judge. Keep your mouth shut nigger an' let the old woman do the talkin'!"

Unable to restrain himself, Tom stepped forward. Jim saw his look; the harsh stare and tight jawed expression he bore when agitated and his feelings were roused. The same grim, ardent expression he had shown when he'd confronted Parker for insulting Brewster.

"There's gonna be no more talk like that." Tom's voice was low and steely. "These good people don't need protectin' by anyone other than us. We're their guardians."

Tom flexed his gun hand.

There was a pause of silence.

"What the hell you mean?" the unshaven one demanded, his voice breaking it.

Tom gripped him with an intrepid, malevolent stare. "You leave here an' never return is what Aa mean!" Ire strained his voice. "Because if you do, Aa'll hunt you down and Aa'll shoot every finger of your hands then every toe off your feet before Aa put a bullet into your big mouth so it splashes out the back of your stupid head." Every word was uttered clearly, with chilling precision.

There was a strict silence.

Muted by the threat, the two younger front riders glanced sideways at each other.

"He ain't no cowboy," a voice came from behind them. "Come on."

"Aa'm ridin'," another muttered and turned his mount and rode off. Without another word, the rest rapidly followed, the two front men now at the rear of the party.

Tom remained static, watching them depart.

Aunt Mae stepped closer and sinking to her knees she gripped his hand. "Dear God, thank you, thank you for this man," she cried. "Aa thank you, Lord."

Tom lifted her to her feet and comforted her in his arms. She sobbed, her face resting against his chest and there were tears in his eyes when he squeezed them shut, inhaling deeply.

Jim beckoned the rest of them away, leaving the two together; one shadow on the ground.

The next morning they left Jacob with his family and rode south. Tom, riding 'Rusty', wouldn't speak about what happened and in his presence no one did.

Secretly, Scott had told Jim he would never forget what Tom had said and the way he had said it. "M-made me nervous but p-proud as well."

Jim had smiled. "Me too."

Though unplanned, the day's delay with Jacob's folk gave the horses and riders the break they needed. In a grey dawn light well before the sun turned fierce they pushed on, intent and true; a spring of exuberance in their stride.

They moved onto a lower plain, flatter and treeless, the short grass bent over, lifeless. The only sign of habitation being an abandoned dwelling alongside a narrow gulch with a vanished stream. After another hour's ride, a slow drink and a change of horses, they veered towards hillier country once more. Towards noon, they stopped by a tree shaded creek with a trickle of water for the animals to recover from their exertion.

Tom took out his map to study it again with Jim and Scott looking over his shoulder. "We got to be around here," Tom pointed. "Just north of Lampasas, here. If we bear right we could make the Colorado River to rest up."

"Another hour's ride?"

"No more than an hour, Jim," Tom assured him.

Scott raised both arms and stretched his back. "Be real good t' have the river t' f-follow down."

"Yeah. An' be able t' jump in every time we feel hot an' weary," Jim added with a wry grin.

Tom's expression never changed as he continued to examine the map. "Like to think w' can get down t' where the Llano runs into it, by nightfall." he indicated.

Jim studied the map again and nodded. Scott had wandered away, looking for a find. Tom put the map away and flexed his limbs. He and Jim went to the tiny stream and, removing their hats, managed to splash water over their heads. When they stood up, Tom was slower, making more effort. Their faces shone in the burning sun.

"Ribs still sore, Tom?"

"Some, but gettin' better by the day," Tom answered brightly.

Jim hesitated. "If it makes y' happy, Aa believe you."

Tom allowed himself a little smile and put his hat on before strolling away. Soon after, they were off again.

The sun passed midday. Since their previous, brief stop they had only paused once to slug down water near an empty shell of another homestead that had been recently abandoned. It had a look of sadness. They viewed it grimly; another victim of the drought.

It took longer than the hour they had anticipated, but they came down at last towards the Colorado and whooped in delight as if they'd seen a friend that was waiting to welcome them. The great river ran smoothly. Bush and full grown cedar-elm and oak trees lined its banks. At once they dismounted and throwing off their boots and clothes, down to their underwear, they splashed into the water's edge up to their knees and sat down to bathe their sweat-stinking bodies. They chuckled merrily at the whiteness of their skin that the sun had never touched.

"Cow's belly, it feels good," Jim declared, throwing water over himself.

Shortly, they stood up dripping and retreated from the edge. Staying in their underwear to dry off in the warm air, Jim prepared a fire while Scott and Tom unloaded the baggage and set the horses free to graze.

"Aunt Mae gave us enough f-ood to last a w-week," Scott said, uncovering dry fruit, beans, potatoes and smoked beef that had been leaf-wrapped and sealed in cheesecloth.

"She's a fine woman. Kindness itself," Tom reflected.

"You were kind t-to her," Scott said. "Aa mean, what y' did, Tom."

Tom shrugged. Exhaustion lined his face. "Did what was right."

Scott nodded. "S-ure you did, Tom. Scared 'em off." He saw that Jim had lit a small fire which was burning fiercely as more dry sticks were added. "Time for c-coffee, Aa guess," Scott suggested, bringing the subject to a close.

As their underwear dried, they drank, ate and rested with satisfaction. Leaving Tom dozing on the ground, Jim and Scott, carrying their rifles, wandered to a rock by the river and sat down staring at the water's flow.

"Got plans, when we reach Kerrville?" Jim asked.

"Take a few days rest then j-join up, maybe, with an-nother outfit," Scott replied casually. "Won't be the same, though."

"Nope. Mathias was a top boss."

"Yeah. But he gave Tom c-redit. He told me Mr Brewster called it 'Tom's T-rail'"

Jim gave a slight chuckle. "Might just tell him that, one day."

Scott looked pleased.

When they started out again, Tom rode 'Locust', Jim sat on 'Sugar' and Scott on 'Blue Coat'. Staying on the left bank, they travelled down stream at an easy canter as if the river's gentle current pulled them along. On the open prairie they'd set their sights on skyline features. Following the course of the river they looked at stages, such as oncoming bends, banks, trees, slopes, straights, to measure their advance. This momentum continued for many miles, swayed not only by the Colorado's flow and its physical markers, but by an increasing awareness that tomorrow evening they could be sitting in a bar on Kerrville's Main Street. It was a golden thought.

Past mid-afternoon, they changed mounts and quenched their thirst. To prevent the horses from over drinking, they hurriedly set off again, rounding a series of rocky bluffs before returning to the river's side. Jim riding 'Mack' assumed the lead with Tom on 'Munch' and Scott on 'Sage-brush' riding together, four lengths behind.

When Jim slowed on the crown of a small rise to a walking pace, they came alongside. "Look ahead, over the river," he urged. "One of 'em spotted me already."

On a bare sandy strip a small band of Indians were squat-ted, except for the one standing up, pointing in their direc-tion. Slowly, the others rose, clutching their rifles. Tethered to trees, there were at least thirty horses.

"Looks like they been thievin', huh?" Jim commented.

"Well, there's only nine of them," Tom said decisively. "And Aa reckon they got enough horses to look to without comin' after ours." Tom paused. "Now, we ain't runnin' an' we ain't stoppin'. We'll stay wide, spaced apart, but we'll keep our eyes on them with rifles ready, okay?" he advised solemnly.

Tom led the way. The Indians stared at them as they calmly walked their horses on the other side of the river, and in a show of defiance, they stared back, undeterred. It was a long, straight stretch so they maintained their walk and vigi-lance. For a time, the Indians remained standing, watching the Texan cowboys and their horses go by, unhurried, and seeing they posed no threat, one by one they squatted down again.

Out of view of the Comanches, Tom gave 'Munch' a nudge and they continued their run again. Wary of being followed they increased their pace over the next few miles, occasionally looking over their shoulders to be certain there were no pursuers.

Late afternoon, they crossed the river and rode into Bluffton, a small settlement situated beside the river, opposite a grand wall of cliffs on the east bank. The place consisted of a saloon cum store, a blacksmith's and a tiny church and several log homes. A notice board claimed there was a population of one hundred and thirty nine. Entering the store, the three cowboys decided they should notify the residents to the party of Indians they'd passed upstream. The storekeeper, a sombre, elderly man, told them they'd heard of a band of hostiles in the vicinity but hadn't seen them or been troubled by them.

"You boys plannin' on stayin' here overnight?" he enquired.

"No. We're aimin' to reach the Llano River before sundown," Tom replied.

"Mmm." The storekeeper sounded disappointed. "Thought you might want a place to stay here." He hesitated. "Anyhow, thanks, Aa'll let folks know about the Indians."

Tom paid for his tobacco while Jim and Scott treated themselves to some homemade cookies. They bought a beer at the bar and sat down for a short break, chatting with two older men at the next table. Outside, they climbed onto their mounts and set off again.

The final stretch of the journey lasted half an hour. The smaller Llano River joined the bigger Colorado and after crossing it they found a sheltered place for themselves to set up camp for the night. They ate well and drank coffee in an upbeat mood, delighted with their long day's run and how, barring mishap, they could be in Kerrville by tomorrow's evening.

Tom's demeanour had brightened at the notion of their journey's ending. He smoked his pipe and talked openly again and gladly recounted their many experiences. He produced the note for the bank that Mr Mathias had given him and handed it to Jim to examine.

Jim's face glowed. "Havin' a spare copy of it was the best thing you did, Tom," he admitted, referring to the incident with the robber who had burned the other.

Tom fumbled inside his tobacco pouch and happily produced another note. "This here's an original note too, Jim. Mr Mathias an' me signed all three."

Jim chuckled. "Aa'm your partner an' you never said y' had another."

"Can't be too careful, Jim," Tom explained, eyes shining with humour.

They laughed together, then merrily tossed coins, gambling over who should do first night watch.

Over excited about their final day's ride to reach Kerrville, their sleep was thwarted.

"Keep th-thinkin' all night 'bout them C-comanches starin' at us ac-cross the w-wa-ter," Scott muttered with more hesitation that they'd heard for a while.

Jim yawned. "Worst night ever for creatures callin'," he moaned. "Owls nearby whistlin' like they wanted t' punish us for bein' there."

Gaunt looking, Tom chewed his biscuit and to help his swallowing he raised his mug of coffee to take a gulp. He wiped his mouth. "Best not think about it. Only makes it worse."

Jim observed the glumness in his older friend's lined face.

"Why, Tom, we got a lot to be grateful for. Sure, it's been a long hard trip, but now we're near the finish, we got more good memories than bad ones."

Tom shook his head as if he cared little. "All I know is we're worn out, we're stinkin' an' we're filthy. The sooner it's over and w' get home safe is all that concerns me. Perhaps, in a few week's time we'll look back an' talk about it with some pleasure. But not now."

Jim glanced at Scott and shrugged helplessly.

The weight of fatigue slowed their movements as they prepared to leave, packing and loading the horses. However, a cold wash in the river stimulated an urge to mount up and get going. Leaving the Colorado River where it turned left to snake its way in a south-easterly direction, they settled into a steady rhythm before the heat of the morning made them blow.

Across rough, baked terrain, they targeted a south-westerly route towards Fredericksburg, a small community marked on the map which Tom had underlined.

Later, pausing to change horses, they sipped water from their canteens, then set off again, wending their way through hilly, wooded landscape. Scanning ahead, they searched the distance for a prominent hilltop to the north of the township where, supposedly, a wooden missionary cross had been erected. "Sure wish w' had Jacob's s-spyglass," Scott said in frustration as his eyes strained against the dazzling sunlight.

Further on, from a vantage point, they spotted the distant cross and pushed on, eager to reach the place for their midday break.

Reaching Fredericksburg, they discovered that it was, almost entirely, a German speaking town of roughly six hundred folks dependant upon agriculture and a wood mill that brought in trade. Lined alongside a creek, the wide main street comprised of log built homes and huts that were spaced apart. The central building was a round shaped Meeting Hall behind which two large storehouses stood. Being a strict, religious community, there was no saloon connected to the General Store. In broken English, the keeper invited them to sit at a table and served them coffee and rye bread which they dipped into a bowl of syrup. Needless to say, the three cowboys were not inclined to dwell, deciding instead to ride along the creek until they found a spot where the horses could graze and they could relax, sitting on the bank side.

Now that their mood was uplifted by the prospect of a

final afternoon's ride to Kerrville, they talked gladly of it with a sense of occasion.

"Gonna get a room for the night, wash up, then buy some new clothes ready t' ride home fresh in the mornin'," Jim decided.

Tom chuckled. He lowered his pipe. "Slow down, Jim. You ain't there yet an' we don't know what time we'll get there. Anyways, we got friends would let us stay."

"Yeah, but bein' worn out w' won't feel like botherin' them."

"Aa w-want t' soak in a tub someplace sippin' a b-beer," Scott mused.

"Is that all?" Jim teased.

"Do t' begin with, J-im. But why you not h-headin' straight home?"

"It's another sixteen miles, Scott, an' it'll be dark gettin' there."

"What 'bout you, Tom?"

"Same. Got some in-laws an' friends in town, but Jim's right about botherin' them. A good night's rest in Meg's Boardin' House would be just fine. Then, in the mornin' after a full breakfast, we can visit the Bank. After that, Scott, Aa'll be homeward bound - back to my home and darlin' family." His eyes reflected the glow in his voice.

They rested and snoozed for an hour and a half, reviving their energies, before Jim rose and went to gather the horses. Tom and Scott joined him and finally loaded up, they climbed onto their saddles and wearily set off over baked, stony country.

———————

Passing by a huge grist and saw mill on the bluff, they arrived in Kerrville late afternoon and wearily walked their horses down the street. Three times the size of Fredericksburg, it was a busier town, and with the heat of the day subsiding more people were out and about. They stopped now and then to be greeted by acquaintances, but were eager to escort their horses to the livery for the night. At Meg's boarding house, they were shown their tiny rooms that were clean and simple. While they ventured out to buy clothes from the general store, Meg, a bright, breezy woman, promised to heat water for them returning later.

Strolling along the street that was familiar to them, they felt the blessing of their return. Their quiet excitement, however, was matched by numbers of folk heading towards a small, noisy Fairground on the edge of town. Curious, they followed, wandering between two exhibition tents and three stalls selling wares. However, the main attraction was surrounded by a group of cheering spectators watching two men fighting.

The challenger, a local man, swung punches recklessly at his burly opponent who dodged them with ease, and counter punched with force. It proved a one-sided contest with the 'champ', named Brown, quickly clubbing the other onto the ground. Raising his hands, the winner claimed victory, while the groggy loser was aided onto his feet, cheered, and then helped from the ring.

An announcer, in hat and military style dress, invited others to attempt to last three-minutes without going down against his prize fighter to win a prize of four dollars. "Dollar-and-a-half-a-go!" he urged. "Bets are on over there for any of you wishin' t' gamble." He pointed at an assistant outside the cordoned off area.

Scott stepped forwards. Tom and Jim gawped in disbelief.

"Don't be a fool, Scott. He'll knock your brains out!" Jim warned.

Scott paid no heed and gave the man his money and rolled up his sleeves for his hands to be bandaged.

Tom shook his head in dismay as the crowd started to clap in thrill and admiration of the tall, young man's daring. Bets ranged on how long he'd last.

Once the betting had ceased, the announcer, acting as referee, loosely instructed both contestants before waving them to begin fighting.

The burly fighter came forward eager for a quick finish. Scott threw a series of left jabs, circling to the right then whipped in a right cross. Brown rocked back, his upper lip spouting blood. In desperation, he closed in and they went into a clinch. Adroitly, Scott wrapped up the other's arms so he couldn't strike. The referee broke them apart. Jabbing and moving, Scott's longer reach was telling. The champ sprang forward. Scott's guard held, deflecting the blows with his arms. He skipped away then stepped forwards delivering a perfectly timed left hook into the man's cheek. The amazed crowd cheered. Scott ducked beneath a powerful right and countered with a sharp punch into Brown's solar plexus. Brown emitted a gasp and as his hands lowered, Scott smacked him with two lefts then a straight right and Brown's head jerked back. Sensing victory, Scott turned aggressor and walloped him again with a short combination and the champ went down onto his seat and stared up vacantly. At once, with a fighter down, the bout was ended. The spectators yelled and whooped at the young cowboy's victory. The announcer handed over four dollars. "You been taught t' fight!" he declared grudgingly.

"Sure have, m-mister. For good r-eason."

Tom and Jim were overjoyed, patting his shoulders as the bandages were removed from his hands. "Boy, oh boy. Y' never told us y' could use your fists like that!" Jim exclaimed. "We could've won a fortune!"

"Told you b-before, Jim, an old Mexican showed me how w-hen Aa was young. He said it was im-portant for me. Aa could tell Brown weren't t-trained p-roper. Just a s-slugger."

"Well, Scott, w' got to admire you. Come on. We'll get us some new clothes first then Aa'll buy you a beer," Tom said, his face beaming with admiration.

Later, in the Lone Star Saloon, they could have dwelled all evening with a succession of customers wanting to congratulate Scott and buy them drinks. They weren't tempted. After one beer they left early and returned in dusk to the boarding house to eat, wash and enjoy a long night's comfortable sleep on soft beds.

———————

Next morning, they rose bright as the sun, feeling refreshed. Dressed in clean, new working clothes they breakfasted, drank coffee and amiably recounted the fight, praising Scott's speed and skills.

Meg informed them of how serious the drought had become. She understood that a number of farmers were selling up, intending to move back east. "Trail herds leavin' every day now at bottom price," she bemoaned.

Her words confirmed the choice that Tom and Jim had made, selling their cattle early, but they took no satisfaction in others' misfortune.

Scott had decided to spend a couple of days in town before joining another trail. Tom and Jim wished him luck and invited him to visit their valley next time he returned to Kerrville.

"Been a real h-honour t' know you both," he said graciously.

Saying farewell, they shook hands and left him sitting at the table.

Outside on the street, without delay, Tom and Jim visited the bank to verify their payment then went to collect their horses. The livery man wanted to talk about Scott's performance, beating the champ, but with their minds set on riding home they didn't care to loiter. Saddled up on 'Rusty' and 'Star', with their spare horses in tow, the two of them trotted their steeds out of town to join the river's side.

"At last. The end run!" Tom glowed at his partner, as they stared at the road ahead to Ingram. Overwhelmed by emotion they paused together, pondering their reunion with their loved ones.

"Been an adventure we won't forget," Jim quipped. "Yeah, it was Tom's trail alright," he voiced to himself. "Was, an' always will be!" With a whoop, he galloped off at pace, ahead of his old friend.

"Huh?" Tom uttered, then his frown lightened. He drew a deep breath, exhaled slowly, and drunk with joy, he spurred for home.

The End

Printed in Great Britain
by Amazon